Also by Elaine Robertson North

I Can't Tell You Why

Bring Me To Life

I'VE BEEN WAITING FOR YOU

Elaine Robertson North

Text copyright © 2023 Elaine North
All Rights Reserved

The characters in this book are entirely fictional. Any resemblance to actual persons living or dead is entirely coincidental.

For Cameron and Rory

PART ONE

1

It was a moment before Esther realised the terrible cry that could be heard up and down the surrounding corridors had come from her. She had no idea she was capable of making such a terrifying sound, but then she'd never been faced with such a harrowing sight before.

She was only vaguely aware of voices at the door and the hushed tones of Detective Constable Carpenter, reassuring whoever was outside that Esther was fine and needed to be left alone. She hoped she would remember to thank her for her kindness later.

Esther had been staring at the ceiling for long enough to know that at some point she would have to find the courage to properly look at Abi. While she waited for that moment to come, she stood as close as she could, one of Abi's hands between her own. A hand that was pale and unnaturally cool. Any sense of time had been lost as Esther took one breath, two breaths and then on the third, forbade herself to exhale until her eyes settled on the face of her friend. She shuddered as she took in the horrible greyness around Abi's eyes and the waxy creaminess of her skin. It made her feel nauseous, bile creeping up the back of her throat. She swallowed hard.

In contrast to Abi's eerie stillness, Esther was now in full flight mode. She was aware of her own rapid breaths, fear making it impossible to do anything but take tiny gulps of air at a time that sent her heart racing and a sense of panic rocketing. Her head hurt too, confusion pounding against her forehead, making her feel dizzy. And yet, despite the instinctive desire to flee, her feet remained fixed to the floor.

The physical reactions were draining and while she struggled to find a sense of calm, a single tear fell silently on to the crisp white sheet that Abi lay on. And then there was another, and another, until a small area of the material became sodden with the only visible evidence of Esther's despair.

"Miss Harrison?"

Esther didn't stir as DC Carpenter appeared just inside the door. "We've spoken to Jamie. He's going to meet you at home. He's on his way there now so if you're ready, we'll take you back." The officer waited for a moment but Esther didn't even flinch.

"Esther?" she tried again, more informal this time. "I really think it's time to go."

Esther exhaled slowly and deliberately, her chest tight, her head still pounding, her cheeks hot with tears. Wiping them away with her sleeve, she reluctantly looked up and gave a small nod. Then she turned back to Abi and bent down to kiss her forehead, fresh tears blurring her vision as she stroked her cheek, still squeezing Abi's hand tightly as she did so. She was suddenly terrified to let go, struck by the realisation that this would be the last time she would ever see or touch her friend. As the thought sunk in, it threatened to overwhelm her, her mind and body flooded with such immense sadness and a terrible sense of injustice that rumbled deep in her gut. She took another deep breath and squeezed her eyes shut, searching every inch of her body for enough strength to leave and then, without looking back, she gently released Abi's hand and forced herself to walk away.

2

Two months earlier

Esther threw open her front door and was immediately tempted to shut it again. A rush of adrenalin caused her eyes to water and her heart to flutter uncomfortably in her chest. Oblivious, her brother, Matt, was over the doorstep without a second's hesitation and as he wrapped his arms around her, Esther silently chastised herself as she instinctively reciprocated. It was never long before that sense of belonging overwhelmed any feelings of foreboding. She folded into him, the perfect fit as always.

"Hi Esty, how are you?"

"A brief call now and then or the odd text and you'd already know the answer to that." Esther pulled away and looked into his eyes. He was the best part of a foot taller than her which put a sizeable dent in any sense of authority she might try to exert. He was older too which also didn't help with the balance of power. Regardless, her sarcasm was lost on him.

The lack of parity didn't end there. His frame was broad, hers more slender. His hair blonde, hers dark. She liked to dress with at least a splash of colour, he was monochrome all the way. She was open and interested while he remained closed with a clam-like efficiency. Their unusually green eyes were the only attribute they shared.

"Who is it Esther?" Jamie appeared in the hallway and Esther watched his jaw visibly stiffen as he saw Matt whose hands were still casually resting on her shoulders. His eyes lowered and he dragged his bottom lip between clenched teeth. Esther could only imagine what words he was trying to contain, words she was sure he would love to hurl at Matt with a ferocity befitting the contempt he made little attempt to hide.

Esther held her breath until Jamie looked up again. "Esther?"

"Matt just needs somewhere to stay. Just for a couple of days." She threw a glance at Matt to check she had that right before she turned back towards Jamie, bracing herself for his reply. When nothing was forthcoming, she nudged Matt. "Go and make yourself a drink. I'll be in in a minute."

Matt did as he was told, smiling a little too smugly at Jamie for Esther's liking as he squeezed past him.

"It's just for a couple of days Jamie," she said again as soon as Matt was out of earshot.

"When are you going to learn to say no? For months now you've been telling me you think you're being watched, and then low and behold the prodigal son turns up again."

"Why would you think that has anything to do with Matt? The only thing that matters here is he's my brother and there isn't anywhere else for him to go."

Jamie sighed. "That isn't a good enough reason any more. I'm sorry but it just isn't."

For a moment they just stood there, Jamie searching Esther's face for a flicker of anything that suggested she knew he was right; Esther studying the floor, her eyes wide in an attempt to stop the tears that flooded them from spilling onto her face.

"Well, I'm going home. I can't stay, not while he's here. I might just kick the shit out of the rotten selfish bastard." He lifted his coat from the rack behind her, aware of Esther flinching at the threat of violence but he refused to be put off. "Wouldn't that be ironic? If I was the one who ended up in a police cell?" Esther made no reply as Jamie opened the door. "I'll call you tomorrow," he said with his back to her. And then he was gone.

Esther turned to face the mirror on the wall beside her and took a moment to wipe her eyes and compose herself before facing Matt. She wondered for a second what he'd been up to and then swallowed hard. It was probably better not to know. And then she turned around to face the picture on the wall opposite. It was a portrait of her late mother that she'd painted herself. She was very proud of it, believing it to perfectly capture the gentleness, the kindness and the beauty that she associated with her. Friends had asked why it wasn't hung somewhere more prominent than in the hallway and her answer was always the same; she liked it to be the last thing she saw every time she went out, and the first thing she saw when she returned.

Esther only took one step into the kitchen before she stopped again. A loaf of uncut bread had been attacked crudely with a knife and both now lay abandoned, a spray of crumbs strewn across the floor. Various contents from the fridge were also scattered about the worktops and the large island, with a bottle opener tossed into the middle of it all. She followed the trail of crumbs through the archway, past the dining table, on through to the lounge and then towards the sofa where they stopped. There was Matt slouched in the corner, his feet on the coffee table, a clumsy sandwich in one hand and a beer in the other. His eyes were already glued to the television where the programme she and Jamie had been watching had been replaced by a noisy action movie, the room now filled with the sound of rapid gun fire.

"Has Jamie gone? I heard the front door shut," he said without looking up.

"Yes, he's gone."

His eyes were immediately on her at the flat tone of her voice and he smiled apologetically. "Sorry Esty."

"It's been over a year Matt. Another long spell of not knowing where you are or if you're okay." Matt quickly turned away again. He took a large bite of his sandwich and chewed slowly, his eyes staring at the television but seeing nothing. "I don't understand why I can't even have a number for you. I know you've got a phone." His head whipped round, eyes suddenly wide. "Oh come on Matt, I'm not stupid! You think I don't hear the whispered conversations? Or see you shoving it in your pocket when I come in the room? And who doesn't have a phone?" She shook her head. It was the same conversation they had every time he turned up. "I just want to…" and then she stopped. What was the point?

"I'm sorry Esty, I really am."

Esther was already heading for her studio. Without turning to face him she put her hand up to stop him. She'd had enough platitudes to last her a lifetime. She certainly didn't have the stomach for any more tonight.

Sitting down at her drawing table, Esther felt her shoulders slowly relax. She was working on some illustrations for a local children's clothes shop and was really loving the job. It didn't feel like work at all, unlike some of the more corporate design work she normally picked up. Not that she ever complained. The boring stuff paid well and meant she had time for the occasional passion project although the canvas sitting on an easel behind her, with the barest outlines of a sketch on it, was a constant reminder that she hadn't had much time for the work she really loved for a while now but that was the way it always worked. There would be a quiet spell soon enough and she would happily fill her time painting.

Esther picked up a soft pencil and started to draw. Before long, she was totally immersed in her work and it was hours later when she finally decided to give in to her tired eyes. She wandered back into the lounge and was immediately greeted by the annoying banter of some graveyard television show. Matt, meanwhile, was fast asleep on the sofa, three empty beer bottles on the floor beside him and his chest covered in breadcrumbs. She started to clear up and then sat down next to him for a moment and just watched him sleep. He looked so peaceful. "What am I going to do with you?" she whispered as she gently stroked his forehead, easing his floppy blonde hair away from his eyes. He looked as if he'd lost weight, not that there was ever much spare flesh on him. As Esther studied his face, it was impossible to avoid the scars, each with their own hideous story attached. She shivered as she felt the dark memories of the past start to circle and she immediately stood up. There was nothing to be gained from looking back and stopping only to put a blanket over him, she quickly headed to her bedroom. He could move into the spare bedroom tomorrow.

When Esther left for some meetings the next morning, Matt was barely conscious. She toyed with the idea of waking him properly and then decided it would be easier all round just to leave him exactly where he was. She had some important appointments today so trying to sort Matt out would just have to wait until later.

She flew from one meeting to the next with barely a moment to spare. There were two hectic days to get through, checking in with current clients and meeting a few potential new ones and the only thing that kept the fixed smile on her face was knowing that it would be some time before she would need to do the rounds again.

When she left her final meeting, Esther was more than happy with the day's achievements. All her current projects were comfortably on track and she'd picked up a couple of new briefs too. As she stepped out into the early evening air, she finally took a moment to look at her watch. "Shit!" she muttered under her breath. She was late for Abi and frantically waving for a cab, she headed home.

As Esther opened her front door, she was immediately greeted with the sound of chatter and laughter and her heart sank. She was too late and as she walked into the lounge, her worst nightmare was revealed. There were Matt and Abi chatting away, Abi's eyes bright and alive, Matt playing the perfect host.

It was Matt who saw her first. "There you are! I was just keeping Abi company while she waited for you. Just as well I was here or she'd have been sitting on your doorstep."

Esther threw down her coat and her bags. "Sorry Abi. I lost track of time. I'll just be a minute getting changed and then we can go out."

Abi smiled, and far too widely for Esther's liking. "No rush. I'm being well looked after."

Esther had never moved so quickly in her life. She raced to the bedroom and in almost one perfect movement, she threw off her clothes and replaced her shirt, trousers and jacket with the pair of jeans and jumper that were closest to hand. She pulled on some boots and was back in the living room within minutes.

"Come on then, let's go. I haven't eaten all day and I'm starving. You'll be okay Matt?"

Matt recognised the look in Esther's eyes and smiled mischievously. "I'll be fine. Don't you worry about me."

"I won't." Esther grabbed her bag and practically dragged Abi from her chair, propelling her towards the door before she had the chance to invite Matt along, aware that was exactly what Abi was desperate to do.

Esther and Abi had already agreed on dinner at a little Italian restaurant just around the corner so there was no need for a discussion on where they should go. Instead, they walked in silence, Esther intent on doing nothing but putting distance between them and Matt. It wasn't until they sat down at their favourite table near the window and a bottle of wine arrived that the conversation started.

"So are you going to enlighten me or do I really have to ask?"

"Ask what?"

"Oh come on Esther! I've known you for nearly a year now and this is how I find out you have a brother?"

Esther took a large gulp of her wine. "It's a long story."

"Well I'm not in any hurry." Abi waited. "Esther?"

Esther sighed. "I don't want to talk about him. I'm sorry that you had to meet him at all and to be honest, I'd prefer it if you just forgot that you had."

Abi looked bemused. "Why?"

Esther fixed her eyes on Abi. "Every time he turns up, I have no idea where he's been, how long he's going to stay, or when he might be back. Or whether he'll even be back at all. So I prefer not to talk about him. The chances are you'll never see him again which is why it would be better to just forget you ever met him. So, what are you going to have?"

Esther used her menu as a shield and quietly braced herself for Abi's protest. Her ears pulsed as the seconds ticked by and then a hand slowly pushed the large menu down until their eyes met again.

"Maybe you should talk about him?" Abi said with an encouraging smile. "You never know, it might feel good to share and I'd like to try to help if you'll let me."

Esther didn't know how to express a deep-rooted fear that if she started to talk about him, she had no idea where it might end. Or what might come out. Revelations that she would never be able to take back. So she simply smiled. "I appreciate that. Honestly I do." She paused for a moment. "But I really don't want to talk about him."

When Esther got home, having dissuaded Abi from coming back with her, Matt had gone out, the usual chaos left in his wake but his absence was probably a blessing. She was angry with him for inflicting a horrible awkwardness on her evening with Abi that had weighed heavily on the conversation all night, the lightness the pair normally enjoyed substituted by long hollow pauses and clipped frustrated words with one of them remaining tight-lipped and the other wishing those tight lips would loosen. If he'd been home, she would have shouted at him, he would have looked hurt and she would then have felt guilty so it was a relief to have been spared a fight.

Tired from a busy day, Esther decided to ignore the mess that surrounded her and headed straight to the bedroom. She had another long day ahead of her tomorrow and had neither the energy nor the inclination to spend the next two hours cleaning up after her brother when she could be fast asleep and dreaming about deserted tropical islands, or hosting the first gallery showing of her art, or having her flat back to herself again. She stopped for a moment, despising herself for even thinking that. She'd waited such a long time to see him and wanted to make the most of what time they had together if that was at all possible. If she'd known he was coming she would happily have rearranged her meetings. And her dinner with Abi. But he hadn't given her the chance to do that and already his visit had been marred by petty conflict which she hated.

It was still early when Esther went to leave the next morning so she was surprised to find Matt already in the kitchen.

"Want some coffee?" he asked as he saw her.

"No thanks, I don't have time. What are you doing up so early?"

"I have stuff to do."

Esther went to ask him what kind of stuff and then decided not to even bother, concentrating instead on getting herself ready for the day ahead. She turned away from him to gather together the various things she needed.

"So how was your evening?" Matt asked her.

"Fine thanks," she said without turning around.

"That's good." He paused for a moment. "Abi seemed nice." Esther's back stiffened but she said nothing. "She didn't even know I existed Esty!"

Esther swung round to face him. "Don't look at me like that! What am I supposed to say to people? 'Oh I have this great brother. I don't have any idea where he is or what he does but you really should meet him the next time he decides to show his face.' What am I supposed to say Matt? Tell me what you've been up to, tell me something, anything about your life and then maybe I'll have a reason to talk about you."

Now it was Matt who turned away. Esther waited for just a moment and then quietly shook her head. "Fine," she said as she picked up her bag. "I'll see you later then. And if you don't have any more pressing business, perhaps you could clean up the mess you've made? You're an absolute nutter when it comes to neatness and yet you always turn my place into a complete pig sty."

"You should be flattered. Being with you is the only time I ever relax," he said, putting his hand out to stop her leaving. "Give me a hug before you go." Esther stood where she was. "Esty, please."

Esther looked at him, looked at the pathetic plea in his eyes and then reluctantly she put down her bag and took him into her arms. "You stupid great lump."

Matt squeezed her tightly. "Tell me you love me."

"You know I love you."

"I don't mean to cause you any trouble, you know that don't you?"

Esther's mind was immediately awash with the long line of questions that always remained unanswered. She'd ask them again if she thought there was even the slightest chance they would be addressed but she knew they would just hang in the air between them like they always did.

They stood in silence for a moment longer with Matt still wrapped around her until Esther wriggled herself free and picked up her bag for the second time.

"I really have to go. I'll see you later."

This time she didn't wait for a reply.

Esther threw herself into her day, refusing to allow herself to indulge in thoughts of Matt. She spoke to Jamie briefly and promised to catch up with him before she went home and as she looked at her watch, she realised that time was already nearing. As she headed for his office, Esther was aware that her heart was starting to accelerate. She hoped he wouldn't be too cross as she struggled with the heavy glass doors and stepped into the swanky reception. The security guard smiled as he saw her approach.

"Afternoon Miss Harrison. Looking for young Jamie are you?"

Esther smiled. "Yes please Mike."

"Take a seat. I'll let him know you're here."

As Esther sat down, her eyes were drawn to the large glass-fronted cabinet opposite her bursting with trophies and awards that glistened proudly. The team that Jamie had pulled together to launch The Club, an online men's magazine, had already won multiple accolades and she loved the fact that the logo that appeared on all of them was the one she'd designed right back at the very beginning when the magazine had been little more than a pipe dream. The connection between her and Jamie had been instant and on her last day on the project, Jamie had invited her out for dinner. That had been nearly four years ago.

Esther stood up, the anticipation of seeing Jamie suddenly making her feel the need to move rather than sit. She started to pace, covering the full width of the reception area a number of times as she waited for him to appear, aware that the only time they seemed to have anything close to an argument was whenever Matt turned up.

She stopped as she heard the sliding doors behind the security desk glide into action and smiled as Jamie strode towards her.

"Hi darling," he said as he reached her and then with a brief kiss, he took her arm and led her towards the door. "Come on, let's grab a drink."

A few moments later they were sitting in a nearby bar, a large glass of wine in front of Esther, a beer in Jamie's hand.

"I wasn't sure if you were still speaking to me."

Jamie looked at her, a sense of anguish immediately flooding his eyes. "Of course I'm speaking to you! I'm sorry I left the way I did but I've just run out of things to say where Matt's concerned. I know you always want to protect him but I'm just trying to protect you."

"I know you are and I love you for it but I can't turn my back on him. I won't turn my back on him." Esther shrugged her shoulders. "That's just the way it is."

Jamie looked at her. "So how far does he have to go before you realise that he's going to hurt you? And who knows how badly?"

"That's a risk I'll just have to take. And why do you always assume the worst of him? Just because we don't know what he's up to doesn't automatically mean he's some kind of terrible criminal mastermind, mixing with the worst of the worst and sitting right up there on the Met's most wanted."

"It doesn't mean he isn't though, does it? And what if I'm right? I just have to stand by and wait for him to finally destroy you, one way or another?"

"Yes, you do."

Their eyes locked, neither blinking until Esther finally made a move, laying her hand on Jamie's. "Please try to understand. Whatever he has or hasn't done, I have to try to help him."

"But you're not helping him! That's the point. He's just using you as an occasional pit stop to recharge his batteries before he disappears again to do who knows what. Perhaps if you were tougher with him, he might just open up a little?"

Esther sipped at her drink, feeling as if the weight of the entire world was resting on her shoulders. A perfectly formed globe sitting at the nape of her neck, pushing her down, down, down, until her back started to buckle under the pressure. Perhaps Jamie was right? She did let Matt walk all over her but sometimes she didn't see him for months or longer. It made it hard to have any real influence on his life. She sighed. "Okay, I'll go home now and talk to him."

Jamie took hold of her hands. "Do you want me to come with you?"

"No, it's better if I'm on my own."

"What are you going to say to him?"

Esther stood up and after she'd gathered her things together, she looked at Jamie and shrugged. "I have absolutely no idea."

Esther took her time getting home then all too soon she was standing outside her front door. She paused for a few moments, still unsure if helping Matt meant throwing him out or asking him to stay and then, taking a deep breath, she headed inside.

As she walked into the kitchen she momentarily thought she was in the wrong place. The room was completely spotless, positively gleaming, with not a single item out of place and every surface cleared and wiped. She walked through to the lounge to see the sofa and cushions had been perfectly puffed up, just how she liked them, with the coffee table neat and tidy and the wooden floors swept.

"Matt!" she called as she headed back into the hallway towards the spare bedroom, the silence now starting to unnerve her. "Matt!" Louder this time as she walked into the room and then she stopped. The bed was perfectly made and there wasn't a single item of his to be seen anywhere.

Esther felt her head drop and her heart sink along with it.

He was gone.

3

The loud knock at the door had Esther up and out of her chair like a shot. She raced through the flat and threw the door open, a wave of expectation propelling her forward and then she stopped, expression frozen, breath tightly held.

"Lovely to see you too," Abi said, dipping under Esther's arm which was still attached to the front door and heading straight for the kitchen. Esther slowly closed the door and followed her.

"What are you doing here?"

"Well that's a fine way to greet someone who's just bought you a delicious lunch."

Esther watched as Abi opened and closed cupboards, pulling out plates and cutlery. She then unwrapped various packages to reveal an array of salads, quiches and a variety of cheeses along with a huge loaf of freshly baked bread and spread it all out across the large kitchen island. She couldn't help but notice that Abi's eyes were everywhere, scanning the place as she busied herself, obviously not as discreetly as she imagined.

"Looking for someone?" Esther asked.

Abi looked at her and attempted a relaxed smile. "I just thought Matt might be here."

"Well he's not."

"So where is he?"

"No idea."

Abi paused and Esther could sense a seed of irritation. "So will he be back?"

"No idea about that either."

"So he's gone?"

"Yes, as I said, he's not here." Esther looked at her, her expression belying her own growing frustration and anger. "So does that mean you're taking your lunch away again?"

"Of course not!"

Esther pulled out a stool but before she sat down she grabbed a bottle of wine and a couple of glasses. "I don't know about you but I need a drink," she said, opening the bottle and pouring two glasses without waiting for a reply.

They sat down opposite each other and Esther took a few large mouthfuls of the chilled wine in an attempt to drown, or at least numb, a growing sense of exasperation. She knew it wasn't fair to take it out on Abi. It was just bloody typical of Matt to disappear when she had things to talk to him about. She was furious with him for just vanishing, again. It was so selfish! He is a completely selfish bastard, she thought, who cares for no-one but himself. Selfish, selfish, selfish! Bastard, bastard, bastard!

Esther forced herself to look up. "This looks great, thanks. I probably wouldn't have bothered with lunch but I'm starving."

Abi just about managed a smile. "It's my pleasure."

Esther doubted that but decided she might as well enjoy the unexpected feast and tucked in but, after a few delicious mouthfuls, she put her knife and fork down and looked at her friend. "Look, I'm really sorry Abi but I genuinely don't know where he is. I did warn you that he just turns up and then disappears again just as quickly and every time he does, he leaves with a string of unanswered questions chasing after him which always leaves me wound up like a coil. It's why I told you to forget you'd ever met him."

Abi looked at her. "Well I might have done if he hadn't turned up to meet me after work yesterday."

Esther choked slightly as she fought to swallow a badly-timed mouthful of salmon and broccoli quiche. "He did what?"

"He was waiting for me at Charing Cross station yesterday. Took me for a drink, chatted to me, flirted with me, promised he'd see me again and then....." She shrugged, unsure how to finish as Esther put her head in her hands and rubbed her forehead roughly.

"I just knew something like this would happen!" She shook her head, the heat of her frustration now causing her neck to redden. She clawed at it.

"You thought I was him at the door didn't you?" Abi asked.

"I got back last night and he was gone," Esther said with a sigh. "I wanted to talk to him so yes, I did hope he'd decided to come back." Esther looked at Abi and the very obvious disappointment in her eyes. "He really got to you didn't he?"

Abi nodded and then shrugged again. "Oh well, probably better off without."

"Believe me Abs, that's the first sensible thing you've said since you got here. And do yourself a huge favour. If he turns up again, walk away in the opposite direction. And fast. As if your bloody life depended on it."

It had been almost three weeks since Matt had left and they were always the toughest. That awful limbo period after a visit when Esther constantly wondered if he might just reappear. Despite how frustrated she got with him, Esther loved having him around and the sense of loss when he left was always acute, particularly in those first few weeks.

Sitting at her desk, and knowing she'd now reached the point where it was unlikely he'd be back any time soon, she was struggling to concentrate which meant she'd done nothing all morning other than wonder how long it would be before she saw him again. She had far too much work to do to be wasting so much valuable time but even the threat of several deadlines looming hadn't been enough to shake off this self-indulgent slump she found herself wallowing in.

Esther struggled through the day but by late afternoon, when she had absolutely nothing to show for the immense effort she'd expended just trying to stay focused, she decided to give up. For the next couple of hours she tried to occupy herself with some household chores and then leapt as the silence was shattered by the sound of her phone ringing. A quick glance revealed a withheld number and her heart rate started to quicken.

"Hello?" Nothing. "Hello? Who is this?" Still nothing, just a faint humming on the line that made Esther shiver. She waited for a second longer and then swiftly ended the call, her body chilled, her hands now clammy. She closed her eyes for a moment, standing rigid with fists clenched. She'd lost count of the number of similar calls she'd had, each one leaving her more unsettled than the last. And then she gave herself a shake and forced herself in the direction of the front door, grabbing her jacket as she went.

After walking for twenty minutes Esther started to feel better. There was a gentle breeze on her face and with her feet bouncing rhythmically on the pavement and her heart pumping along to the beat, it wasn't long before she felt her shoulders relax, a smile spreading across her face. Arriving at the nearest collection of shops and bars to her flat, she was suddenly surrounded by bustle which suited her renewed energy. She dipped in and out of the shops that were still open, treating herself to whatever she felt would continue to enhance her mood which today meant cheese, the freshest bread imaginable and cake. Lots of cake.

And then just as she felt recharged enough to return home, she stopped suddenly, blinking several times to be sure her eyes weren't playing tricks on her. Was that really Matt she could see? What was he doing here? And then she gasped as she saw Abi catch up with him. They were very close to each other as they walked, chatting and laughing as Matt then took hold of her hand, unable to take their eyes off each other as they disappeared inside a bar.

For several moments afterwards Esther stood exactly where she was, mouth still slightly open, brain struggling to work out exactly what she'd just seen. They weren't two people out together, they were a single item, a couple. Eventually she forced herself to turn around and she slowly walked home, dumping the goodies she'd just bought in the first bin she passed, the thought of eating them now making her feel physically sick.

Once she was back in her flat, Esther had no idea what to do with herself, unsure exactly what was upsetting her most. Was it the fact Matt and Abi had looked so intimate? Or was it that, given a choice, Matt had chosen to turn up on Abi's doorstep rather than her own? And worse, had then decided not to contact her, not thinking for a minute that she might like to know he was still around. And no wonder Abi had been so quiet over the last couple of weeks! Clearly her attentions had been concentrated elsewhere despite Esther's warning to steer well clear.

The one thing she did know was that she felt totally unnerved by the idea of them together. She tortured herself wondering what he might have told Abi. There was so much about their past that remained a mystery to her, and the idea that Matt might open up to Abi in a way he refused to do with Esther was so far beyond what felt right and just, it was enough to make her feel faint.

It was a couple of days later before Abi started calling. It started on Sunday evening and it was clear Abi had no intention of stopping until she'd got Esther to pick up. Esther was refusing to comply, rejecting every call and diverting them straight to voicemail. She quickly became irritated by the overly jolly messages and so stopped listening to them. The thought of some overexaggerated role playing – Abi ignoring the fact that she'd seen Matt, and Esther ignoring the fact that she'd seen Matt and Abi – was simply too much.

It was seven o'clock on Thursday when Abi switched to a text. 'I've got a great bottle of wine just begging to be drunk,' it read. 'Be with you in half an hour.'

In the moment, the skills to make a polite decline had escaped Esther and they had now been sitting making idle chit-chat for what felt like hours to Esther but was probably ten minutes at most. Abi was extremely animated while Esther was finding it increasingly hard to be civil.

And then Abi went quiet for a moment and Esther braced herself. "So have you heard from Matt at all?" Abi asked her.

"No, I haven't." Esther watched Abi as she played with her wine glass, obviously trying to find the right words to explain that she had.

"I have." And there it was. Two simple words and it was out. "He turned up at work again. I didn't mention it because like you said, I didn't know how long he'd stay around," Abi continued, stumbling over her words now under the intensity of Esther's stare. "And I've seen quite a lot of him since." She paused for a moment. "I just wanted you to know that he's around and he's doing really well."

At this point, Esther put both her hands up. "Stop there. Just stop right there." She looked at her friend for a moment, chewing the inside of her cheek as she tried to collect her thoughts. She'd known this moment would come eventually so had all sorts of responses planned, from calm and collected, to smart and cutting, to screaming with rage, all practiced and ready to be used depending on what felt most powerful in the moment. And yet, despite her careful preparation, she was surprised to find she had absolutely nothing to say. Instead, she simply stood up. "If you don't mind Abi, I've had a really slow few days and I'm way behind. I really need to get back to work."

Abi was unable to hide her surprise. "You're not going to say anything? Don't you want to talk about it?"

Esther thought for a moment and then shook her head. "No, I'm not, and no, I don't."

"But Matt has pretty well moved in with me. He's living just down the road. Don't you want to see him?"

"I did see him. I saw him out with you over a week ago. It was pretty obvious that you were more than just friends so the reality is you haven't actually told me anything I hadn't already worked out for myself."

"Oh Esther I'm so sorry," Abi gasped. "I thought Matt would tell you and then when I realised he hadn't, I tried calling you. That's not how I wanted you to find out."

Esther took the biggest breath she could manage but was only able to count to four before she burst and the words started to spew out, none of which were part of her planned repertoire. "You amaze me! Listening to the way you talk about him, I..." Esther shook her head as she struggled to align her thoughts amidst a swelling anger. "I tried to tell you what Matt was like but no, you knew best. One flutter of his eyelashes and he's in your bed, in your flat, already embedded in your life for fuck's sake! And don't you dare sit there and tell me how well he's doing! You know nothing about him. Nothing at all!"

"I know everything I need to know. And why does it make you so angry? Why can't you just be happy for us? You're not being very rational about this."

"Rational? Are you fucking kidding me?" Esther squeezed her fists tightly together until she could feel her nails piercing her skin. She mustn't lose control. If she was honest, she didn't actually know why she was so angry, thinking it was most likely born out of fear. Or perhaps fear and hurt would be more honest. She may have reprimanded Jamie for always thinking so badly of Matt but the truth was she really had no idea what he was up to or how he spent his time and here was Abi, jumping in with her eyes tightly shut. The last thing Esther wanted was to be stuck in the middle when it all inevitably went wrong. Then her friendship would be in tatters and her brother would visit even less than he did already, never mind her anxiety about what he might share with Abi along the way.

And her feelings had been hurt too. Matt had been nearby and neither of them had thought to tell her. Childish as it sounded, she'd been made to feel left out and people making plans behind her back was something she was particularly sensitive about.

She sighed. "I won't be drawn into this. You're making such a huge mistake Abi but that's up to you. I'd just prefer to be left out of it."

Esther walked away and busied herself by the sink, waiting, waiting, waiting, until finally she heard Abi stand up. For a moment she felt her hover and then slowly admit defeat.

"I'll call you tomorrow," Abi said and then, when it was obvious Esther wasn't going to engage further, she headed for the door.

Esther didn't turn around until she heard the front door open and then close. The minute she was alone, she immediately stopped what she was doing and sat down again, her head in her hands, her eyes tightly closed but not enough to stop a river of tears squeeze their way through.

And there she stayed until she felt the frustration, the fear, the horrible sense of disquiet, drain away with her tears, and then she stood up, wiped her eyes and headed back to her desk.

4

"Esther!"

Matt did his best to weave through the waves of human traffic without bumping into anyone as he slowly closed in on her. When there'd been no answer at her flat, he thought it was worth a stroll through the village-like collection of shops and bars that sat just a short walk away and it hadn't been long before he'd spotted her unmistakable gait, to him at least, her long hair swinging rhythmically from side to side with every step.

"Esther, wait!" he shouted again, dodging a buggy before negotiating a group of meandering teenagers.

"Esty!"

Finally she stopped, turning just at the moment he reached her. "Didn't you hear me?" he panted. "I've been trying to catch up with you for ages."

"And now you have."

Matt chose to ignore the less than enthusiastic response and instead took hold of Esther's arm and half led, half marched her towards the nearest bar. "Let's have a drink," he said, his hand already reaching out to open the door. He ushered her inside. "You find a table and I'll go to the bar."

Matt watched her head for a quiet table in the furthest corner where he joined her a few moments later, placing a large glass of wine in front of her before sitting down himself, beer in hand. Her eyes remained fixed on the table.

Matt took a few large gulps of his drink while he studied her keenly, waiting patiently until eventually she looked up.

"What?" she snapped.

The return of the petulant teenager he thought with a warm smile. He remembered her well.

"Stop staring at me like that. You're making me uncomfortable."

"Sorry. And I'm sorry Abi spoke to you before I did. It's all happened so quickly I…."

Esther put her hand up to stop him. "I don't want to know."

"I really like her Esty. It's the first time, possibly ever, that I've actually wanted to be with someone for more than just one night."

"Did you not hear me?" Esther cut in. "I don't want to know. About any of it."

Matt sat back in his chair. "I thought you wanted me to be around more?"

"Well if you thought this is what I meant by that then you're an idiot. And even more selfish than I thought you were, which is pretty bloody selfish just to make sure that's clear."

"Why not like this?"

"Because Abi's my friend. And it's all moving so ridiculously fast. It sounds like you've moved in already but what if you change your mind? What do you think will happen to my relationship with Abi when you decide to disappear without warning? And I gave her an incredibly streamlined version of our childhood. What are you planning on sharing when she starts asking you to open up? What will you tell her about what you actually do with your life? Because I don't know the answer to that. And there's so much else you won't tell me. Is she going to end up knowing all sorts of stuff that I don't? Things about me? About Mum?" Esther stopped for a moment. "Well the look on your face means that of course you haven't given any of this even the slightest thought which is exactly why I wish it was anyone but her. Selfish. Idiot."

Esther sighed and then looked at her watch. She quickly drained her glass. "I have to meet Jamie and thanks to you I'm now going to be late. But thanks so much for the chat," she said, her voice dripping with sarcasm.

"I'm sorry Esty, really I am. Your feelings are hurt, I get it. I should have spoken to you before Abi did." Esther raised her eyebrows. "I mean I should have spoken to you before you saw us out together." Her eyebrows shot up even further. "I should have let you know I was back straight away." He shrugged. "I messed up."

Esther rolled her eyes. "You say that like this is an isolated incident."

"I know it's fast but that's because I've never felt like this before. None of this was planned Esty! When I met her from work after I left you it was on a complete whim and then when I came back, I never intended to stay but I just want to be with her all the time. I know that probably sounds alien to you. You and Jamie have moved at a much more sensible pace."

"Don't make this about me! And if Jamie and I are moving slowly it's because I have trust issues. I wonder why that is?"

Matt stood up and pulled her up out of her seat and into his arms. He squeezed her tight. "I'm sorry Esty. I never meant to hurt you."

She sighed and then released herself from his grip enough to be able to look into his eyes, pushing his hair to one side to make that possible. "You're a bloody idiot," she said with a wry smile.

He smiled back at her. "Yeah, you said that already."

Jamie watched Esther shovelling large spoonfuls of sticky toffee pudding into her mouth, a blissful look on her face. She had indeed been late to meet him despite having taken every opportunity available to shave minutes off her journey across London, paying the price with a dewy complexion and the discomfort of her shirt sticking to her back when she arrived. She hadn't even sat down before she was regaling Jamie with news of Matt and Abi's coupling but the stress was now melting away with every delicious toffee-fuelled mouthful of the largest pudding Jamie had ever seen.

"I must say you seem remarkably calm about it all."

"I was really hurt and angry and worried about how ridiculously fast they're moving with it all," she said between mouthfuls, "but watching his face when he talks about her," she shrugged, "it's pretty obvious that unless I want to completely push him away, I have to accept he and Abi are a couple and that's that."

Jamie immediately sat forward. "Or you could just push him away?" he said with a smile, quickly warming to the idea. "Or better still, we could be the ones who disappear without a trace for a change and just leave the lovebirds to it."

"Very funny. What's actually going to happen is we're all going to be the best of friends and to get that ball rolling, I've invited them round for dinner."

Jamie looked at her. "Just so I'm clear on a couple of things, would that be just the three of you or am I expected to take part in this madness?" Esther glared at him. "Okay, that'll be a yes for my participation then," he said. "And secondly, how long did you say this has been going on?"

"A matter of weeks."

"And he's moved in already? What, with just the shirt on his back?"

"You ask as if you suddenly expect me to know all about how and where he's been living when, as you well know, I know absolutely nothing about his life."

Jamie watched her eyes go down and he immediately took her hand. "It'll be fine love, I promise. We'll be the perfect hosts and I promise to be on my absolute best behaviour. Unless he upsets you, in which case I'll probably thump him but he'll have asked for it so I'll be totally blameless." He smiled at her and squeezed her hand until he saw her expression lighten.

"You're going to hate every minute of it, aren't you?" she asked.

"Abso-bloody-lutely."

A few days later Abi and Matt were in the back of a taxi on their way to Esther's with Matt staring out of the window and Abi staring at Matt. She looked at his knees clamped together, his hands clasped tightly on his lap, his mouth firmly closed. She was no body language expert but to conclude he was a little tense seemed more than reasonable. She was suddenly aware of her own shoulders sitting uncomfortably close to her ears. She forced them down and then gave them a little roll. If this evening was going to go well, and it absolutely had to if her relationship with Esther was to get back on track, any potential hostility had to be squashed before it had a chance of joining them at the dinner table.

Abi broke into a wide smile, hoping it would translate into her voice. "So, what's your relationship with Jamie like?"

"He hates me," Matt replied without hesitation or expression, his eyes still fixed firmly away from her.

"Oh," Abi said. "Maybe that's just because he hasn't had a proper chance to get to know you? Well tonight could be the start of a beautiful friendship."

Matt turned to look at her, his forehead furrowed to form the perfect facial question mark. "I think that's highly unlikely."

Abi swallowed hard. The truth was she'd only ever spent snatched moments with Jamie herself so had no real relationship with him either but if Matt wasn't prepared to give him a chance then she certainly would despite instinctively feeling that Esther deserved so much better. Someone kinder and warmer for a start, but that was one opinion she wouldn't be sharing over the beef Wellington Esther had promised.

Two hours later, there were no traces left of what had indeed been an incredibly impressive beef Wellington.

"Esther that was amazing," Abi enthused, slumping back in her chair to take the pressure off her waistband. "I'm surprised you're not twice the size Jamie with such a talented cook for a girlfriend."

Not for the first time that evening, Jamie looked at Abi through narrowed eyes but said nothing. Abi had often thought of him as a silent observer but it felt particularly out of place this evening. It would be intimidating if she let it.

"Thanks Abi," Esther said, her words louder than necessary as if volume were needed to fill the void left by the absence of a response from Jamie. "You don't seem to have much to say?" Esther then added, turning her attention to Matt.

"Just taking it all in," he said, locking eyes with her.

Abi looked from one to the other, the heat in her cheeks slowly rising. "You still enjoying the magazine Jamie, or is it time for a new challenge?"

Let the siblings face off, she thought, choosing instead to stay focused on Jamie who was looking at her with either irritation that she was still trying to engage him in conversation or mild disdain, she really couldn't be sure which.

"I'm fine where I am for now." His eyes narrowed again. "And what about you Abi? I'm not sure I've ever heard you talk about work."

Tempting as it was to lower her gaze, Abi refused to break eye contact. "That's because it's quite dull to talk about. I love it, but business consultancy doesn't make for great dinner party chat."

Abi felt herself starting to buckle under the intensity of his stare, and then he swiftly turned his attention to Matt. "So, what have you been up to since you last graced us with your presence Matt?"

For a split second Abi had been relieved Jamie had chosen to move on until she watched Matt slowly straighten himself up. It was a small gesture but significant enough to make her feel nervous but before he could answer, Esther was on her feet.

"Anyone for dessert?" she said, immediately gathering up some plates and heading for the kitchen. "Bring the rest of them for me Matt," she added without looking back.

Abi let out the breath she'd been holding as she watched Matt hesitate for just a second then he stood up and started to stack dishes haphazardly into his arms before following Esther. "Just you and me then," she said to Jamie, punctuating her words with the warmest smile she could muster.

"Careful!" Esther chastised Matt as he half placed, half threw his armful of dishes onto the kitchen counter. He quickly organised them into a neat pile and then turned to look back through the archway where Abi and Jamie still sat at the dining table.

"What do you think they're talking about?" he asked her quietly, eyes squinting as he tried to lip read what Abi was saying. They were only separated by a short distance but the music playing in the background made it impossible to hear the words being spoken.

Esther stopped what she was doing and came and stood beside him. "Oh I don't know. Perhaps they're discussing how morose you've been all evening and how rude you've been to Jamie."

"No I haven't!"

"And don't look at me all innocent in that spectacularly annoying way," she said without looking at him, the hushed tones they'd both adopted doing nothing to lessen the anger in her voice. "As if you being rude to Jamie was the most inconceivable thing in the world when you've been nothing but belligerent and unpleasant all night."

Matt was about to object then remembered it was Esther he was talking to. "He's the morose one. He's barely spoken and when he has, it's either been rude, patronising or provocative. He's the one you should be telling off."

Esther turned around, dragging Matt with her to the furthest point of the kitchen and then she looked at him with

41

pleading eyes. "Please Matt," she said, her voice still hushed. "What's the point of you being around more if the four of us can't even have a civil dinner together? If I'm prepared to give you and Abi a chance then you have to go easy on Jamie. Please? For me?"

Matt turned back towards the table and looked at Jamie. He could only see him side on but everything about the way he sat, the way he held himself, the way he took frequent slow sips from his wine glass, seemed to spell trouble. He sighed.

"Fine."

The sweetness of dessert brought with it a renewed sense of calm and the conversation finally relaxed. Or maybe it was the amount of alcohol consumed that had finally broken down the barriers that had been so firmly in place when they'd first sat down. Jamie was desperate to know the details of the little tête à tête between Esther and Matt that had so deftly changed the mood around the table. The strong connection between them made him uneasy at best.

"I think I'll make a start on the washing up." Jamie stood up and gathering a few bowls, headed to the kitchen. He could only stomach the saccharin-coated chat for so long. A few minutes later, he felt Abi's presence and then watched out of the corner of his eye as she picked up a tea towel and started drying dishes. "I won't put them away," she said to him. "Esther won't be happy if everything's in the wrong place."

"Yes, she does like everything in order." Jamie stole another glance and then offered no further response, happy to let an awkward silence take hold.

"Thanks for tonight," she eventually offered. "It's been a really lovely evening."

Jamie smiled. It seemed the safest option rather than risking actual words. 'Uncomfortable', 'awkward' and 'never to be repeated' would be first out if he let them. Quickly followed by 'isn't it time you left?'. As far as he was concerned, it had been exactly the torturous experience he'd anticipated, believing you'd have to be ridiculously thick-skinned not to notice how stilted and fake the conversation had been, with Esther doing her best to behave like she fully supported the idea of Matt and Abi's blossoming relationship, Abi being overly sycophantic, desperate for the evening to go well and for everyone to be the best of friends, and Matt, typically, giving absolutely nothing away, his steely eyes as impervious as ever. Jamie hoped he had got his contribution just right. Enough to have kept himself out of trouble with Esther, but not so much that Matt might think for one minute he was happy to have him around.

"I'm so pleased Esther's more comfortable with Matt and I being together now." Jamie could feel Abi's eyes on him but made no visible reaction. "And he's really starting to relax and even open up a little," she added. Then another hesitation. "They don't like talking about their past much though do they?" Abi waited again but Jamie said nothing. "Does Esther talk to you about it?"

"About what?" he asked.

"About the past. About their childhood. Their parents. Any of it."

Jamie stopped what he was doing and looked at her. "You ask a lot of questions Abi."

"How's it going in here?" They both turned to see Esther. "You look flushed Abi. You okay?"

Abi smiled. "Too much red wine!"

"Probably time we left then." Matt appeared beside Esther and rested an arm around her shoulders. He kissed her cheek. "Thanks Esty. I really appreciate tonight."

Abi put down the saucepan she'd been drying and as Matt grabbed their coats, she gave Esther a hug. "Thanks Esther. It's been a really lovely evening. And thanks to you too Jamie," she said as Matt returned with her jacket.

Jamie waved a soapy hand in their general direction and was still elbow deep in suds when Esther returned from seeing them out. She joined him at the sink and quietly started to dry the final dishes. They worked in silence and after a few moments, Jamie stopped to look at her. She tentatively glanced up and their eyes met.

"Don't say a word," she said.

Jamie squeezed his lips shut and turned his attention back to the roasting tin in the sink, scrubbing it long past the moment it was clean.

5

Esther gently pulled Matt to the side of the pathway as a wayward toddler came hurtling towards them with his mother in hot pursuit. She smiled. This was her favourite park, filled with sights and sounds that always gave her a beautiful sense of peace, from the squeals of delight from the playground, to the tinkling of teacups and the sounds of chatter and laughter that drifted on the breeze from the café, to the large open spaces that offered room to just breathe. And to be ambling through it in the middle of the afternoon with Matt felt as close to perfect as she'd felt for some time.

"Ironic isn't it that you're living within a few miles and yet I still never see you?"

Matt looked suitably aggrieved. "Yes you do! It's only been a couple of weeks since we were over for dinner. In fact it's been less than that."

"The only thing that hasn't changed is that you still just turn up unannounced and expect me to drop everything."

Matt stopped walking. "If now wasn't a good time you just had to say so."

Esther reached for his arm and gave it a tug, pulling him back into step with her.

"Don't be so sensitive," she said, slipping her hand through his arm. "I'm still adjusting, that's all."

Esther steered them towards a coffee truck and got them both a drink. Getting comfortable having Matt around was proving to be much harder than she could ever have imagined. Of course she loved spending more time with him but there was something awkward about having Abi in the mix now. Time on her own with Matt was so precious but she couldn't help feeling there was something clandestine about it. Esther wondered if Abi knew they were meeting, imagining she wouldn't want them to get together without her in case she missed out on something. As the thought took hold, Esther knew it was ridiculous but forgiving Abi for stealing a huge part of her big brother, and behind her back at that, was something she was finding it particularly difficult to do.

"It makes me really nervous that we still haven't discussed how much of our past is appropriate to share," she said as they settled back into a comfortable rhythm, coffees in hand. "If it's not too late already, can we please at least talk about it?"

"If it matters that much to you then yes, of course we can."

"So what have you already told her?" Esther asked.

"That Dad was violent towards Mum and me. That he went to prison for burglary and while he was inside, Mum died. That Dad moved away when he came out and we lost touch several years ago." He shrugged. "That's about the sum of it."

Esther chose to ignore the edge to his tone and the exaggerated deep breath he'd taken before starting his answer. It all sounded so inconsequential the way he recounted it when the reality was so very different. Matt, beaten within an inch of his life time after time, horrible memories of him whimpering in his sleep, his whole body permanently black and blue and throbbing with pain. Or their mother crying out as she was pummelled and slapped and thrown around like a rag doll. And then, of course, there was the most awful guilt that plagued her every waking moment as she asked herself again and again why, in the midst of all the horrific chaos, had she been left untouched?

"It's more than I've ever told her but thankfully not contradictory in any way," Esther said, snapping herself back to the present. And then her head went down for a moment.

"You okay Esty? I don't understand why it bothers you so much. What are you so worried about?"

Esther slowly looked up at him. "Do you know the first thing I remember when I think back to when Mum died?" Matt shook his head. "Whispering. Constant hushed tones. And secrets. Lots of secrets." She stared at him, searching for anything in his eyes that he knew what she was talking about but he said nothing. "Quiet conversations behind hands between you and Pete," she continued, "that always came to an abrupt end the minute I walked into the room."

"Pete was just there to help, you know that. He may have worked with Dad but he was sympathetic to us too. He was a real friend to us."

"To you, maybe. Not us. As I was never included in the conversations, you can't include me in that."

"Esther you were fourteen years old! However you may remember it, the fact is Pete was a massive support to me. He helped me get everything sorted and back on track."

"But that's just it, isn't it? What is this 'everything' he helped you with? And don't tell me you mean Mum's funeral because we both know there was way more to it than that. Well, you know there was. I, of course, know next to nothing."

They continued their walk in silence. After a while, Esther glanced up at him. His jaw was tightly clenched, his eyes staring straight ahead. She really didn't want things to be uncomfortable between them and so she smiled. "Did you tell Abi what an amazing big brother you were to me? How you looked after me and protected me from…" She stopped for a moment as she remembered. "Well, pretty much everything."

Matt put his arm around her and pulled her close, the bubble of tension duly burst. "You were my reason to keep going."

"And I'll always be so grateful. And what about you? What have you told her about your life since all that happened?"

"As little as I can. Abi said you were heading to Mum's grave yesterday?"

"I've never made a secret of the fact I go there."

"Even after all this time? And it must take you hours to get there and back?"

"The passing of time doesn't mean I miss her any less." Esther shrugged. "I like to talk to her. And the trip takes me half a day or so which never feels like much of a sacrifice."

Matt hesitated for a moment. "I'd like to help you move on if you'll let me?"

"The only thing that will let that happen is knowing what really happened to her."

"It was a heart attack. You know that."

"Do I?"

Esther looked up at Matt in time to see him flinch, his brow furrowed, his expression tight. She felt an all too familiar sorrow wrap itself tightly around her.

They reverted back to silence, a noticeable gap between them now as they walked, the sun slipping unnoticed behind a wall of high rise flats in the distance. Esther shivered as its warmth disappeared along with the brightness it had offered to the afternoon and now slowly withdrew.

"Time to go?" Matt asked her. Esther nodded, leaning into him as he put his arm tightly around her again. "Let's not dwell on the past, Esty. There's nothing to be gained from it."

Well of course that would suit you perfectly, she thought, but she simply smiled by way of an answer.

Esther was finding it difficult to motivate herself and it was only Tuesday. She had a flat that needed some love and attention, a ridiculously long to-do list, an air of lethargy due to a lack of sleep, and a sluggishness that she hadn't been able to shake off since she'd seen Matt a few days ago.

Fuelled by endless mugs of strong coffee, Esther struggled through the morning. She stuffed herself with comfort food at lunchtime which only made her feel even more fatigued and by mid-afternoon, she'd ground to a premature halt. Thinking a walk with Matt would perk her up she reached for her phone to call him but instead of the expected ringing sound, she was greeted by an automated voice informing her that the number was no longer available. She looked at her phone to be sure it was Matt she'd called and his name duly stared back at her so, assuming it must have been some kind of technical glitch she tried again only to once again be greeted by the unwelcome robotic message that the number she was calling was most definitely no longer in use. She ended the call and tried Abi. When she got the same automated response for the third time, Esther was suddenly sitting up straighter than she had all day, her brain now buzzing. What the hell was going on? She put her phone down on the desk in front of her and tried to think rationally. Maybe they'd gone away for the weekend and were in a signal black spot? But then surely her calls would just go straight to voicemail? And wouldn't Matt have mentioned an upcoming trip when she'd seen him? Maybe they'd switched network providers and had new numbers? That seemed plausible, at a stretch. Perhaps the switch had happened quicker than expected, before they'd had time to share their new numbers? Esther shook her head, aware how ridiculous and unlikely that sounded.

She made a cup of tea and then forced herself to get back to some work, convinced she was overthinking what would almost certainly turn out to be something and nothing. She managed to pass an hour or so fiddling with new logo designs for a local book shop but eventually the sense of unease returned and refused to be ignored.

Esther checked her watch and then picked up her phone again. She felt her heart rate start to slowly pick up pace as she tried first Matt and then Abi, the sound of the automated responses now prompting a rather unpleasant feeling deep in her gut.

She drummed her fingers on her desk. What could she do? She didn't know any of Abi's friends well enough to have their numbers and she was pretty sure Matt didn't have any mates of his own. Her mind was frantic but there was no clarity to her thoughts and then, in the absence of any better ideas, she jumped up and flew through the flat, grabbing her bag, keys and jacket as she went, before heading out the front door. She would go over to Abi's place, telling herself as she fidgeted at the bus stop that she would casually pretend she'd been at an impromptu meeting nearby and had just knocked on the off chance one of them would be in, confident that one of them would be. At which point she would silently chastise herself for having behaved so irrationally.

Forty-seven long minutes later, thanks to the usual rush hour chaos, Esther was standing outside Abi's building ringing the bell for flat number seven. The ornate facade and traditionally large windows built expectations of period features but a very fresh modern design waited inside, if only Esther could actually get inside. She buzzed and waited, then buzzed and waited again but there was no response. To her relief, someone with a key then disappeared through the large front door leaving it to slowly swing shut behind them, allowing more than enough time for Esther to slip in as well. As the person in front of her let themselves into one of the ground floor apartments, Esther ran up the stairs two at a time to the first floor landing, walked briskly down the corridor and then finally she was knocking on Abi's door, gently at first and then louder and louder.

Just as she was about to knock again the door opened to reveal a man in a suit.

"Can I help you?" he asked.

"I'm looking for Abi."

"Moved out."

"What do you mean she's moved out?"

The man looked almost as confused as Esther, clearly wondering what was so hard to grasp. "Moved out. Left the building. As in, no longer lives here." He went to shut the door but Esther put her hand out to stop him.

"No, please, just a minute. When did she move out? Do you know where she's gone?"

"I know nothing," he said, irritation slowly building, "other than I've got an inventory to check and a full inspection to complete. Pop into the office. It's Marshall and Ward, just on the next corner. Someone in there will be able to help."

As soon as he was confident Esther wasn't about to thrust another hand or a foot in the path of the door, he slowly closed it. Esther tried not to panic and then she quickly headed back down the stairs. She needed to get to the agent's office before it closed.

Once outside, she weaved her way down the busy pavement as quickly as she could but when she finally reached the large glass door with the names Marshall and Ward elaborately etched into it, it was already locked. The lights were still on and she shook the door handle vigorously in the hope it was just a little stiff. A woman then appeared at the back of the office to see who or what was causing all the noise, her coat already on.

"We're closed," she mouthed to Esther.

"Please," Esther pleaded. "I just need two minutes of your time. No more, I promise."

The woman hesitated for a moment, clearly desperate to say no and then with an exaggerated sigh, she picked up a large bunch of keys and headed to the door. She unlocked it to let Esther in and then quickly locked it again behind her. She didn't want anyone else thinking it was okay to come breezing in when the working day was clearly over.

"Thank you so much, I really appreciate it," Esther said but the woman's hand was already up to stop her.

"Just tell me what you want."

"Abi Wilson. She lived at number 7 James Court, just up the road. Do you know when she moved out? And if she left a forwarding address?"

Again the woman hesitated and then she headed to a filing cabinet. She flicked through a drawer of identical looking files and then stopped, pulling out a wedge of paperwork that she quickly glanced through. "She moved out yesterday." Another pause as she continued to flick. "And no forwarding address I'm afraid."

Esther could feel that rising sense of panic again. "But what about post that arrives? Or if you need to get hold of her if you suddenly find she's damaged something?"

The woman looked at her. "What can I tell you? There's no forwarding address but I'm sure whoever was looking after the letting here will have made sure everything was covered. And it's not as if I'd be able to give you that sort of information in any case. What do you think this is? Some kind of information free for all?" She put the file away and closed the drawer. "Sorry not to be able to help," she said as she headed back to the door. She unlocked it and then stood with it open, waiting for Esther to take the rather unsubtle hint. With a deep sigh Esther thanked her for her time and stepped outside just as the door closed loudly behind her, the sound of the lock turning calling time on the fruitless meeting.

Esther made a quick call to Jamie and then hurried home, her mind whirring, panic now on the verge of overwhelming her. By the time she walked through her own front door, her breathing was shallow, her hands clammy. She threw off her jacket, switched on some lights and then tried to think of something useful she could do. She grabbed the laptop from her office and sat with it in the kitchen. She started searching for phone numbers and within half an hour, she'd called any bar or restaurant she could think of to check if Abi had made a booking or was sitting at the bar. Each time, she told whoever answered the same ridiculous story, that she'd forgotten where she was supposed to meet her friend so would they mind checking their dinner reservations or do a shout out in the bar in case she was already waiting but it was all in vain.

Just as she was struggling to come up with an alternative plan, there was a knock at the door. She scrambled to the hallway and threw open the door only to see Jamie standing there. "Sorry," he said as he watched her shoulders slump. "Only me I'm afraid. I got here as quickly as I could."

He stepped across the threshold and took her in his arms. "It'll be okay," he said as he kissed her head. "They can't just have disappeared."

"That's exactly what's happened," she said as she headed back to the laptop. "This may be the cruellest thing he's ever done to me."

Jamie sat down next to her and took hold of her hand. "And when we find them, this time I'll definitely be punching him very hard in the face, possibly a number of times and I won't be persuaded otherwise." Esther felt her brow furrow and Jamie immediately looked sheepish. "Sorry. Just trying to lighten the mood. How can I help?"

"By not being your normal insensitive self, that's how." Esther watched his cheeks redden, wondering if the sudden spread of crimson was fuelled by embarrassment or anger. She held his eyes for a moment longer and then slowly exhaled, blowing away the temptation to start a fight. She needed to stay focused.

"I'm all out of ideas," she said, her voice strained. "I mean, I didn't even know Abi rented her place. I thought she owned it. I mean why wouldn't she? She earns enough. At least I think she does."

"Have you called her office?"

Esther felt her cheeks flush. "I don't have a work number for her. I always call on her mobile. All I know is she works for a consultancy firm somewhere near Charing Cross. It's not that I didn't ask her about it. She's always said it just wasn't the kind of work that made for interesting conversation so we never really talked about it."

"What's the company called though?" Jamie thought for a moment, struggling to retrieve the correct series of names from deep within his memory, at the same time making a mental note that he really should listen more. "Davies, Bentley and someone else? Or Daniels maybe? Daniels, Bentley and something royal sounding I'm sure." He shook his head. "I can't remember. Daniels, Bentley and Crown?"

Esther sighed. "I'm ashamed to admit I've no idea," she said as she typed Jamie's best guess into a search engine. Nothing even vaguely relevant came up.

"How could I not know?"

"No point beating yourself up about it. Like you said, it's not something she spent any time talking about."

"Can we report them missing?"

"We can, but I just can't see the police getting involved. Two adults who've cancelled their phone contracts, settled up with their letting agent and then left London. There's nothing suspicious about any of it. It looks like they've tied up the loose ends which has to mean leaving was planned. For whatever reason, they just chose not to tell us." He stopped as he watched Esther bite her bottom lip, her eyes swelling with tears. "I know that's really hard to hear love but what other conclusion could there be?"

After a night of tossing and turning, interspersed with terrifying nightmares, Esther was up and about early the next day. Jamie offered to stay with her but she convinced him he should just go to work as normal. She knew she would be twitchy and snappy and she really didn't want to take her angst out on him. He pushed, and then pushed again but the only thing his persistence was achieving was making Esther even more irritable and increasingly angry. Jamie finally admitted defeat and agreeing to meet up with him later, Esther waved him off and headed to Charing Cross.

Coming out of the station and using the map on her phone as a guide, she systematically worked her way around the surrounding streets, her eyes constantly scanning. She searched every face around her, stared through café and restaurant windows and stepped into every doorway to read the names of the companies housed within one building after another. After a couple of hours she stopped for a coffee, sitting outside so she could continue to search and scan passers-by while she gave her feet a break. She bought a large muffin loaded with blueberries but then pushed it away, the fear so alive in her stomach that it swallowed her appetite before she could enjoy a single bite.

Unable to relax, she was quickly up and back at it, pounding pavements, eyes flitting, scouting, scrutinising. Then she peered through the umpteenth doorway and there it was towards the bottom of a list of companies – Daniels, Bentley & Prince. Without hesitation, she pulled open the heavy glass door, striding up to the reception desk with such purpose that the receptionist rolled backwards slightly in her chair.

"Could I see Abi Wilson please? She's with Daniel, Bentley & Prince."

"Do you have an appointment?" the receptionist asked, quickly pulling herself back to her rightful position.

"No, but I'm a friend and it's an extremely urgent matter so if you wouldn't mind calling her for me?"

The receptionist looked at Esther with a fixed smile then scanned the screen in front of her before picking up an internal phone. "Can I have your name please?" she asked as she dialled.

"Esther Harrison."

Esther listened to one side of the conversation, shifting her weight from one foot to the other and then back again. She stopped the minute the call was over.

"Take a seat please Miss Harrison. Someone will be down to see you in a moment."

Esther did as she was told, hoping that the 'someone' would turn out to be Abi. She picked up a magazine and flicked through it, her eyes not really seeing anything but she was grateful for something to do. She put it back and watched a few people come and go, wondering if they were colleagues of Abi's. They all looked very serious so for Abi's sake, she hoped not. Then she picked up another magazine and flicked through it with the same lack of interest or focus.

She was kept waiting for nine very long minutes and then suddenly a man was walking towards her, his face tired but kind looking, his tie a tad squint as if he'd put it on in a hurry. He looked like he was having as bad a day as she was. And then his hand was coming towards her.

"Miss Harrison?"

Esther nodded as she took his hand. He had a firm grip and she felt her body tremble as he shook it. "I'm Adrian Williams. I work with Abi."

"Oh," Esther said, her disappointment obvious. "So she's not here then?"

"I'm afraid not, no." Adrian gestured for Esther to sit down again as he took the seat opposite.

"Has she been in the office at all recently? I haven't been able to get hold of her and to be honest, I'm really worried about her."

"That puts us firmly in the same boat then I'm afraid. She hasn't been in the office for a few days now so I'd hoped you might have some information for me."

Esther felt her shoulders slump.

"Miss Harrison?"

Esther looked up. "I'm sorry. I indulged myself for a moment there that the nightmare was about to be over. And it's Esther, please."

"Has something happened?" Adrian asked. "You don't have to tell me if you don't want to, not if it's personal," he quickly added, "it's just not like her to slip completely off the radar."

Esther paused for just a moment and then decided she had nothing to lose. "She hasn't just slipped off your radar. She's gone completely AWOL. She's a friend of mine but she's also in a relationship with my brother and they've just disappeared. I tried calling both of them yesterday and their phones had been disconnected. I went to her flat and there was some random bloke there who said they'd moved out so I went to the letting agency but they couldn't shed any light either. They apparently left on Monday night but didn't leave a forwarding address."

"This man in her flat," Adrian asked. "Do you know who he was?"

"Said he was doing an inspection so I thought he was from the letting agency but now that you mention it, I didn't actually ask him who he was. Why?"

"No reason," he said with a smile. "Quite the detective aren't you?"

"Well I couldn't just do nothing. I thought about calling the police but as my boyfriend pointed out, it all looks too planned to report them missing. I just don't understand why they didn't tell me they were leaving." Esther took a deep breath as a few rogue tears filled her eyes. Their presence made her stand up. "I've taken up enough of your time. Thanks for seeing me though. I really appreciate it."

"If you do hear from her, would you mind letting me know?" Adrian stood up too and took a notebook out of his pocket. She watched him write his name and number on a piece of paper and then tear it out of the book.

"Sorry about the scrappy bit of paper," he said as he gave it to her. "I'm temporarily out of business cards."

Esther took it from him and then rummaged in her bag for a card of her own. "Perhaps you could return the favour?" she asked, as she handed it over.

"Of course." Adrian smiled at her. "Take care now won't you Esther."

Accepting there was nowhere else for her to look, the next day Esther forced herself back to work. It was a distraction if nothing else but it didn't stop her jumping every time her phone rang, hoping it might be Adrian with some news or, better still, Matt or Abi. To hear one of their voices would be such a relief provided, of course, they had a bloody good excuse for putting her through such hell.

She limped through Thursday and then just as she'd settled herself at her desk on Friday morning, there was a seemingly innocent knock at the door. She opened it to reveal two women who quickly identified themselves as police officers, Detective Sergeant Jane Campbell and Detective Constable Eva Carpenter.

"Would it be okay if we came in for a moment?" the older one asked.

"Of course," Esther said, stepping out of the way to let them in. "Go straight through to the lounge." And then she hesitated. "Actually, would you mind just telling me why you're here?"

The two women stopped and turned around to face her. "Are you sure you wouldn't prefer to sit down?" the younger office asked her.

Esther gulped. "No, whatever it is, please just tell me."

"I'm afraid we found the body of a young woman this morning." It was the Detective Sergeant who spoke now. "She had a mobile phone in her possession that only had one number stored in it which we traced back to you. There was no identification so, as it stands, we don't know who she is." She paused for just a moment. "We wondered if you would be prepared to come with us to see if you can identify her?"

Esther closed her eyes as the colour drained from her face. "Abi," she mouthed, unsure if the word had actually sounded, her head immediately swimming with horrific pictures of Abi laid out on a cold hard slab somewhere. She put a hand out to steady herself.

DC Carpenter immediately stepped forward and gently took hold of Esther's arm. "Do you need to sit down now Miss Harrison? Or I could make us a cup of tea?"

"No, it's okay thank you, I'm fine," Esther said, giving herself a little shake. "Do you know what happened to her?"

"She was shot," the Detective Sergeant said, her colleague wincing at her directness.

Esther felt her mouth fall open slightly. She had heard and understood the words but was unable to make sense of them. "What do you mean she was shot?"

"Are you sure you wouldn't like that cup of tea?" DC Carpenter asked again.

"No, thank you. In fact, let's just go," Esther said. "I need to know who it is." And picking up her keys, she headed straight out the door waiting for the officers to catch on and follow her.

They drove through miserable rainy streets but Esther was numb to the cold. She was vaguely aware of reassuring voices but she heard nothing, lost in a trance, caught between never wanting to reach their destination and feeling desperate just to know if it was Abi. But the torment was short-lived. It was only a brief journey and all too soon Esther found herself in a soulless room looking at the lifeless shape of a body lying on a table beneath a bright white sheet. DS Campbell walked confidently to the far side of the table and waited but Esther couldn't move. It took all her effort to force one foot forward where it waited patiently for the other one to join it. Then another small shuffle forward with one foot and a beat before the other one again reluctantly joined it.

"Here, take my arm."

Esther looked to her side to see DC Carpenter standing next to her, her arm held firmly up like an imitation support rail. Esther took a strong hold, aware of some comforting words floating somewhere close as she continued to slowly move forward. And then she stopped. She was still a metre or so from the table but that was as close as her feet were prepared to take her.

Esther held her breath, heart pounding, palms sweating, eyes fixed and staring as DS Campbell leant across the table and pulled the sheet back to reveal the face of her dear friend. Or was it? Abi's complexion wasn't pale and waxen, her hair wasn't lacklustre and flat, her lips didn't have a purplish hue. Esther stood in disbelief, clinging to a denial that was already slipping away from her. She looked again and she gasped.

Do you know who she is Esther?" DS Campbell asked her.

Esther simply nodded.

"Why don't we give you a moment?" DC Carpenter headed for the door and held it open until DS Campbell followed her.

As the door gently closed behind them, Esther stood where she was for a moment, her head tilted backwards, eyes fixed on the ceiling. And then she let out a cry. A tortured, painful wail as the reality of what was happening, and the fear of not knowing why, took hold of her with a vice-like grip. She forced herself to look at Abi. She touched, stroked and held a cold hand, her heart breaking. And then she cried.

Esther was terrified of leaving Abi. It would feel like turning her back on her forever and she simply didn't feel strong enough to make such a definitive move. It subsequently took several gentle attempts before DC Carpenter was finally able to persuade Esther that it was time to go, taking her home and delivering her into the arms of Jamie. He had raced to the flat the minute the police had called him and now held Esther so incredibly tightly as if trying to literally hold her together.

Esther's silent tears dampened his shoulder. "I know love, I know," he whispered, keeping his arms firmly wrapped around her until she finally let her body relax. "Come on, I'll make some tea," he said, steering her towards the sofa before heading to the kitchen. "With a large whisky to wash it down," he added over his shoulder.

As he joined her a few moments later, Esther took in the contents of the tray he placed in front of her – a mug of tea, a glass of whisky, a large bar of chocolate and a selection of biscuits. She reached straight for the whisky, downing it in a single gulp. Jamie was immediately on his feet and heading back to the kitchen, returning a few moments later with the bottle. He poured her another and she downed that too. Esther watched him hesitate for just a second and then he poured her a third. This time she sat back with the glass in her hand and took just a sip, her senses duly anaesthetised. She was aware of Jamie watching her as they sat in an eerie silence, unspoken questions waiting to be asked.

"You okay?" he said the moment she lifted her head high enough for their eyes to meet.

"I don't know what to think," she said, her voice small and vulnerable.

"What did the police tell you?"

"They didn't know much at all. They didn't even know who she was. They just got my number from a phone left in her pocket. It was all so shocking I couldn't think straight so they're coming to talk to me tomorrow."

"Well I won't be leaving your side that's for sure."

"What the hell happened Jamie? Someone shot her! Someone pointed a gun at her and shot her dead. Who would do that? Why would they do that?"

"I have no idea. But I'm here for you, you know that don't you?" Esther did her best to pull off a smile but was aware of her left eye twitching.

"Esther, what is it?"

"Where the hell is Matt?"

PART TWO

6

Two months earlier

When the door to Esther's flat opened to reveal Matt, Abi's only worry was that she might immediately give herself away, so jubilant was she to finally see him in the flesh. She was tempted to prod him to check he was real although he appeared real enough, his eyes sharp and alert with just a tantalising hint of mischief. The immediate adrenalin rush was so staggering she felt herself rock backwards slightly, senses on high alert, a knot of nervous excitement in her gut.

"You're not who I was hoping to see," she said, loving the fact the joke was totally lost on him.

"Well I'm very sorry to disappoint," he said, that hint of mischief slowly starting to engage. "I'm Matt, Esther's brother. Esther's not back yet but you're welcome to come in and wait for her."

"Her brother? Well aren't you an unexpected surprise!"

Matt looked at her for a moment, his eyes suddenly narrowed. "And you are?"

"Abi," she said as she stepped inside. "And a glass of wine would be lovely, thank you. And then you can tell me all about yourself."

Abi had been desperate to let her team know that Matt had finally shown himself but she'd been forced to wait a couple of hours until she was half way through dinner with Esther before she could share the momentous news. The minute Esther made a trip to the toilet, Abi had grabbed her phone and sent a brief message to a WhatsApp group called Tuesday Yoga. "Def see you for next session. Will be bringing a friend." A huge smile had spread across her face as she'd typed, her nervous energy barely containable, knowing that a flurry of pings would now be sounding around London followed by a series of eyes popping, faces flushing and anticipation rising. Eleven months undercover and she'd finally been able to send the agreed message that would let everyone know they were game on.

In the briefing room the next morning the excitement was palpable. Abi had been in the office super early and was already seated at the front of the room when her colleagues started to filter in on a wave of high fives, fist bumps, loud whistles and even the odd cheer. They were a small but noisy bunch.

"Okay, okay, that's enough." The unit's boss, Detective Inspector Liz Baker, entered last and the room immediately fell quiet as she strode to the front. Everything about her was efficient. The short hair that required minimum attention. The plain navy suit and white shirt, the sturdy navy brogues, the reusable coffee cup, all perfectly reflected her no frills, no-nonsense approach. "Right, let's get started," she said turning to Abi. "Why don't you fill us in? This is the first time the team's been together for a while and we've got some new members so it would be good to start with a brief resumé of the story so far."

Abi stood up. "This is Matt Harrison," she said pointing at a picture at the centre of a large white board. "He's the son of Dave Harrison," she added, pointing this time to a picture to the right of Matt. "Dave Harrison did time for a professionally planned commercial robbery but that was twenty odd years ago. His wife shopped him but he had a smart lawyer who shot holes in the key evidence and got him to invoke marital privilege which meant his wife couldn't testify so despite running the operation, his sentence was ridiculously short and he was out in around three years. It was thought she was a victim of domestic violence but she couldn't be persuaded to press charges. Too proud, maybe." Abi paused for a moment. "Anyway, there were all sorts of rumours at the time of Dave's trial of jury tampering and possible bribes but, without proof, nothing could be done. He completed his probation period and then went to ground and no one's seen him for years which is why the picture we've got is so out of date. But, despite his elusiveness, there's been plenty of chatter and we're convinced he's been responsible for a whole host of stuff since, we've just never been able to prove it. It's been predominantly highly planned robberies but also assaults of varying severity. There are some who believe lives may have been lost along the way, either directly or indirectly, including that of his wife who died while he was in prison." Abi paused for a moment. She'd got to know Esther well enough that saying that out loud choked her slightly. She took a deep breath. "He commands incredible loyalty from his nearest and dearest and became über careful from the minute his prison stint was over. Whatever he's threatening people with to ensure they don't turn on him is clearly far worse than any punishment we can administer. The robberies over the last few years have been highly sophisticated which is where Matt comes in. He's a tech genius and seems to be able to hack his way in anywhere. The problem is that most of the companies they've targeted online don't want their customers to know they were rendered vulnerable so the crimes rarely get reported. Just another reason why Dave Harrison has been so hard to catch out."

"So this operation, as most of you know, is part of a wider drive to infiltrate organised crime groups," DI Baker interjected. "The aim is to not just nibble at the ankles of an organisation but obliterate it all the way to the very top. Dave Harrison heads up a substantial gang so suffice to say the potential here is huge." She paused to let that sink in and then turned back to Abi. "Sorry Abi, back to you."

"The aim was to get in at the bottom of the food chain, gain trust and move up from there," Abi continued. "Matt was on our entry hit list, mainly because there's no violence in his past that we know of and therefore he felt like the safest way in but, as it turned out, it was his sister, Esther, where it all started," Abi said, pointing back to the white board to the picture on Matt's left. "We'd been keeping a lazy eye on her for a while and I took the chance to approach her at a craft fair where she was selling some of her paintings. We seemed to hit it off so I used it as an opportunity to start a relationship with her."

There was a wolf whistle from the back of the room followed by a few childish giggles. "For fuck's sake Tim," DI Baker shouted. "Do that again and I'll have you put on one of HR's 'how to stop being a complete knobhead when it comes to dealing with women' courses. And if you think I made that up you can look it up on the station's intranet."

DI Baker nodded at Abi to carry on while a scolded Tim sat uncomfortably with his head down. "That was almost a year ago," Abi went on, "and I'm now fully immersed in Esther's life but despite how close we've become, she's incredibly closed off about talking about her past other than a few snippets – violent father, dead mother – but there'd been no mention at all of a brother. It's been a long wait but he turned up at her place last night completely out of the blue and we had half an hour or so on our own before Esther got home. I didn't want to bombard him with questions so can only hope my flirting was sufficient enough to mean he'll stick around for a while."

"No opinions required thank you!" the DI bellowed in response to a flurry of loud whispers. "Great work, Abi, thank you," she said, her voice now returned to a more normal level. "Right everyone. Time to get focused. Tim?"

"Yes Guv."

"Make sure the office set up for Abi's cover is watertight. Check that Daniels, Bentley & Prince is still on display alongside the other companies in the building. And who gets the calls?"

"I do Guv."

"Great, well someone test it and make sure Sarah answers it correctly," she said with an encouraging wink in the direction of the team's newest recruit. "Abi, make sure you always enter and leave through the cover entrance from now on please. We can't afford to get caught out now by silly mistakes. And get tech to make sure your laptop has suitable emails and documents on it in case you get close enough to Matt that he decides to take a look. Ade, you head up the surveillance on Matt. Now that we've found him, I want permanent eyes on him so get over to Esther's place straight away. Anything else?" She scanned the room. "No? Okay, I don't need to remind you we've waited a long time for this moment so let's stay sharp people. Dave Harrison is an extremely dangerous man and we need him off the streets." A brief pause to make sure that statement had been heard and understood. "So what are you waiting for?"

The room burst into life, the break they'd been waiting for energising every member of the team.

"Not you Abi!" the DI shouted above the noise as Abi went to leave the room. Abi immediately turned back to face DI Baker. "A word please," she said, signalling to her office next door.

Abi followed her out of one room and into the next. "Sit down," the DI told her. Abi did as she was told and waited for her boss to take the seat opposite her. "So we need to talk about how your relationship with Matt might develop," she said, not wasting any time on niceties.

"We covered this already didn't we?"

"But it's actually happening now so I want to go over the guidelines one more time. We always knew this was going to be a tricky one but I am absolutely not authorising you to have an intimate relationship with him. Is that clear?"

"Yes Guv."

"That said, sex can be justified if refusal to take part could jeopardise your safety. But if it happens, what must you do?"

"Report it to you straightaway Guv." Abi's hands suddenly felt very clammy. She was immediately reminded of watching sex scenes on the television with her parents in the room and then quickly decided this was actually a great deal worse.

"I need you to be sensible and stick to the rules. Your goal is to take the relationship slowly and get results quickly. Can you do that?"

"Yes Guv, I can."

When Abi left work that night, she took a lift to the ground floor then, instead of leaving through the main entrance, she went to the back of the reception area, punched in a code on the keypad beside a plain door and crossed into the reception area of the serviced offices behind the police station. Her eyes scanned the huge sign behind the reception desk listing the companies that were in residence which included Daniels, Bentley & Prince, a fake company used when required for undercover officers like herself. Its name was chosen for its adaptability so that the officer involved could pretty much determine the nature of its services to suit their own experience. So far it had been a firm of accountants, of team of architects and a creative agency but for the foreseeable future, Abi had decided it would be a business consultancy, confident she could sound knowledgeable enough if necessary thanks to a business studies module taken as part of her degree course. The aim was to keep the lie as simple as possible so there were no social media accounts and no company website, just a holding page explaining an update was underway and any visitors should check back soon. In whatever guise it was used, it was always a small outfit that the officers involved would claim traded on reputation and personal recommendations with no need for any noisy marketing.

As she stepped outside, she stood for a moment to let the cool evening air sweep over her. The heating in the office was either on or off with nothing in between and it had felt particularly stuffy today so the light chill that greeted her was very welcome indeed. After a few calming moments, she was about to set off for the tube station when her phone rang. It was Ade.

"Did you tell Matt where you worked?"

"I might have mentioned I commute in and out of Charing Cross. Why?"

"We weren't at Esther's long before he was on the move and we've followed him back here. He's loitering near the underground station."

"Wow. I'm clearly much better at flirting than I realised!"

"Circle round a bit and approach from the left otherwise you'll miss him."

Abi did as Ade told her and when she stopped to cross the final road before reaching the station, there was Matt standing on the opposite side, smiling and now waving at her. When the traffic lights changed, Matt was first off the mark so Abi waited where she was for him to reach her, instinctively clenching her stomach muscles to crush the sudden influx of unwanted butterflies. She felt her face flush with the effort, overwhelmed by a feeling unlike anything she'd ever experienced. She was reminded of a time she'd stumbled across a film crew in a quiet London street and had stopped for a moment, transfixed by the excitement of it all. "Camera rolling!" she had heard someone cry, quickly followed by a very assertive, "Action!" She heard those words in her head now and channelling her inner actress, she slipped into character, held his eyes and smiled.

"Matt! What are you doing here?"

"I have a nasty habit of turning up when I'm least expected."

"So, what are you doing here?" she asked again.

"I just wondered if you'd like to grab a drink?"

She smiled at him. "There's a really good bar just a street or so away."

Matt gestured for her to lead the way and within a few minutes they had settled themselves at a table and ordered some drinks. It was a comfortable place with laid-back staff, the wooden tables and upholstered chairs positioned to create a sense of space, and the music set at just the right volume to create an atmosphere while still making conversation easy. Matt sat opposite her but was immediately leaning forward, the subtle scent of his cologne caressing Abi's nose. She watched as he turned up the cuffs of his shirt, worn over a plain white t-shirt, making two neat folds in each sleeve. His hair was thick and blonde and it fell forward as he worked, forming a veil over his eyes. He pushed it to one side to reveal their familiar colour, a green that married the brightness of an emerald with the depth of the most intense forest. They were the one feature that irrefutably connected him to Esther. Satisfied his cuffs were neat and symmetrical, Matt took the first long sip of his drink.

"So how did you know where to find me?" Abi asked. "Or was running into me just a bizarre coincidence?"

"I remembered you mentioning Charing Cross station when you talked about work. I was nearby so thought it was worth hanging out there for a while just in case you were heading home. I'd forgotten how busy it gets though so I can't actually believe I found you."

"Well I'm glad you did." Abi smiled, aware that without Ade's intervention, he absolutely wouldn't have. She also noted how easily he lied about being in the area.

Matt looked back at her with a real intensity. "Yeah, so am I."

Abi held his stare, ignoring the prickling heat that irritated her neck. "So what brought you into town today?"

"Oh nothing much."

"Well something brought you nearby?" Abi narrowed her eyes slightly, her mouth curling into a wry smile. "I promise not to tell."

"The only interesting thing about my day is that it brought me here to this bar with you." Abi held her breath as he leant in even further, his eyes wide and hypnotic. And then he picked up her empty glass. "Fancy another?"

A couple of hours flew by unchecked and then Matt started repeatedly checking his watch, his relaxed demeanour ebbing away with every glance. Abi was just about to ask him if he needed to be somewhere when he cut in ahead of her. "I'm really sorry but I'm going to have to go," he said before draining his glass. "I'll see you again though?"

Abi smiled. "I'd like that."

Standing up, he bent down and kissed her gently on the cheek. "I'm so sorry to just run out on you but I'll see you soon," he said quietly into her ear.

Before Abi could ask when, where and at what time, he was already walking away from her.

Despite the lack of plans to meet up again, Abi couldn't believe she was off to such a great start so when Ade called her that night to let her know they'd already lost Matt, it was impossible not to fly into a panic. She just felt so stupid! She'd let him walk away from her without even getting his number and who knew how long it would be before he reappeared?

Esther was her only hope but when Abi turned up unannounced at Esther's flat the next day, loaded with lunch for them both, there was no sign of Matt there either. To discover that he'd disappeared without a word felt like a physical blow to the stomach.

When Abi confessed that she'd seen Matt the previous night, Esther's anguish was obvious. "I just knew something like this would happen!" she cried at Abi.

Abi watched Esther, her body language screaming how distressed she clearly was and, in that moment, Abi suddenly understood what it must be like for her to have her beloved brother appear from nowhere, seemingly without a care in the world, and then disappear again just as abruptly with no warning, no explanation, and without any means of contacting him once he'd gone.

Abi immediately softened, her own frustration now swallowed by the compassion she felt for Esther.

"You thought it was him at the door didn't you?" she asked, wincing as Esther explained that yes, she'd hoped he was back so they could have a well-needed chat.

Abi did her best to reassure Esther that the only reason she was there was to surprise her with a lovely lunch, and that seeing Matt again would just have been an unexpected bonus. She then focused hard on keeping the conversation moving and the atmosphere light and was hugely relieved that they parted with any awkwardness banished. She had to keep at least one of her Harrison relationships on track or her special ops career was as good as over before it had even started. She would be the perfect friend, other than adhering to Esther's parting plea that she should quickly walk away should Matt turn up to meet her again. There was absolutely no way she would be doing that.

For the next week or so Abi remained vigilant, often doing an extra loop around Esther's flat and the office too, all in the hope that she might suddenly spot Matt again. See him bounce towards her with a huge smile on his face saying that he'd been trying desperately to get in touch with her but must have written her number down wrongly. But then he hadn't actually asked for her number. She even got into the habit of approaching the station from the same direction she'd bumped into him that first time, basically doing anything she could think of to increase the chances of another encounter.

At work she had no choice but to carry on playing her part in other ongoing cases while she waited for her own leading role to be back in play, working hard, as she did so, to keep her relationship with Esther on track. Esther had been slightly cold for at least a week after lunch-gate and it had taken some careful handling to slowly warm her up again. Then just when she'd convinced herself that Matt had surely gone forever, Abi left the office one evening and there he was, standing outside the train station again, leaning against a wall without a care in the world. She tried to ignore it but she knew her heart had just sprouted wings and taken flight, tickling her chest until she coughed. She felt her cheeks flush, quickly telling herself the physical reaction was nothing more than adrenalin and the thrill of the operation being on again, and absolutely nothing at all to do with how instinctively happy she was to see him again. Abi stood where she was as Matt looked up. She could already feel the warmth of his smile as he walked over to meet her.

"Hi Abi," he said as he kissed her cheek.

"Hello stranger," she replied, immediately aware of his hand on her arm.

Matt looked at her through smiling eyes. "I did say I'd see you again and I'm always true to my word. Fancy some dinner?"

Abi looked at him for a moment. It wouldn't do to give in too easily but then allowing him to think she wasn't interested was a far riskier game to play. "Sounds great," she said, taking the hand he was now offering.

"Then I know just the place," he said, leading her away.

After a brief walk, Matt stopped at a small intimate French restaurant and as they settled at a quiet table, Abi took a moment to reacquaint herself with this most intriguing man. His hair was hiding his eyes again as he studied the menu giving her plenty of time to explore the scar on his chin and another one that sat high on his left cheek. She'd noticed them last time and had spent many a quiet moment since wondering how he'd got them. This was definitely a man who had been in a few scrapes which reminded her how little she still knew about him, no thanks to Esther who guarded their past like a national secret.

"I take it you've decided what you're having as you have so much time to stare at me?" Matt looked up at her through his fringe and smiled as Abi turned a delicate shade of crimson.

"You really are a total pain in the arse aren't you?"

Matt shrugged. "Loveable at the same time though, don't you think?"

Abi raised her eyebrows and was grateful for the arrival of a waiter, relieving her of the need to find a suitable retort.

With their orders given, Abi paused for just a moment to enjoy a few sips of wine and then decided to just jump in. "So where've you been?"

"Just around. Nowhere special."

"Doing what?"

He shrugged. "This and that."

Abi sighed. "What is it about your family? Did your parents spend hours teaching you how to be evasive? How to avoid the most simple of questions?"

Abi's tone was pitched to make it clear she was only playing with him but she needed to find a way to get him to open up. Having lost him once already, she was keen not to let the evening go by without having something useful to report back. She felt her heart start to quicken as she watched Matt's expression change. He seemed to struggle for a moment as painful memories stirred before he looked up, his eyes suddenly serious.

"Actually, my father spent most of his time beating the hell out of me, and my mother too, so conversation of any kind wasn't really our family's strong point. And then my mother died and I'm afraid any notion of keeping communication channels open was buried along with her."

"Matt, I'm so sorry," Abi gasped. "Esther mentioned your dad was aggressive on occasion but I had no idea how bad it was but she did tell me your mother died so that was incredibly insensitive of me." She reached for his hand. "I really am very sorry."

He smiled at her. "No need. It was all a very long time ago."

"Esther's clearly not comfortable talking about her past. Or her family in general to be honest."

"Clearly! You didn't even know I existed!"

Abi squeezed the hand she was still holding. "That must have been strange for you?"

He shrugged. "It was a bit of a blow if I'm honest. I've spent years protecting her from…" And then he stopped.

"Protecting her from what?" Abi held her breath. She watched him stare into the distance for a moment, clocked the increased blinking like the shutters on a camera as if he was mentally scrolling through one image after another, each one more disturbing than the last.

"Matt?" He slowly brought his gaze back to rest on her. "Protecting Esther from what?"

He gave himself a shake and smiled. "This conversation is getting way too serious for my liking!" He turned to look for the waiter. "What's happened to our food?"

Abi sat back and tried to squash her disappointment that she'd smashed into a conversational brick wall so quickly.

"Ah, here it comes!" Matt turned back to face her with a wide smile as the waiter placed two plates of delicious looking food in front of them.

"Wow, this looks amazing," she said, her smile mirroring his own. "See you on the other side!"

They tucked in, the conversation light-hearted and once again sprinkled with just the right amount of flirtation. When every last mouthful had been devoured, Abi slumped back in her chair, clutching at her swollen stomach. "I can't believe I just ate all that."

"Neither can I! You must have hollow legs."

Abi laughed. "Not anymore I don't!"

"So do you want some dessert or is that pained expression on your face an admission of defeat?"

"No room for anything else I'm afraid."

"Come on then, I'll see you home."

Matt insisted on paying the bill and a few moments later they stepped outside. Abi shivered and Matt immediately put his arm around her as they headed for the nearest station. A shaky old tube train that rattled and rolled on the tracks made conversation impossible so they sat in an enforced silence for the ten stops it took to get them within a short walk of Abi's flat.

"Well, here we are," she said as they reached the door of her building. "I think I could manage a coffee now if you fancy coming in?"

A spontaneous smile burst across Matt's face. "Sounds good to me."

Abi opened the door and Matt followed her across the entrance hall, up a short flight of stairs, along a corridor and then finally into her flat. She turned the lights on to reveal what was essentially one really large loft-style room with stripped floorboards covered in places by huge rugs in deep, rich colours. There was lots of open brickwork and it was all framed by two enormous windows and dramatically high ceilings. The two sofas that faced each other were dark blue and sat around a low wooden coffee table, matched in style by a dining table in the far corner opposite an open plan kitchen, a carefully placed breakfast bar separating it from the rest of the room. The space was then peppered with a careful collection of items from a set of ornate candlesticks on the fireplace, to a beautifully elegant chair beneath one of the windows, to a vase that sat proudly on the dining table. There were two doors on the side of the room, one leading to the bedroom, the other to the bathroom, both presented with the same taste and style.

"How do you like your coffee?" she asked, heading straight for the kitchen.

Matt took off his jacket as he followed her and then sat on one of the stools at the breakfast bar. "White please. No sugar."

"Coming right up."

"This place is amazing," he said, his eyes slowly taking it all in.

"Thanks. It works well for me."

"Own or rent?"

"Rent." Abi grabbed some mugs from one cupboard and a milk jug from another while she waited for the coffee machine to wake up. "What about you?" she asked, glancing over at him as the machine finally decided it was ready to go, raising her voice slightly to be heard above the chugging and gurgling as she made the coffee.

"I love the idea of buying and settling somewhere but I haven't worked out where that should be yet. So how long have you and Esther been friends?"

His ability to seamlessly steer the spotlight away from himself was mind-blowing but Abi let it go. Instead she thought for a moment before answering his question, putting down two mugs of coffee and making one last trip for a bottle of Amaretto and two glasses before sitting on the stool next to him. "Almost a year I think." She held up the bottle as she spoke and Matt nodded his reply. "We met at a craft fair. Her stall was overrun, obviously, so I stepped in to help," she told him as she poured, and then pushed a glass towards him. She shrugged. "We just clicked. You know that way you do sometimes when you just immediately get someone, when it's just really easy with no effort required at all. It already feels like we've been friends for much longer."

There was a pause while Matt took a moment to enjoy his coffee-liqueur combo, giving Abi the chance to keep going. "So are you ever going to tell me what you do with your time or is it to remain one of life's great mysteries?"

Matt smiled. "There's no mystery really. I was always fascinated by computers and coding. It was the only subject I paid any attention to at school and then I'd shut myself away as soon as I got home, building programmes and just messing around really. I spent any money I could get my hands on on new equipment, constantly upgrading my kit. Over time I developed quite a skill for it and became a bit of a….." He hesitated for a moment. "I suppose the only word to use is hacker."

Abi's eyes widened. "You mean breaking into people's systems?"

Matt laughed. "'Fraid so. I never did anything bad. I just enjoyed being able to take on a firewall and win. It gave me a feeling of power." He thought for a moment. "It was the first time I'd ever felt in control of anything and it was a feeling I really liked so I kept going, slowly getting better, faster and smarter."

Abi looked at him with a wry smile. "I'm not sure I want to hear what's coming next."

"No, stick with me, it gets better! I met this guy a few years ago in a bar, one of those chance meetings, and he said he had terrible problems with his computer system at work, a virus he thought, so I said I'd take a look. It took me a few days but I cracked the problem. Then I realised people were prepared to pay ridiculous amounts of money to have similar problems solved. Before long, my name and number were being passed around and it all kind of grew from there. The work became pretty constant and I just went with the flow."

"It sounds really exciting."

He winked at her. "Keeps me out of trouble."

Abi seriously doubted that. Actually she didn't doubt it at all. She knew for a fact that the truth was the complete opposite. His computer prowess was what kept him *in* trouble. It was bizarre hearing him spout half-truths, bits of what he was saying falling somewhere vaguely close to honesty, the rest a great fat pack of lies. They suspected his computer wizardry was used primarily to disarm alarm systems as well as hacking bank accounts, intercepting emails, tapping phones and accessing voice mails. The potential list of chargeable offences was endless but what mattered was that he was talking to her. She had never imagined Matt would open up about himself so much in one long outburst, even if it was as much fiction as fact.

"I suppose that would explain why you're never in the same place for long?"

"Something like that, yeah. Different job, different location."

"So where's home?"

"Nowhere really."

"You must have a base somewhere?"

Matt attempted a smile but it was obvious he was starting to feel uncomfortable with all the questions so he leant forward and kissed her. A soft, gentle kiss that rendered Abi completely helpless. His hands were immediately on her face, his touch warm and delicate. Instinctively she reciprocated, leaning closer, her hands reaching for his shoulders, her only thought that she didn't want him to stop.

When finally they pulled apart, their eyes remained locked together. Abi felt the most discreet shiver ripple down her back. A connection had definitely been made and not just on the surface. The physical attraction was obvious but already she felt it went deeper than that. The shiver rippled back up again making the hairs on the back of her neck stand to attention. And then she had a decision to make. And fast. He had no base of his own to go back to so if she let him leave, where would he go? The answer was she would have no idea where and she simply couldn't risk losing him again.

"So are you planning to do another vanishing act or can I persuade you to stay the night?"

Matt smiled at her. "No persuasion necessary."

"Promise me you won't go without leaving your number."

"Abi, stop it! You really are going to have to learn to trust me."

"Esther said she hadn't seen or heard from you for the best part of a year. You can't blame me for being just a little wary."

Matt kissed her again. They had talked enough for one night.

Abi had no idea what time they had finally given into sleep. She'd only been aware that her body was exhausted, her mind was alive and the level of adrenalin coursing through her body was making her heart beat dangerously fast which had kept her awake long after Matt had drifted into a peaceful slumber. That, and thoughts of the conversation she knew she now had to have with DI Baker.

When she woke the next morning, panic swallowed the immediate feeling of warm contentment in one ugly gulp as she slowly took in the empty space beside her. She sat up with a jolt and then grabbing for a t-shirt that she clumsily pulled over her head, she was out of her bedroom in three large strides. And then she stopped, immediately trying to look casual and relaxed as she saw Matt on the sofa, engrossed in a phone call. As he saw her, he smiled and bringing the call to an abrupt end, he quickly slipped the mobile back into his pocket and put out his hand to her. As she reached him, he pulled her onto his lap and kissed her.

"Good morning. Did you sleep well?" he asked her, his arms now folded around her.

"Yes but not for long enough. What time is it?"

Matt looked at his watch. "Just after seven."

"Who on earth were you talking to at this time of the morning?"

"No-one important."

She smiled. "Coffee?"

"Or we could go back to bed?"

Abi stood up. "Some of us have regular day jobs I'm afraid," she said as she headed to the kitchen. "What are your plans today?"

"I've got a meeting later and then depending on how that goes I may need to go away for a few days at the end of the week but until then, I'll just be kicking my heels." Walking over to join her, Matt sat at the breakfast bar, watching her while she made them coffee. "Maybe I could hang out here?"

Abi stopped what she was doing and looked at him. "Just for today? Or stay here till you go away? And won't Esther be expecting you?"

"Esther doesn't know I'm back yet but I was thinking I could stay here till I go away. But only if you want me to?"

Abi smiled at him, her mouth suddenly very dry. "Stay as long as you like."

Two hours later Abi was sitting in DI Baker's office for an update.

"Well that's quite a turn of events," DI Baker said once Abi had filled her in, her expression giving nothing away.

"It's been incredibly frustrating since we lost him but I really feel like he's interested in me enough to stay put for a while which will give us all the time we need to gather significant intel," Abi rattled off.

DI Baker looked at her, really studied her and Abi felt herself start to fidget. She immediately then focused on nothing but sitting still. Now more than ever, she needed to hold her nerve.

"Well that may be true," DI Baker eventually said, "but you've presented me with quite a dilemma."

"But I had no choice!" Abi said with earnest. "And surely this is the best possible outcome? It may be unorthodox but tracking him will be so much easier while he's staying with me."

"Unorthodox." DI Baker said the word slowly, letting it just float between them for a moment while she ruminated. "It's quite a bit more than that don't you think? By having sex with him you've put yourself in an incredibly grey area where the rules are concerned. So much so that I'm going to have to take advice." Abi's eyes widened. She might as well take out a bloody ad in a national newspaper just to be sure no one missed the news she'd slept with Matt. "And if we're allowed to move forward," the DI continued, "I imagine some time constraints will be put on us, along with some guarantees that your contact with Matt will be terminated the minute we get close enough to reel Dave in."

DI Baker continued to study Abi while she spoke. Every few words caused a physical reaction that Abi was simply unable to control. A blink, a bite of her lip, a rub of her nose.

"Are you okay Abi?"

Abi pushed her hair behind her ear, only to shake it free then immediately place it back there again. "I'm fine. Absolutely fine. I'm just finding this all a little awkward."

"I'm sure I don't need to remind you that the counselling sessions are non-negotiable," the DI told her. "Developing this kind of relationship can mess with your head so if I hear you've missed even a minute of therapy, I'll pull you straight out. Is that clear Abi?"

Abi summoned up the strength required to still every inch of her body before holding the DI's eyes with her own impenetrable stare. "Crystal."

"The only thing he's been plotting today is what to make you for dinner."

Abi could see Ade and his partner Eddie in a car across the road from her building as she walked the last stretch from the tube station with her phone held tightly to her ear. Having clocked them, she quickly looked away, partly because she didn't want to draw attention to them and partly through necessity. She needed her eyes to negotiate her way through the constant stream of people darting past her towards the station, her body swaying left and right as she navigated her way through, her nose twitching as it adjusted from the staleness of those who'd spent the day cooped up in an office to those on their way out, sprayed liberally with an array of colognes and perfumes.

"You're a bit obvious aren't you?"

"Well parking isn't exactly plentiful around here. We had to take what we could get."

"So anything else interesting to tell me?"

"Nope. All he's done today is go food shopping."

"What about the meeting he mentioned?" Abi quickened her pace as she spoke, keen not to be held up by traffic lights as she nipped across the road just before the signal changed.

"He went to a library half an hour away, sat on a computer for a while and then left. He didn't speak to anyone, never mind meet someone. And before you ask, tech have been all over the computer he used but he covered his tracks. They got nothing."

"Well it wouldn't be any fun if he made it too easy for us now would it?"

"Easy works for me," Ade said, without a hint of irony. "We'll catch up with you tomorrow. Have a fun evening."

"Not too much fun though!" Eddie shouted in the background.

"Did you hear that? Eddie said…"

Abi had already heard enough and swiftly hung up. She let herself into her flat and then immediately stopped as she struggled to take it all in. The lights had been dimmed and there were candles everywhere. The table was set for two and the smells coming from the oven immediately set her mouth salivating and her stomach rumbling. She headed for the kitchen, dumping her bag and jacket along the way to join a smiling Matt, wooden spoon in one hand, glass of wine in the other.

"You need to come and stay more often!" she said as she kissed him.

"I've had a lovely afternoon browsing markets and thinking about what to cook for you after a hard day's work."

"Well whatever you decided to make, it smells amazing. And you certainly look very at home."

"Ready in fifteen minutes," he said, pouring her a glass of wine and then handing it to her. "Go and relax till it's ready."

Abi accepted the drink and then headed for a sofa. She put the glass on the table and then before sitting down, she headed for the first large window and closed the blind, moving on to the second one and doing the same, just in time to see Ade and Eddie drive away as she did so.

"So how was your day?" Matt asked as she finally sat down.

"Same old same old. The thing about working in the kind of consultancy I do is there are never any interesting anecdotes to share. How was your meeting?"

"Cancelled."

"So are you still heading off at the end of the week?"

"No. My next job's been delayed for a bit."

Abi watched as Matt busied himself stirring, tasting, adding some salt and then tasting again. She clamped her teeth tightly together. It would be so easy to invite him to stay with her but she didn't want to rush him or risk scaring him off. As the silence stretched out in front of her, taunting her, she was determined to hang on to her resolve.

"Maybe I could hang around here for a few more days until I know what I'm doing? Or is that too much? It's absolutely okay to say no. I don't want to put too much pressure on us when we seem to be off to what certainly feels to me like a really great start." He shrugged. "I just really like being here."

Abi smiled, releasing the tension in her jaw. She loved the fact he looked slightly uncomfortable, showing a vulnerability she hadn't seen before.

"I told you already, you can stay as long as you like," she said, her smile flowing into her eyes and making them glisten. "Especially if I'm going to be this well looked after! Have you let Esther know you're back yet?"

"No, but I will."

"Matt you must. She should definitely hear it from you and not me and I feel really awkward not being able to call her until she knows you're here. Please say you'll call her tomorrow?"

"I'll let her know I promise." With a flourish, Matt then folded the tea towel he'd been holding and draped it over his arm as he bowed his head. "In the meantime, dinner is served."

The next morning, Abi headed off for work as normal. She disappeared into the tube station, waited for ten minutes and then came straight back out again. Keeping away from the main road, she then worked her way back towards home and jumped into the back of Ade's car.

"How long have you been here?" she said, pushing the array of food wrappers, empty cans and water bottles as far away from her as possible. "It's disgusting in here by the way. And it stinks."

"Lovely to see you too," Ade said, "and we just got back about half an hour ago. So what's new?"

"It'll have to wait," Eddie cut in. "He's on the move."

All eyes were suddenly on the door to Abi's building which was now swinging shut behind Matt. They watched him stop to check his watch and then put his phone to his ear. It was a brief conversation and as he slipped his phone into his pocket, he stepped to the edge of the pavement scanning the horizon for the light of a taxi for hire. Abi slid down as low as she could until he was out of her sight line.

"What's he doing?" she asked as Ade started the engine and slowly pulled away.

"He's just got into a cab. Put your seatbelt on. We're going for a ride."

After twenty minutes, Ade held back as the taxi pulled over and Matt climbed out. He stood for a moment while he got his bearings and then headed for a nearby café. Ade parked up and Eddie was immediately out of the car. He picked up a newspaper from a vendor on the pavement and then followed Matt inside.

Eddie took a table as close to Matt as he could, ordering a coffee as he passed the counter and putting the headphones that had been around his neck up over his ears as soon as he was seated; anything to make it look like he wasn't interested in his surroundings. He tapped his fingers on the table as if listening to music and then pulled the newspaper he'd just picked up out of his coat pocket. A waitress did a full circle of the place, putting a coffee down in front of Matt then depositing the second drink she was holding in front of Eddie before returning back behind the counter in one perfect fluid movement. Matt had chosen to sit where he could see the door and his eyes were firmly fixed on it. Eddie sat side on to him, watching Matt's left eye twitch periodically as he waited, his left knee bouncing in time below the table. He had no idea what the right side of his body was doing, wondering if it too was in perpetual motion.

Eddie glanced up briefly each time the door opened, his eyes immediately falling back to his newspaper when it turned out to be no one of interest. It was a long time since he'd sat with a coffee and a paper and he'd forgotten how much he enjoyed the feel of newsprint in his hands. And the smells! The blend of coffee and ink was one thing but the sizzling pops and crackles that accompanied the unmistakable aroma of bacon cooking was on another level altogether. Eddie could feel his stomach rumbling. It wouldn't hurt, would it? Tucking into a bacon butty would just make him look even more authentic, wouldn't it?

Eddie was about to raise his hand to attract the attention of the waitress when he sensed Matt moving. Eddie's eyes were instantly fixed on him, watching him now as he sat up straight, pulling his chair in, pushing his hair out of his eyes only for it to fall forward again, crossing his legs, then uncrossing them. Eddie looked towards the door and waited, his own nerve ends now tingling with anticipation.

A large man came in, of significant enough stature that it felt like he only just made it through the door. Or perhaps it was just something about the way he carried himself that made him seem so formidable? He headed straight for Matt and sat down, leaning in before he started talking to him in a low growl.

Eddie sent a text to Ade with just one word in capitals: DAVE. He then set his phone to record and slipped the right headphone back off his ear as casually as he could, hoping his phone was able to pick up more than he was. While the man's words may have been hard to decipher, his body language and expression could not have been more eloquent, expressing in no uncertain terms his frustration, his dissatisfaction and the seriousness of their current situation. Punctuated by a series of distinguishable words and phrases – 'postpone again', 'time you got your shit together' and various threats to remove body parts, and

Eddie suddenly understood why Matt had been fidgeting so nervously in his seat at the thought of even just a few minutes in the company of this monster of a man.

The meeting was over at speed and, without any discernible pleasantries, the man left as abruptly as he had arrived. Eddie watched Matt slump back in his chair, his whole body decompressing as if he'd been holding his breath and had finally released every last puff of air in one accelerated blow. He then massaged his forehead with both hands, his head heavy and down, his left leg still bouncing under the table. Eddie slipped his headphone back over his ear and slowly turned the page of his newspaper as Matt stood up, rummaged in his pocket for some money and left more than enough for his coffee on the table. He then pulled on his jacket and left.

Eddie was just a moment behind him. With the briefest of nods towards Ade and Abi, he then kept walking, being careful as always to keep a comfortable distance. With just Matt to follow, he and Ade would regularly swap places with each other to avoid becoming a regular fixture over Matt's shoulder but Ade now needed to follow Dave. They'd have to stay on their toes today to make sure they remained unseen.

"Did you get a picture?" Abi asked Ade, still slumped down in the back seat of the car, her head raised just enough to be able to see what was going on.

"Not one that will win any awards but something more up-to-date than the one we've got at the moment at least," he said as he perused the series of shots he'd taken as Dave had left the café. They'd watched him walk to a car and then get in but as yet, the car hadn't moved. "He's aged quite well all things considered."

"And judging by the look on Matt's face when he left, he's as terrifying as he ever was."

Ade pulled on his seat belt, his eyes drawn to Dave's car which now had an indicator blinking as it prepared to pull away. "Now get lost," he said without turning around. "I need to go."

Abi quickly got out of the car and turned away while first Dave's car and then Ade's disappeared off down the street. Once she was sure they were out of sight, she stood on the pavement for a moment, suddenly feeling a little surplus to requirements. Eventually she swung her bag over her shoulder and headed for the nearest tube station and the quickest route back to the office.

7

When Matt told Abi that night that he was still waiting for some clarity on his next job, it came as no surprise to her. If there were problems, it would certainly explain why Dave had been so aggrieved during their meeting, an encounter that had left Matt twitchy and unable to fully relax.

"Did something happen today?" she asked him a couple of times throughout the evening but each time he insisted he was fine.

Early the next morning, Abi left for work as normal, ducking in and out of the tube station again and then taking a different route back to where Ade and Eddie were waiting.

"Any clues as to his plans today?" Ade asked as she slipped into the back seat.

"A vague hope of a meeting coming off later but nothing more specific than that."

"Seems he's in business earlier than planned then," Eddie said as he started the car engine.

They all watched as Matt stood on the pavement for just a minute or two before a car pulled up beside him and then quickly moved away again the minute he was inside. Eddie was able to pull out a vehicle or two behind with Ade already making a call to get the number plate checked. The name of the registered owner was a hire car firm so Ade immediately tasked Tim with finding out more then they all sat back and waited to see where they were headed.

After half an hour, it became clear they were leaving London, heading out past Hammersmith towards the motorway that would take them west of the city. At this point, Ade started to feel uncomfortable.

"We're too obvious sitting behind them after such a long time especially now the traffic's starting to thin out. We need to get someone else to take over before we hit the motorway."

He made a call and within ten minutes Eddie clocked two motorbikes winding their way through the traffic behind them. He turned off the main road and while one of the bikes continued past them, the other followed them into a side road. Ade jumped out of the car, put on the helmet the biker held out to him and then in a loud smoke-belching roar, they sped off.

Eddie headed back to the main road, driving in the direction of the city for the briefest moment before turning into the first side road he came to. He turned the car around and parked up, redundant for the time being.

"Now what?" Abi asked Eddie.

"We wait until they're on their way back," Eddie told her.

"What here?" she said, looking around her for a café or at the very least, a corner shop where she could buy some snacks. "I'm going to see if I can find coffee," she said as she opened the back door of the car.

"Don't go far," Eddie warned her. "I'll go without you if I have to."

"Charming," she muttered, closing the door behind her.

Ade's driver radioed the first motorcyclist to let him know they now had him in sight and then watched him peel away leaving Ade's bike to fall into position. They were like a seamless tag team, ensuring the view from the rear-view mirror of Matt's car continued to change. Ade looked around as best he could, watching every road sign as he tried to work out where they could be going. Up ahead to the left, he then noticed a large warehouse style building. As they got closer, he could see there was another behind it and another one beyond that. It was obviously some kind of industrial park and moments later, they followed Matt's car off the motorway and on to a quiet road that wound its way through the mass of shapeless characterless buildings.

Ade tapped the driver's shoulder and pointed towards the third building. As they pulled over, they watched Matt's car follow the road around to the right and then stop. Ade dismounted and walked into the reception, keen to make it look like he had legitimate business there. He watched through the glass-fronted entrance as Matt got out of the car, crossed the road and disappeared down the side of another one of the large buildings. He was gone for a minute or two at most and then headed straight back to the car. Ade wondered if Matt's driver was taking pictures but he couldn't imagine what of, and Matt had clearly needed to check on something relatively simple but something that could only be done in person. Ade watched as the car turned around and headed back out of the park.

"Can I help you?"

There was a pause and then Ade realised the receptionist was talking to him.

He started to walk towards her and then patted his pockets. "I've left my phone in my car," he then said, rolling his eyes at his own feigned stupidity. "I'll be back in a moment and then yes, you definitely can help me."

Abi had been back in the car for just a few short minutes when Ade called to say Matt was on his way back.

"Perfect timing," she said with a smile, reaching forward from the back seat to put a coffee in the cup holder beside Eddie and hand him a bar of chocolate. "I figured you were a Mars bar kind of guy."

Eddie started the car and pulled up to the end of the road so he could watch out for Matt. It would be a little while yet before he reached them. Long enough to enjoy at least a few sips of coffee and definitely enough time to enjoy the chocolate.

Ignoring the speed limit, Ade was past Matt in minutes and quickly back with Abi and Eddie.

"Thanks mate," he said to the motorcyclist as he dismounted and handed back the helmet. The response was a simple nod and then he sped off, leaving Ade ruffling his hair with his hands and wiping the sweat from his forehead.

"So what happened?" Abi asked as Ade slipped into the passenger seat.

"Not much," Ade replied, twisting around to face Abi. "Industrial park. Bland buildings with very little branding. Matt dipped into a building for the briefest of moments and then they left."

"Here they come now," Eddie said as he slowly rolled forward, ready to rejoin the main road once Matt's car had gone past.

"So what were they doing?" Abi asked, her confusion obvious.

"I have absolutely no idea," Ade said. "No idea at all."

Over the coming days, Matt didn't go anywhere of particular interest. He would often head to a café for a coffee and a moment to just sit back and watch the world go by then wander to various different markets and independent stores to buy ingredients for one delicious dinner after another. The only place that stood out slightly was a pawnbroker's that he'd visited three or four times in a short enough space of time that it had caused the raise of an eyebrow. They were still looking for where Matt kept his computer equipment so this felt like as good a place as any to consider. Someone from the tech team was duly dispatched to investigate.

Now they had eyes on Dave, another surveillance unit had been assigned to watch his home, an enormous gated property in south east London that had more security than the Bank of England. There was a small core group who were continuously in and out of the place which meant information was slowly coming together on his trusted inner circle, one of whom had now been identified as the man who had driven Matt out to the industrial park.

"You really don't have to go to so much trouble every night you know," Abi said as she tucked into a perfectly cooked duck breast. "And where did you learn to cook like this? I thought you might have a couple of signature dishes but you've already gone way past that. Once again, this is amazing!"

Matt beamed, clearly loving this rare opportunity to show off his culinary skills. "Sometimes in between jobs I take holidays but it can be a bit boring on your own so a few years ago I started doing cookery courses abroad in some really stunning places – beautiful chateaus in France or the most palatial villas in Italy and Spain. I find it really relaxing and over time, it's turned out I've become quite good at it."

"Good? You're way past good. Never mind settling down somewhere, you should open a restaurant."

"Maybe one day. But I'm happy just to cook for you in the meantime."

"Well beans on toast in front of the telly was my norm until you rocked up so that definitely works for me but it's Friday tomorrow so why don't we go out? My treat though," Abi insisted. "It's the least I can do to say thank you."

"Sounds good to me," Matt said as he stood up and took his plate to the kitchen.

"Leave the clearing up to me," Abi said as she passed him. Matt then yawned loudly, stretching his arms out wide as he did so. "Why don't you go and relax in the bath? I'll even share my special relaxation music with you," she said, picking up her phone to access one of her many carefully collated playlists, pausing for just a moment to let Matt kiss her before he happily headed for the bathroom. "Turn the speaker on!" she shouted after him and then waited for the sound of the first suitably soothing track.

Abi busied herself as she listened to the steady sound of water pounding into the bath as it slowly filled up. After a few minutes, the sound of crashing water stopped and she heard Matt get in. She waited for another minute to slowly tick by and then she grabbed for his phone that he'd left on the breakfast bar. Initially, it was as if it had been superglued to his person but over the last few days, he'd become much more relaxed about leaving it lying around. A couple of times since then Abi had stolen the chance to take a look, cracking his passcode to unlock the device with just five attempts. Unbelievable to think that someone with his technical savviness would chose zero eight to represent Esther's birthday and one seven for his own but it hadn't mattered. To her disappointment, he clearly deleted everything as a matter of course. There had been no emails, sent or received, in fact no messages of any description, no browser history, nothing but it didn't stop her trying again. With the sound of Matt singing tunelessly along to a 90s power ballad, she quickly unlocked it and then let out a small gasp at the sight of a lengthy text conversation yet to be wiped. There were no names and it was all a bit cryptic at first glance but she took a picture of the screen with her own phone, her eyes constantly flicking in the direction of the bathroom and then sent it to her tech team for them to work their magic.

By the time Matt reappeared, Abi had finished clearing up and was relaxing on the sofa.

"Have you spoken to Esther yet?" she asked him as he sat down next to her but his sheepish look made it immediately obvious that he hadn't. "Matt! For goodness sake! Well it can't wait any longer. She'll start to think I'm not speaking to her. I'm going to call her myself."

Abi had soon lost count of the number of times she'd tried to get hold of Esther but she knew it had been too many. Why was Esther avoiding her? Abi couldn't think of a single reason so could only assume Esther had her head down, lost in work and drowning in deadlines. It wouldn't be the first time she'd disappeared into a work-shaped hole, the only cure for which was a bottle-shaped lifeline. So, when she reached the point where she'd run out of chatty innocuous messages to leave, Abi changed tack and sent a text to say she was on her way over, bottle in hand.

When she arrived at Esther's and shared the news that Matt was at her place, she'd never imagined for one minute she would be met with what started as some kind of bizarre disinterest and then quickly morphed into a barrage of insults, coated in a raw and aggressive anger that burned from Esther's eyes and made her body rigid. Neither had Abi expected to discover that Esther already knew. She could have killed Matt in that moment, wondering for the millionth time why he hadn't just told Esther he was back. She endured Esther's wrath as best she could until she was driven out by a terrible awkwardness that she clearly wasn't capable of dissipating.

By the time Abi got home, she was really angry. "Well that was fun," she said, her tone perfectly contradicting her words. There was a loud clatter as she tossed her keys into a large china bowl before striding towards the kitchen where a nervous Matt waited. "Why on earth couldn't you just tell her you were here? She saw us out together last Friday so instead of just being angry that we're together, we've managed to hurt her feelings too by not even bothering to let her know you're back." Abi shook her head. "It was horrible watching her trying to hide how pushed out she feels and the worst part is it was all completely avoidable!"

Matt looked at her for a moment and Abi felt her heart skip a beat. His expression was completely blank, the look in his eyes suggesting his thoughts had taken him a long way away. "Matt?" Abi waited but he said nothing. "Matt?" He jolted, her raised tone snapping him back to the moment.

"I'm sorry. For all of it. This is why it's better when I just stay away." Abi watched as he picked up his jacket. "I need some fresh air," he mumbled as he headed for the door and then closed it loudly behind him.

Abi was immediately rummaging in her bag for her phone, her movements all the more frantic the longer it took to find it. With a small yelp of relief, she finally laid her hands on it and quickly dialled Ade. "He's on the move!" she yelled the minute he answered. "Do not lose him!"

If Abi hadn't been out for the evening leaving Matt home alone, Ade and Eddie would have left hours ago so she was hugely grateful they were still around. She stood for a moment tapping her phone against her palm, horribly aware of the silence although she was sure she could still feel the final reverberations from the front door shutting somewhat firmly behind Matt. She then sat down on the nearest sofa, legs crossed, arms folded tightly, one foot bouncing in mid-air. And there she stayed, desperately trying not to think about the possible repercussions of her so spectacularly triggering Matt. What was she thinking coming in with all guns blazing? It's not like she didn't know how sensitive the relationship was between him and Esther. She shook her head, unable to comprehend her sublime stupidity. And then she jumped as her phone signalled the arrival of a text from Ade. Matt was in the pub at the end of the road, sitting at a table with a beer and his thoughts for company. Her limbs immediately unfolded as she let out a sigh of relief, convinced that if he was planning to bolt, he would surely have gone further before stopping for a drink. She rested her head back for a moment and closed her eyes, willing herself to be more careful in future as she regulated her breathing and gave herself permission to relax.

It was just over an hour later when Ade sent a second text to say Matt was on his way back. Knowing he would walk in at any moment made it easier for Abi not to react when he came through the door. Instead, she sat with her laptop at the breakfast bar in the kitchen as if busy catching up on work, slowly looking up as he approached, quietly bracing herself for whatever was coming.

"I'm so sorry Abi but this is all a bit overwhelming for me," he said, as he pulled out the stool next to her and sat down. "Caring for people has never worked out well for me in the past. Every time I leave Esther I tell myself it would be better for her if I just stayed away but I never can. And I've never allowed myself to even consider having a relationship and yet here I am." He hesitated for a moment, obviously choosing his words carefully. "This is such uncharted territory for me, and for Esther too, which is why I just couldn't tell her. She's never seen me in a relationship, never known me to want to just stop for a while and be with someone and I just knew she would react badly." He paused again. "It just feels so good to be connected to you," he said, taking hold of her hands, "but that doesn't mean it's not terrifying for me at the same time. I'm going to make mistakes, that part goes without saying, but I want the chance to try to get a few things right too."

Abi leant towards him. "Make all the mistakes you like," she whispered as she wrapped her arms tightly around his neck.

When Abi got home from work the next day, Matt came in just behind her. "I've seen Esther," he said with a large grin. "We're all good. In fact, she's invited us for dinner."

8

"Don't turn round but I think there's someone following you."

"You know all I want to do now is look over my shoulder?"

"Well don't. Cross the road to that coffee van up ahead and get yourself a drink."

"I don't want a drink."

"Abi, for fuck's sake!"

"Where are you? And who is it?" she asked, never tiring of how easy it was to wind Ade up, waiting for a moment for a car to pass before stepping off the pavement to follow his instructions.

"We're parked up behind a van half way down the street. And we've no idea who he is. I got a picture of him a minute ago that I've just sent to the team in case anyone recognises him but in the meantime we need to be extra careful. No jumping in the car near your flat in the morning. We'll arrange to pick you up somewhere. And I'll swap cars too for tomorrow just to be on the safe side."

"What made him stand out?"

"I just felt like I'd seen him before so we've been keeping an eye on him. It didn't take long to realise he was tailing you but I've a feeling I recognise him. I'm sure I've clocked him near Matt so it maybe it's really him he's watching. Either way, we need to stay alert."

"Where is he now?" Abi asked as she paid for her coffee, her phone held tightly to her ear.

"He's stayed on this side of the road. He's looking in a shop window so I'm guessing he can see you in the reflection."

There were a couple of tables and chairs around the coffee truck so Abi sat down. "I see him," she said. "Now what's he going to do? If he turns around he'll be looking straight at me."

"Go home then. You're almost there and he'll probably head off once you go inside then Eddie can follow him for a while to help us work out who he is."

Abi stood up again and started walking the last stretch to her flat. "Before you go, tell me where Matt's been today."

"We think we've found where he keeps his computer equipment. He was back at the pawnbroker's again but out of sight somewhere. We got Milo from tech to join us with some fancy kit and the broadband readings were off the chart so we're finding out who owns the place and checking out who works there."

"And what about the messages I found on Matt's phone? Have tech managed to do anything with them yet?"

"Not yet. I've put someone from the team on it and they know there's a full briefing with the Guv on Monday so hopefully something will come through later." Ade thought for a moment, reminding himself where he'd got to recounting Matt's day. "Yes, so Matt was at the pawnbroker's most of the morning and then he went for a walk with Esther."

Abi felt her jaw stiffen slightly. She couldn't help wondering what the two of them talked about, primarily in case they covered anything that might move the investigation forward but also because she knew they would discuss her relationship with Matt. It shouldn't bother her. She didn't want it to bother her. But the reality was it did.

It was Monday morning and the team had gathered for a briefing. "Right, come on let's get this done," DI Baker shouted above the chatter. There was a flurry of activity as everyone took their seats and conversations were simultaneously brought to an end. "Ade," she said as her eyes found him. "Let's start with you."

"We've been struggling with some seemingly unconnected bits of information but as of this morning, I think we can now confidently say that it's all starting to make sense. Matt took a ride out to an industrial park but it wasn't clear at all why that was then while we were gathering information on the businesses that are based there, Abi got something." Ade nodded at her to continue.

"Matt's started to relax and has become less guarded as a result. He's left his phone lying around a few times but whenever I've had the chance to take a quick look, there's been literally nothing to see. No messages, no emails, nothing. Then a few days ago there was a lengthy text conversation for the first time that I sent to tech. There was a clear code word repeated a few times and references to somewhere called 'FL'. Then we discovered a company called FutureLab has a major research facility on the industrial park Matt visited."

"But why the visit? I thought their thefts were always electronic?" DI Baker asked.

"That's why we're convinced the next target is FutureLab," Ade replied. "I've talked to the CEO who admitted there's a highly sensitive and controversial project underway that they'd do anything to protect. The research exists online but there's a log book too linked to some scary sounding experiments so we think an actual break-in could be part of the job. To lose the online research would be one thing but for both elements to be stolen would be catastrophic. I sent someone back to the industrial park for another look. It turns out Matt placed a small device on the security camera that covers a side exit that would allow him to control it remotely. The company has an impressive security system but if Matt can isolate certain parts, any breach is far less likely to be detected. The CEO's given us special access so we can monitor any unusual online activity but it's a careful balance from here. We don't want Matt to know we're on to him."

"And what about Dave?" DI Baker asked Stacey, the officer leading his surveillance.

"Activity at Dave's house has definitely picked up," Stacey told the room. "We now have IDs for a number of regular visitors but the security's so tight we can't get in to bug the place. Following some of his team has given us the chance to listen in on conversations though. There's been talk of highly sensitive research, its worth to the company responsible for it, and its potential resale value. Once we heard about FutureLab and got Ade's latest insight, it seems likely that Dave's planning to steal the research mentioned and then do their usual – offer to sell it back to FutureLab or to the highest bidder if they don't pay up."

Stacey nodded to Ade who took the lead again.

"Matt's been spending an increasing amount of time in his hideaway at the pawnbroker's which we now know is owned by Dave by the way, and tech are gradually managing to intercept stuff but it's slow making sense of it all and Matt is of course an expert at putting up impenetrable barriers and wiping stuff as he goes. That said, knowing the focus is FutureLab obviously makes a massive difference."

A loud noise then distracted Ade. It was a special alert he had for messages from Eddie and he immediately reached into his pocket for his phone. "Sorry, that's Eddie," he said. "He wouldn't message now unless it was urgent." And then as he quickly read the message, he was on his feet. "I gotta go," he said, already heading for the door. "Matt's with Dave and it's got physical. I'll send you the pictures."

The closing door clipped short his last word leaving the room in the grasp of a stunned silence. The DI went to say something but Tim beat her to it.

"I got them!" he shouted.

There was a then a huge kerfuffle as everyone crowded around his desk. He scrolled through the images, each one carrying an increasingly shocking picture than the last. Abi gasped as she took them in. Dave leaning into Matt, a threatening finger just millimetres from his face. Dave with his hands gripping Matt's jacket, his lips curled up over his teeth in fury. Dave with Matt pinned against a wall across a number of shots suggesting he had repeatedly smashed him against it. A fist raised, a bloody nose nursed and then finally, Dave walking away and a shot of Matt, crouched down, hands up to his face.

Abi looked at DI Baker. "Go!" she said, shooing Abi away. "But stay connected. Make sure you check in with me later." Abi nodded, already gathering her things together. "Great work everyone. Things are clearly hotting up so let's reconvene tomorrow please," the DI added to the wider group. "By which time I want to know what the hell they were fighting about!"

By the time Abi slipped into the back of Ade's car, he was on the perimeter of a park. "Where is he?" she asked as she shut the door.

"Were you careful about being followed?"

"Yes I was," she said, irritated by the distraction away from Matt. "Tell me where he is."

"Getting some fresh air. Eddie has eyes on him but I've just heard back from someone on Stacey's team who recognised the guy who's been following you. He's been seen going in and out of Dave's house."

"What do you know about Matt?"

"Abi, did you hear what I just said?" Ade repositioned himself so he could look at her. "Dave is having you followed! And most likely Matt too. We might have to pull you out. This is really serious, don't you get it?"

"Yes, I get it," she said, "but can we worry about that once we know what's happened to Matt?" For a moment they just stared at each other. "Please Ade!"

Ade turned back around to face the front and grimaced, digging his fingers into the centre of his ribcage before reaching into his pocket for some pills.

"You okay?"

"It's nothing. Just indigestion," Ade said, popping an antacid.

"So what do you know?" she asked again.

"Not much. As you'll have seen from the pictures, Eddie wasn't close enough to hear what it was all about. We're relying on you for that."

Abi said nothing. She was desperate to know Matt was okay but had to remind herself he had no idea she already knew about the fight. Much as she wanted to message him, she couldn't risk raising suspicion by behaving any differently and texting him at this time of the day would definitely be unusual. Like it or not, she had to just sit back and wait to see where he went next. She wondered what he'd tell her when they finally met up. He'd have to come up with something to explain whatever marks his beloved father had left on his face. She couldn't hope for the truth but something close might be enough for them to piece together what had prompted such a violent outburst. She knew Dave had form but it had felt very much like the physical abuse at least had been left in the past. For a moment, a tiny thought crept into the furthest corner of her mind; that as long as he was okay, it really didn't matter what he told her. She shook her head to dislodge it and forced herself to forget it had ever been there at all.

Abi's wandering mind was interrupted by Ade's phone ringing followed by a brief exchange between him and Eddie. "He's heading out the park," Ade said, already opening the car door. "I'm going to pick him up from Eddie at the exit opposite here." Abi took her cue and got out of the car too. "Stay on your toes today Abi," he shouted over his shoulder as he hurried away. "Stay on your fucking toes!"

Abi watched him go and then looked at her watch. It was four o'clock. There was no point going back to the office. She considered her options for a moment until she started to feel conspicuous, standing on a street corner as she was, looking vaguely troubled, so she forced herself to just start walking. Her feet took her straight towards the nearest tube station and once there, she decided she might as well just go home. If Matt turned up, she would simply claim a meeting had been cut short so she'd taken the opportunity to duck out early.

When she came back out of the underground her phone immediately beeped with a message from Ade. 'Lost him,' was all it said. Abi groaned. Of all the days for this to happen! She quickly text back saying she was almost home and would let him know as soon as Matt appeared. She then typed a second message confirming just that so it was ready to go the minute Matt walked in. This would mean she only had to press the send button as he crossed the threshold rather than fumble with her phone trying to write a surreptitious message with Matt watching her. But when she walked into the flat, Matt was already there, pacing backwards and forwards, the holdall he'd arrived with packed and sitting by the front door.

"Oh my God what happened to you!" she cried as she walked towards him, hitting send as she went, the bag temporarily forgotten and a look of utter horror on her face as she took in the full close-up picture of his wounds. Enough time had passed to give the cuts and bruises all the time needed for the former to congeal into ugly lumps of dried blood, and the latter to explode into a rainbow of distorted swollen mounds. This was so much more than she'd expected despite having seen pictures of the whole sorry event. His father clearly knew exactly how to inflict maximum injury with minimum effort.

"We have to leave."

Abi winced as she studied his face. "I need to clean that for you," she said, looking at a nasty gash above his left eye.

"Abi, you need to listen to me. You need to get packed, and quickly. We have to get away."

His words slowly penetrated and Abi stopped. "What are you talking about? Why do we have to leave?"

"Because it's not safe. For either of us. I'll explain later but please, just put some essentials in a bag and let's get out of here."

Abi took a step back in response to Matt's raised tone. "I'm not going anywhere until you tell me what the hell is going on."

Matt started pacing again, faster now, his body twitchy, his expression pained. "If I tell you, you might not come and I need to be with you. I love you Abi." He stopped and looked at her and Abi took hold of his hands, her heart thumping in her chest.

"I want to be wherever you are," she told him, "but I need to know who did this to you and why we aren't calling the police instead of running away?"

"It was my Dad and if we call the police I'll end up in jail alongside him. Esther and I don't talk about him because he's a thug and a bully, and the worst possible kind. I do work in tech but I work for him, and his line of work is as far away from legitimate as it gets. I've never hurt anyone but I have broken the law but not from choice," he quickly added, his agitated state obvious, his words and sentences clipped as he spoke increasingly quickly in short sharp bursts. "That part I'll have to explain later," he continued, "but I just never thought I could get away from him, or had the energy or motivation to even try. Until I met you. Now I have a reason to break free but it's complicated. And he's dangerous. Really dangerous and he knows about you and he doesn't like the fact I'm in a relationship which means we have to get away. I know it's huge to expect you to just drop everything. I know we haven't been together long enough for any of this to make sense or feel comfortable but this is an unimaginable situation." Matt stopped for a moment, his face full of such a raw desperation. "I just don't know how else to explain it. How to make you understand why there's simply no choice here. I mean it's one thing him beating me up but I can't let anything happen to you. So please Abi! Just pack a bag and let's go!"

"Are you saying he did this because of me? But that makes no sense? What did I do?"

"You haven't done anything but he sees anyone outside his trusted circle as a threat. He thinks I'll tell you stuff and that's a risk he simply won't allow me to take."

"And how long have you been working for him? I thought he'd been out of your lives for years. Does Esther know?"

"No, Esther has no idea. And the rest is way too long a story to share now." He watched Abi stand motionless in front him as if frozen to the spot and his body started to twitch again. "Abi, please!"

"It's a lot to take in," she said, her voice barely more than a whisper. "It would be like being on the run. People like me don't go on the run! Even saying it out loud sounds completely ridiculous."

Abi was struggling to keep up. Everything was suddenly moving at such an accelerated pace.

"Just say you'll come with me?"

"I can't just disappear! Think about what you're asking me to do! Everything's moving too fast!"

Of course she would go with him. She had to. This was a job and she was playing a role but there still needed to be some authenticity to the inner battle that, in different circumstances, the situation would have deserved.

"I get it, Abi, I do," Matt said, taking hold of her hands. "And there'll be plenty of time to talk later but all I can think about now is keeping you safe. And I wouldn't be suggesting leaving if I thought there was any other way of dealing with this."

Abi silently counted to ten. She heard Matt take a large breath and hold it while she worked her way slowly through the numbers, each one acting as cover for the contemplation that wasn't actually needed. When she hit ten, Abi slowly looked up into his eyes and then she smiled. "Of course I'll come with you."

Matt leant down and kissed her, wincing with the pain that came with the physical contact. "If you're okay with it, an old family friend, Pete, will come in later and pack everything up and then put it in storage. Just till we know what we're doing. He's basically the only person I trust. Apart from you. So you just need one or two bags for now. The lighter we can travel the better. And you need to let the flat go."

"What? Surely not? Aren't we coming back?"

"I don't know but it needs to look like we've really gone."

Abi looked flustered now and Matt gently took hold of her shoulders. "I know Abi, I'm sorry, I really am. And somehow I'll make it up to you, I promise. Isn't the letting agent nearby?"

"Yes, it's just a short walk away."

"So we'll put a letter and the keys through the door with enough money to cover any damage or repairs. I'll write something now and then you can sign it."

Abi was about to object and then decided not to bother. She'd have to give up the flat when the investigation was over so she might as well let him take care of it now. It would be one less thing to worry about further down the line.

"Well the large furniture isn't mine so make sure he doesn't take that," she said, taking her phone out of her bag and heading towards the bedroom.

"Better give that to me."

She turned around to see Matt with his hand out, nodding towards her phone. "Why?"

"Abi, you're going to have to trust me." Taking the phone from her hand, Matt dropped it on to the floor and stamped on it repeatedly until it was nothing more than a pile of mangled plastic. He then picked up the SIM card that was now visible and already slightly misshapen, took a penknife from his pocket and cut it into small pieces. Abi gasped.

"Don't worry. We can pick up new phones later. And don't pack your laptop or anything else electronic."

Abi disappeared into her bedroom and then stopped the minute she was out of sight. Her mind and heart were competing against each other in some kind of sprint race and she needed to put the brakes on, and fast. She needed to pull herself together. She needed to think. They were heading off to who knew where and she now had no way of letting Ade know what was happening and without her phone, he wouldn't be able to track her either. And did Dave's reaction to their relationship mean he was on to her? She wanted to believe that was inconceivable but was it? This wasn't some petty thief. Dave was in a league of his own and the consequences of underestimating him could be catastrophic. Think, think, she urged herself.

With her brain still a frenzied blur, she grabbed a large holdall from the top of the wardrobe and as mindfully as possible started to throw things in it, not stopping until it was full.

"Five minutes," she said to Matt as she passed him on her way to the bathroom, emerging a few moments later with a stuffed toilet bag, casually collecting her handbag on the way back to the bedroom. She rammed the toilet bag into the holdall and then taking her make-up bag out of her handbag, she slipped a small device into a compact before putting everything back in its place. She took a deep breath. Without her phone, the emergency tracker she'd been given was the only lifeline she had.

Abi picked up her bags and headed back to Matt. He was already standing with his jacket on and immediately took the large bag from her. "You ready?" he asked with a nervous smile. Grabbing her coat, Abi nodded and then with a quick glance around the room, she started switching lights off.

"No, don't do that," Matt said. "If anyone comes by, I want them to think we're in."

Quickly turning them back on again, Abi then followed him to the door, her mind whirring. If she could just keep breathing, she could convince herself she was still in control of this madness because that's what it was. Total utter madness.

Matt locked the door behind them and then she watched him as he removed an air vent to the left of where they stood. He pulled an envelope from his pocket and then adding the keys Abi had only recently had cut for him, he pushed it into the open space before replacing the grille.

"Instructions for Pete," he said as if his actions were the most natural thing in the world.

"How will he get in the front door of the building?" Abi asked him.

"I've given him that key already," Matt replied without a beat. He really has thought of everything, Abi mused as they started to head off, and then she stopped. "What about Esther?"

"We can't tell her. It'll only put her in danger too."

"But we can't just leave her?"

"We have no choice," he said, a sense of panic now creeping into his voice. "Please Abi," he said, taking hold of her hand and gently encouraging her forward. "No more delays."

Matt and Abi strode off down the pavement just moments before Ade and Eddie pulled into the road. The traffic getting across London had been a nightmare so Ade was relieved to have finally made it back. Almost as relieved as he had been to get Abi's text telling him Matt was at home. To have lost sight of him at such a crucial moment was simply unacceptable and would have given him night sweats for weeks if Matt hadn't reappeared. He parked the car and then looked up to see the lights on in Abi's flat. He stared at the windows, hoping to see some sign of movement. Anything that would reassure him that everything was okay. The back of his neck prickled and he dug his fingers into it in an attempt to make it stop. There should have been an update from Abi by now and her silence was starting to make him uncomfortable.

By ten o'clock nothing had changed so Ade called DI Baker. She hadn't heard from Abi either. "It's a little disconcerting," she said, "but if everything looks quiet, we've nothing to gain from storming in there just to make sure they're both tucked up for the night. Let's gather first thing and take it from there."

Ade ended the call, his eyes sweeping back to Abi's flat, scanning the windows from left to right, and then from right to left and back again.

"Please tell me we can go home now," Eddie said, watching Ade as his eyes continued to scan, dragging his teeth across his bottom lip as he did so until he flinched at the self-inflicted pain. "Sarge?" Eddie waited. "Ade?" he then tried. Ade finally looked at him. "You okay?"

Ade turned the key in the ignition and the car purred into action. "I'm fine," he said. "Just try calling Abi before we go."

It was unusual to call rather than text but Eddie did as he was told. "Straight to voicemail," he said. "Not much more we can do sitting here is there?"

Ade sat for a moment and then without saying another word, he pulled away, turning on the radio as he did so in an attempt to drown out his growing sense of unease.

When Pete pulled up in a small van an hour or so later, the first thing he did was a careful walk up and down the street to check there was no one suspicious hanging around. He took his time. He knew what he was doing and knew that haste was always the enemy.

When he was convinced there was no one lurking, he went back to his van to pick up some flat-packed boxes and then let himself into Abi's building. A few moments later he'd retrieved Matt's envelope and was stepping inside the flat. He had a quick look around and then wasted no time getting to work. He needed to move fast and clear the place as quickly and as orderly as he could.

He knew Matt described him as a family friend but he was so much more than that. He loved Matt like a son and would do anything for him but that didn't mean he placed no value on his own life. He'd grown up with Dave and working so closely with him made looking out for Matt tricky at best, suicidal at worst. Despite that, he'd willingly taken numerous chances for Matt over the years but these last few weeks, the level of risk-taking had been taken to a previously unimaginable high. He wanted the best for Matt, he really did but there had been moments recently when he'd thought he might as well write his own death certificate. All the more reason why he had to execute Matt's plan as efficiently as he possibly could.

With a film of sweat gluing his t-shirt to his slightly overweight body, the sun was already nudging its way above the horizon by the time Pete was done. It took him countless trips up and down the stairs to clear out the boxes, his eyes frantically flitting this way and that every time he took the short walk from the front door to his van and back again, each time feeling slightly more exposed as the light of the new day slowly took hold. And then finally it was done. He'd followed Matt's instructions to the letter and with his eyes still on the clock, he quickly headed for a storage unit to fulfil the final request. There was a young lad in situ for the graveyard shift so he slipped him fifty quid and the boxes were behind a bolted steel door in record time.

Pete got back into his van and checked his watch. He had just enough time to nip home for a shower and change and still be at Dave's by eight as expected. He smiled as he pulled away, silently congratulating himself on a job well done.

Matt and Abi had stayed on foot, sticking to smaller quiet roads where possible. After dropping an envelope into the letting agent's office, they jumped in a cab and headed to the pawnbroker's. Matt whisked Abi through the shop and into an office at the back which housed the most incredible suite of computer equipment she had ever seen.

"Bloody hell!" Abi marvelled at the multiple screens and the array of consoles, hard drives and all sorts of other fancy looking stuff she had no hope of identifying. There was no response from Matt who was busy pulling a suitcase out of a cupboard which he then opened.

"Move your stuff into here," he said. Abi didn't question him, just blindly did as she was told, knowing that he was thinking about CCTV cameras and doing his best to change their appearance. By the time she'd finished the transfer, Matt was handing her a new coat and a woolly hat. He'd already changed his jacket and added a baseball cap.

"This is starting to feel anything but spontaneous," she said, packing her own coat and putting on the new one.

"I knew if my Dad found out about us there'd be trouble but I also knew I couldn't give you up. I thought I should put some plans in place, just in case."

Abi wasn't sure how to respond to that so instead took a slow breath to regulate her heartbeat which was suddenly flip-flopping about like a fish out of water. It was shocking how little she still knew about him. She'd seen kind and vulnerable. Now she was seeing calculated and controlling. What traits, good or bad, was he still to show? She felt a knot form in her stomach and then tighten.

"So what's next?" she asked stretching her torso in an attempt to untangle it.

"I've got a car waiting in a garage about an hour out of town. The quietest route is by bus, a train and then a bit of a walk I'm afraid but once we're in the car we can relax a bit. And I've found somewhere perfect for us to go." He hesitated for a moment. "I know I'm expecting a lot of you. It's a massive upheaval without any notice but it won't be forever. I'll work something out but I need to know you're safe in the meantime. And the only way to be safe is to disappear."

"You're right, this is huge. And I'm not going to be able to relax until you've told me everything so I can really understand what the hell is going on, and I do mean everything." She waited for some reassurance but he said nothing. "I mean it Matt. If for any reason you can't or won't give me a full explanation for all of this, I'll be coming straight back, danger or no danger."

"You have my word. In fact, you can have as many words as you like once we get away but one thing at a time," he said, hurrying her out of the back of the building and off to a nearby bus stop.

There was little conversation for the next hour and a half. Abi remained somewhat in awe of the level of planning. First a bus took them to a quiet station off the main commuter trail, then on to an even smaller station that she'd never even heard of. How had they not known what he'd been up to? Not even the slightest detail had slipped out anywhere. It was quite unbelievable. She could only hope that any questions from the Guv about exactly how far into the sand their heads had been buried would evaporate the minute she delivered the complete life and times of Dave Harrison that Matt had promised to share.

As they'd headed off from the second station on foot, it had only taken a few minutes before the houses started to spread out, the gardens getting bigger, the roads quieter, the street lighting more spaced out and the night sky darker as a result. Then, just when she started to think they'd left all civilisation behind them, she saw a petrol station up ahead and a small row of garages. Matt unlocked the far one and opened it to reveal a newish nondescript car no doubt chosen for its overall blandness. He opened the boot and looked relieved to see a holdall already there which was stuffed to the brim with cash. Abi gasped.

"It's too easy to track activity on cards. It's cash only for the time being," Matt said, lifting her suitcase into the boot and throwing his own bag on top. Then he opened the passenger door for her. "Time to go somewhere beautiful and turn this horror show into something amazing," he said with a warm smile.

Abi felt a sharp pain in her chest as if a hand had burst through her ribcage and taken hold of her heart and then squeezed hard. The levels of adrenalin coursing through her body were beyond intoxicating. She felt light-headed, fearful, excited, exhilarated even. As if she was free-falling. As if life was suddenly terrifyingly fragile. And it was impossible not to feel something for this human being, whether pity for the terrible life he'd lived, sadness for the relationships he'd tried desperately to protect, fear for what might lie ahead, or love for the man he'd become. The truth was she didn't know what to think or how to feel so instead she just slipped into the car and waited to be told what was coming next.

"Have a look in there," Matt said as he pulled away, gesturing towards the glove compartment.

Abi pulled out a handful of papers that she quickly identified as the details of a cottage. It was a beautiful place, full of character and charm.

"The good news is we're not actually going that far," he told her. "I thought about Scotland, or even Ireland, but then realised that as long as I was careful, there wouldn't be a trail to follow so distance was strangely immaterial. My Dad won't have a clue where to start looking."

Unlike my team, Abi thought, who would be hot on their heels the minute they started following her tracker which meant it was Matt's meticulous planning that would turn out to be completely pointless. Abi stared out of the window. Nothing was familiar and she wondered if she should be truly scared. She knew members of Dave's gang had been following them both but, if Dave's plan was to take her out, surely he'd have done it by now? Knowing what he was capable of was enough to send a spine-tingling shudder rippling through her body leaving her feeling hot and cold at the same time, her palms suddenly damp, her legs twitching. But there were positives too. She'd earned Matt's trust and he was set to tell her everything which she was confident would turn out to be so much more than any of them was expecting. It would be mind-blowing, headline-grabbing and, without doubt, career defining.

Abi felt a vein pumping uncomfortably in her neck. What if Ade got spooked and came bursting in before Matt had the chance to offload his mine of incriminating secrets? He could be close already for all she knew but she couldn't rush Matt. She needed time to make him comfortable enough to share the full unedited, raw, no holds barred version. What if she wasn't given enough time to make that happen?

Abi reached for her handbag and keeping her hands deep within it, she opened her make-up bag, felt around until she found the compact and then the tracker and pressed the small button that would take it from on to off. She then put everything back as it was and placed the bag back in the footwell.

"You okay?" Matt reached over to take hold of her hand.

She smiled. "The adrenalin's wearing off. I'm just tired."

"We'll be there in an hour. Why don't you close your eyes?"

However tempting, Abi felt she should stay awake but her eyelids suddenly felt incredibly heavy and it wasn't long before she lost the battle to keep them open.

The next thing she knew, the car had come to a stop and Matt was turning off the engine. She took a moment to wake herself up and then she peered through the car window to see the cottage that was more beautiful than it had appeared on the printed page, even in the dark. Matt had pulled up at the side of the house but Abi could clearly see a series of garden lights that paved the way to the front door that was perfectly framed by a deep pink begonia.

"Come on," Matt said as they got out of the car. "Let's get inside."

"It's stunning." Abi didn't know where to look first as she followed him through the front door, struggling to take it all in. The house was very traditional on the outside but super modern on the inside. The ground floor was open plan with a living space leading to a dining area then on to the most phenomenal kitchen she'd ever seen. Upstairs, Abi found a huge master bedroom and decided she had no need to go any further. She collapsed on to the bed and Matt was only a few beats behind her. For a moment, they just lay there, both staring at the ceiling, taking the chance to just catch their breath. Then Matt rolled on to his side. Aware of him looking at her, Abi did the same until their eyes met. Ever so gently, Abi put her hand to Matt's face. "It looks so painful," she said as she allowed her fingers to assess the damage.

"It'll heal," Matt said with a smile. "And at least now I have you all to myself, twenty-four seven. So, every cloud."

Abi smiled back as he moved close enough to kiss her, his arm pulling her towards him until their bodies were perfectly blended together.

"I love you so much Abi," he whispered.

Her arms moved tightly around him and she held him close. "I love you too."

9

Ade had insisted he and Eddie were back at Abi's flat the next morning as close to seven as possible. His thinking was they would wait for Abi to leave for work and then give her a lift to the station. That way, they could get a full debrief on the way to joining DI Baker and the team.

As Eddie pulled up, Ade's eyes fixed on Abi's windows. Immediately he was unbuckling his seat belt and opening the car door. "The lights are still on," he shouted at Eddie as he jumped out of the car and rushed across the road. Instinctively, Eddie was only seconds behind him although he had no idea what had prompted the sudden need for alarm. Ade reached the building and started rummaging in his pocket for his set of Abi's keys. Sweaty palms left him fumbling to unlock the front door. He needed to calm down but there was nothing he could do to quell the firm belief that something terrible had happened, a feeling that had sat deep in his gut ever since they'd left the evening before.

"What's the panic?" Eddie asked as he caught up with him.

"The blinds were open when we left last night which bothered me," he said as he finally opened the door. "They're still open and the lights are still on. Either the blinds should be shut now or the lights should be off."

It sounded like a riddle to Eddie who was struggling to catch up but Ade's concern was infectious. They hurried across the entrance hall, up the stairs, along the corridor and then stopped at Abi's door. Ade knocked loudly.

"Abi!" he shouted.

"What are you doing?" Eddie hissed, wondering how on earth they were going to explain themselves when Abi, or worse, Matt, suddenly opened the door.

"Abi! Abi!" Ade yelled now, still banging on the door.

"Sarge, stop!" Eddie urged him.

"Something's seriously not right," Ade then said, shaking his head.

"Open the bloody door then!" Eddie waited for just a moment and then snatching the keys from Ade's hand, he opened the door and quickly stepped inside. As Ade followed him in, Eddie moved swiftly through the flat. It was obvious there was no one in the lounge or kitchen. The place looked stripped bare, every lamp, soft furnishing and ornament gone. Eddie swiftly checked the bedroom and the bathroom before coming back to face Ade. He shook his head. "Everything's gone. Abi's gone."

Ade looked at him, a sense of dread sweeping so quickly through his body that it made him sway. Then filling his lungs with as much air as he could, he shouted at the very top of his voice. "FUCK!"

It was another hour before the team had gathered. For the first time ever, the room was close to silent, the only sounds coming from tapping feet, scraping chairs shifting under fidgety bodies, and the occasional exhalation of a deep jagged breath.

"Tech say we've got a location somewhere close to Rochester Airport and then nothing," DI Baker said the minute she burst through the door. "Still no word from

Abi?" she asked as she made her way to the front of the room.

All eyes were immediately on Ade. "Nothing. Her mobile's now saying it's been disconnected and the number she gave us for Matt has been disconnected too." His head went down. DI Baker may have told him to leave Abi's flat the night before but he still felt responsible. A burden he would carry with him until they found her. His heart burned painfully, his hand immediately in his pocket searching for his antacids.

"I don't need to tell you all that time is of the essence," DI Baker continued, now addressing the room from the front. "All we know is that Dave beat up Matt and then within hours, Matt and Abi disappeared. We know Dave's had both Matt and Abi followed so what did Dave know? Was he just nervous of Matt having a girlfriend or does he know she's a cop? Either way she's not safe until we know where she is so I want eyes on Dave around the clock. We can't track all of his associates but let's use our intel efficiently to pick up on anyone he might assign to track them down. And how much pre-planning did Matt do? He obviously has all the necessary skills to cover his tracks unless the escape was panicked in which case he may have been careless. Your thoughts Ade?"

"We need any CCTV footage from around Abi's flat for starters," Ade said. "It also struck me that maybe they weren't alone. Maybe Dave has them somewhere? And we need to see what Esther's up to and decide if she knows anything. Is Rochester Airport significant? What flights have left since the tracker went dead? We last had contact with Abi just after five o'clock yesterday afternoon so that puts us almost fifteen hours behind them."

Ade stopped abruptly. It was the first time he'd admitted that out loud and the sound of his words was terrifying.

"That's a lot of questions that need to be answered," DI Baker said. "So why are you all still here?" she yelled, prompting a cacophony of scraping chairs and instructions being shouted from one side of the room to another while the door continuously opened and shut as people hurried out. "Keep in touch and meet back here at six. And I want hourly updates until then!" she shouted over the noise.

Ade and Eddie headed back to their desks with Tim. Ade checked his watch. "Let's gather all the CCTV footage we can as quickly as possible," he said to Tim. "Check if any shops or bars around Abi's flat have cameras and access the traffic cameras in the area too. And pull in some people to help you. We need to know if they left the flat on their own or if someone was with them. And see what tech can tell you from the tracker about the route to the airport and any places they stopped."

Tim headed for his desk, gathering up some support as he went.

"What about us?" Eddie asked as he watched Ade put on his jacket.

"Let's go back to Abi's flat and have another look around," Ade said. "If they left in a hurry, maybe we missed something."

Ade and Eddie had been combing through Abi's flat for almost an hour when the first breakthrough came.

"I've got them walking away from the flat," Tim told Ade the second he answered his phone. "And they were definitely on their own. They went to a letting agency and dropped something through the letterbox. I've got someone heading there now to find out what it was."

"Do we have anything useful from the airport?"

"Not that I know of. I'll see what I can find out and let you know."

By the time the team reconvened it was closer to eight o'clock and the picture of what had happened was coming together as slowly as a thousand-piece jigsaw. There had been no contact details left with the keys at the letting agency, just a wedge of cash that was way more than was needed for any repairs or replacements. They still had no news on the taxi but had looked around the pawnbroker's place and had acquired new footage of them going inside but then the trail went cold again. Rochester Airport, where Abi's tracker stopped, was a tiny site used mainly by private planes but no flights had left in the last twenty four hours so there were no leads there either.

When Ade's phone rang in the middle of a very eloquent rant by DI Baker even she knew he had to answer it. They couldn't afford to miss a potential lead so she waved him away to take the call. He answered as he stepped outside the room but when he heard Abi's voice, he immediately stepped back in again.

"Abi!" he said loudly, his heart pounding against his chest. The volume in the room plummeted to zero at the mention of her name. "Are you okay? Where are you?"

There was then a silent flurry of activity as Tim dived for a phone to try to get the call tracked.

"I've only got a minute," Abi said. "I'm fine. Matt's going to talk to me and tell me everything so I couldn't risk you crashing in."

"So you dumped the tracker? You fucking idiot!" Ade bit his lip, immediately regretting the outburst. "I'm sorry," he quickly corrected himself. "It's just been really scary not knowing what happened to you."

"I know and I'm sorry but I just had to go with it. The beating was because of his relationship with me. Dave clearly has no desire for him to make new friends, never mind have a relationship but Matt's promised the full background so you've got to give me some time."

"Where are you exactly?"

"I thought you might panic and come barging in before he'd opened up. You do understand why I had to stall you?"

"Abi, just tell me where you are." Ade was working really hard to keep the panic he was feeling out of his voice. If Dave Harrison didn't want her around, she was incredibly vulnerable and as far as he was concerned her safety came before whatever information Matt was suddenly keen to share. He was aware of DI Baker now standing right beside him.

"Abi, tell me where you are," he said again, shouting this time.

"Give it to me!" DI Baker instructed, gesturing for him to hand her his phone.

"Abi!" Ade shouted one last time and then his head dropped. "She's gone. She's fucking gone!" he spat through gritted teeth.

A gasp shot around the room and then all eyes were immediately on Tim, the only other person who was on the phone. They waited, breaths held until he looked up and then slowly shook his head.

"They couldn't locate it," he said.

In just a few large strides, Ade shot out of the room, antacids already in hand, slamming the door behind him.

10

Several hours before making the call to Ade, Abi was waking up on her first morning in the cottage. A clock on the wall opposite surprised her with the news she'd slept until just after nine which was unheard of for her but then the previous day had hardly been an average one. Matt's arms were still loosely around her, his head facing her, his breathing low and even. Not wanting to disturb him, she just lay there, making the most of the quiet moment to reflect.

Yesterday had been quite a day. She replayed her memory of it at speed, her heart rate increasing at points when she'd experienced genuine fear. By contrast, some of it had been quite exhilarating. In fact, it had been one long adrenalin rush from start to finish, like a rollercoaster ride that simply wouldn't end. Although the day had, of course, ended and with Abi telling Matt she loved him. Abi shifted uncomfortably as she remembered but they were just words. Words that were totally inconsequential, said purely because they'd been required in the moment.

Abi looked at Matt's battered face. She hated that he'd been so badly hurt. She ran her fingers gently down his arm, an arm that had held her close the night before and felt her cheeks flush at the touch of him. She remembered how scared he'd been that she might get hurt, how he wanted only to protect her, how he'd buried his head in her neck, whispering repeatedly how much he loved her already.

Abi felt her heart pounding in her chest, cheeks no longer just flushed but burning as she realised she was feeling things, experiencing emotions that had no place in an operation of this nature. She felt connected to him but then she needed to feel connected to him in order to convincingly pull this off, didn't she?

For a moment she just lay there, stepping back from the swirling thoughts in her head and then chose to simply congratulate herself on playing her part so beautifully that even she was starting to believe it was real.

By the time they were up and showered it was already late morning. "Fancy a stroll into town?" Matt asked her. "We've got to believe it's safe to leave the cottage and I fancy a walk on the beach."

Abi was happy to get out and they both enjoyed the fresh air and the chance to get their legs moving and their hearts pumping. After nearly half an hour, they hit the edge of the town, coming first to a beautiful collection of houses that slowly turned into shops, bars and restaurants and then finally, there was the sea. Abi closed her eyes and breathed in the salty smell. There was something so exhilarating about the sheer expanse of it and the sound of the waves as they tumbled onto the shore. She felt her lungs expand as she gulped in the exquisite air, nerve ends quivering, cheeks tingling.

"It's like being on holiday," she said, beaming. "Feels like we've escaped, doesn't it?"

"Well that was the plan so that's exactly how it should feel," Matt said with a wry smile. "Shall we grab a coffee and something to eat and take a walk along the sea front?"

That sounded perfect to Abi and after a quick stop in a café for coffees and pastries, they walked long enough for the main hub of the town to be nothing more than a few colourful dots on the horizon before sitting on the sand to fully enjoy their breakfast.

"I thought you'd be pushing me by now to tell you how we ended up here," Matt eventually said.

Abi looked at him for a moment, looked at his bashed up face for the umpteenth time and then reached out to take hold of his hand. "Would it make sense if I said I just wanted some time off from it all? A few hours to just be together, behaving like we're a couple on holiday without a care in the world?"

"That does sound pretty attractive," Matt said, his eyes flooded with warm affection.

"It's official then. We're giving ourselves the day off," Abi said with a smile.

With the decision made, they sat where they were to finish their coffee, staring out at sea, hypnotised by the waves, a gentle breeze caressing their faces. Abi felt herself start to really relax. She didn't want to think about Ade and the team, or what Dave might be planning, or how distressed Esther would be the minute she realised they'd gone. In fact, she didn't want to think at all. She wanted to silence the confused chatter in her head and just live in the moment. She just wanted to be.

They took their time, walking and exploring and then stopped for lunch at a small pub before winding their way back, this time with shoes off, their feet loving the texture of the wet sand as they dipped in and out of the surf. Abi rolled up her jeans, wishing she'd packed some lighter clothing but then she hadn't really had time to consider what she might need, deciding just to be grateful for the t-shirt she'd thrown in at the last minute and the fabulous floppy straw hat she'd bought from a beach-front shop.

Conversation was light and they chatted freely as they talked about everything and nothing, the more banal and trivial the better.

"All this sea air is making me permanently starving. Is it too early for dinner?" Matt asked. "We can pick up some food and head back to the cottage or we can stay out. Whatever you like."

"Let's stay out," Abi said without hesitation. "Somewhere casual that doesn't mind sandy feet."

They headed for a small fish restaurant they'd spotted earlier in the day, both feeling exhausted the minute they sat down.

"I can't remember the last time I spent a full day on the beach," Matt said, as they both quickly opted for a traditional plate of fish and chips. "I'm drunk on sea air!"

"It's been a wonderful day," Abi said with a smile. "I feel completely restored and ready for anything."

"Ready for that?" Matt asked as two enormous pieces of battered fish arrived accompanied by a mountain of perfect looking chips and a bowl of mushy peas.

"Absolutely!" Abi said, her knife and fork immediately raised and ready for action.

By the time they'd finished, Abi was starting to feel increasingly uneasy about how worried Ade and the team would be about her. She felt an uncomfortable heat rising up her neck before bursting into her cheeks bringing with it a moment of clarity.

"Anything wrong?" Matt asked as she started rummaging in her bag.

"I must have left my scarf on the beach. You get the bill and I'll run back and get it."

Before Matt had the chance to say another word, Abi was out of her seat and heading for the door. As soon as she was outside, she took a quick look around and then dipped into a nearby pub.

"I don't suppose you have a phone I could borrow?" she said, smiling at the young barman. "I think I left my mobile in a restaurant earlier and need to check if it's still there. I'll happily make a donation," she added, nodding towards a charity box sitting on the bar.

Without saying a word, the barman turned around, picked up a phone from beneath the optics and placed it in front of her.

"You're a lifesaver," she said, stuffing a ten pound note into the charity box which the barman deftly removed and pocketed the minute she turned away, the handset already pressed to her ear, her fingers already dialling.

"Ade, it's me."

Three words that set off a barrage of questions. She hadn't been surprised to hear the relief in his voice then frustration and finally anger but she just wasn't quite ready to tell him where they were. She tried to make it clear she needed time before she started pushing Matt to open up and she was careful not to stay on the line for too long to be confident they couldn't trace her. Ade would just have to be happy to know she was safe.

Tired legs walked them back to the cottage by which point Matt and Abi were both completely beaten. They didn't even turn on a light and instead headed straight upstairs. They were in bed within minutes, sandy feet and all. As Abi then lay with her arms around Matt, their bodies close, a contented weariness in their eyes, she knew she was starting to feel too comfortable but she was too weary to care. She let her eyes close, the tiredness now resting heavily on her eyelids and, without another thought, she drifted off to sleep.

She was the first to wake again the next morning and lay quietly on her back, staring at the ceiling. She felt a horrible numbness, the pure joy of the previous day stolen by sleep, leaving her with nothing but a rude awakening. She carefully shifted her body to create space between herself and Matt, needing the physical disconnection to think clearly.

The day passed with Abi going through the motions.

"You okay?" Matt asked her for the umpteenth time.

Abi forced the biggest smile she could manage. "I'm fine, honestly."

"It's the sea air," she said the next time he asked. "It's completely knocked me out."

They headed back into town, opting to take the car this time to save their weary legs and by early afternoon, they were sitting in a café in need of a caffeine injection and a sweet treat to re-energise them.

The sugar rush came a few minutes later and Abi felt her sense of duty switch itself back on. It was time for a reality check. It was time to make her move.

11

"Ade!" Eddie shouted at him across the office. "Esther's here!"

The words sent Ade flying out of his chair. "What do you mean she's here?"

"She's come into the fake office asking for Abi. What do you want to do?" he asked with his hand over the phone's mouthpiece.

"Say I'll be down in a sec," Ade said, frantically searching his desk drawers for a tie, taking what felt like an eternity to find one. He threw it around his neck and as soon as he had a barely acceptable knot, he headed towards the lift. He was still reeling from Abi's call yesterday and the increasing sense of frustration that they were getting nowhere fast so the chance to see Esther was by far the most interesting development that had happened all day.

As he strode across the reception a few moments later, he was surprised to see how delicate Esther looked. He'd obviously seen her picture but she was prettier in the flesh and looked incredibly anxious as she sat flicking through a magazine at such speed that she couldn't possibly focus on a single word, never mind actually read anything.

"Miss Harrison?" he said, offering her his hand as she stood up to greet him. "I'm Adrian Williams. I work with Abi."

"So she's not here then?" Esther asked him.

As Ade gestured for her to sit again, he told a clearly worried Esther that they hadn't seen Abi in the office for a couple of days. Taking a seat opposite her, Ade then listened as Esther told him what she knew which wasn't too far shy of the information his own team had amassed but his ears pricked up at the mention of the mystery man Esther had encountered in Abi's flat.

"Do you know who he was?" Ade asked.

"He said he was doing an inspection so I assumed he was from the letting agency. But now that you mention it, I didn't actually ask him who he was. Why?"

"No reason," he said with a smile. "Quite the detective aren't you?" he added, making a mental note to check the man was legitimate.

She told him doing nothing wasn't an option and that she'd wanted to call the police but her boyfriend had pointed out it all looked too planned to report them missing. The irony wasn't lost on him.

As they wound up their chat and exchanged numbers, Ade suddenly didn't know what his final words should be. He wondered for a moment if someone should now be following Esther. He'd talk to DI Baker as soon as they were done. He felt a sudden desire to keep Esther safe and wanted desperately to reassure her that the police were in fact doing everything they possibly could to find her brother and her friend. Instead, he just smiled at her.

"Take care now, won't you Esther," was the only appropriate farewell he could come up with.

Ade spent the rest of the afternoon pacing up and down the office, feasting on antacids as he waited for people to report in with what he hoped would be the break they so badly needed but there was nothing. He barked orders and chased anyone and everyone but each call produced a big fat terrifying nothing.

By seven o'clock, the office was almost empty. The administrative staff had gone home and all the available officers were still out desperately searching for leads. Ade sat at his desk refusing to move. Leaving would feel like admitting defeat. It would be like he'd given up on Abi, like he no longer believed they could find her and he absolutely refused to accept that was the case.

When his mobile rang with a withheld number he snatched at it.

"Yes?" he barked, ready to let rip if it was someone wasting his time. And then he heard Abi's voice.

"Abi!" he shouted. "What the fuck?"

"I know," she said. "I'm sorry but I had to go last time and this is the first opportunity I've had to call you back."

"Just tell me where you are. Please!"

"It's a cottage called Daisy's Place," she said as Ade immediately grabbed for a piece of paper and a pen and wrote it down. "There are no street names that I've been able to see but it's about a twenty minute drive outside Deal on the Kent coast."

"We'll be on our way within the hour but then it'll be a couple more hours at least before we get to you. Where are you now?"

"In the main town on a borrowed mobile." Abi smiled over at an older lady who'd fallen for her 'I left my mobile in a restaurant' story and let her use her phone.

"And where's Matt?"

"He's buying food but I can't be away for long."

"Is there somewhere we could leave a phone for you to pick up?"

"I doubt we'll come out again tonight but I could suggest an early morning walk on the beach? There's a café called Angelo's near the entrance to the pier with tables outside. Why don't you wait there and I'll drop in for takeaways. I can pick it up from your table as I pass."

"If you're sure that'll work?" Ade asked.

"Of course I'm not sure but it's the best I can think of. In fact, I could suggest to Matt that we have our big chat as we walk. Any chance you can get a van down here and listen in? That way you'll know everything when I do. I haven't pushed him to talk until I was able to contact you again."

"I'm sure we can get that sorted," Ade said, looking at his watch and hoping that would indeed be the case. "We'll leave a phone and a mic for you. You'll just need to slip it in your pocket."

"Okay, but I don't know what time we'll be there so you'll have to assume early. You may have to hang around for a while."

"We'll be near the cottage in a few hours so we'll be watching but we'll arrive late so leave a light on somewhere downstairs so I know you're okay."

"Will do. And you need to check out a guy called Pete. He's the one who helped Matt get the escape plan in place. I gotta go."

"Be careful Abi," Ade pleaded but the line went dead leaving him unsure if she'd heard him.

Ade took a moment to let the relief that she was okay sink in, and then he picked up his phone again and started making calls. First an update for DI Baker then a call to organise a surveillance van and then finally he called Eddie.

"Pack a bag," he told him. "We're off to the seaside."

12

Matt's face lit up as he watched Abi approach. "Did you get everything you wanted?"

Abi held up a small bag with a smile having feigned a need to visit a chemist. "What about you?" she asked as she sat down opposite him at a table outside a small bar.

"Managed to squeeze in the butcher, the supermarket, the greengrocer, the deli and the bakery. It was like my own mini episode of Supermarket Sweep but with multiple venues! Do you want a drink or shall we just head back?"

"Let's just head back," she said, picking up some of Matt's many bags. "And then tomorrow, we need to have that chat."

As she said the words, Abi felt their blissful bubble slowly deflate. The time to face up to their current reality was now uncomfortably overdue and it had suddenly felt right to have Ade and Eddie listening in. She'd make sure they were up and out early the next morning with the long-awaited one-off performance of the life and times of Matt Harrison starting the minute she'd collected the mic and dropped it into her pocket.

For now, they headed back to the car for the short drive back to the cottage. Abi was out of the car first and as soon as she opened the front door, she turned on the lights and headed towards the kitchen. And then she stopped.

"Finally! I thought you two were never coming home."

Abi gasped and then forgot how to breathe. She turned around to see Matt behind her and beyond him, one of Dave's gang who'd stepped in behind Matt and was now blocking the door.

"How did you find us?"

She knew it was Matt who had spoken but it didn't sound like him. Abi could feel the terror seeping from every pore of his body as he gingerly stepped forward to stand next to her.

"Oh Matty, Matty, Matty," Dave said, his words slow and deliberate. He put his gloved hands on the armrests of the chair he sat in and pushed himself up until he stood at full height, his huge frame casting a deathly shadow across the room. "It didn't take long for Pete to talk."

"No!" Matt cried. "What have you done to him?"

"Oh, he'll be alright," Dave said with a dismissive wave of his hand.

"If you've hurt him, I'll…."

"You'll what?" A wave of anger crashed through Dave, making his back straighten and his fists clench. For a moment they just stared at each other. "Never mind all your posturing," Dave then said, irritation coating every word. "All that matters is that you've stepped so far out of line it's gonna take a bloody satnav to get you back on track. I told you she'd bring you down," he said, nodding towards Abi. "I gave you the chance to work out for yourself what you needed to do, and you threw that chance back in my face."

"I love her. Why is that so hard for you to understand?"

"You've known her for five bloody minutes!"

"Of course you don't understand. How could you?"

Dave smiled at him and shook his head, mocking him, his eyes heavy with condescension. And then he looked at Abi. "Are you going to tell him or shall I?"

Abi felt her face flush so intensely, the sudden heat made her eyes smart and her ears burn.

"Tell me what?" Matt looked from Abi to Dave and back again but they continued to stare at each other, Dave's eyes alive and daring her to speak.

"Abi?" Matt pleaded but she couldn't look at him even if she wanted to, her terrified eyes locked on Dave.

"Dad?" Dave didn't flinch. There was no way he was going to be the one who weakened and looked away.

"For fuck's sake, tell me what?" Matt's voice was suddenly so loud that both Abi and Dave immediately swung their heads around to look at him.

"She's a bloody copper!" Dave bellowed in response. "An undercover police officer with the country's finest Metropolitan Police Service. Isn't that right Detective Sergeant Abigail Wilson?"

Abi went to take hold of Matt's hand but he was already backing away from her. "Don't listen to him Matt. You know he'd say anything to break us up."

Tears stung Matt's eyes. "I thought this was real? I thought you felt the same?"

"It is and I do, I love you Matt, more than you could ever know."

"How can that be true if you're a cop?"

"It doesn't make any difference to how I feel about you!"

"So it is true?"

Abi hesitated for just a second but it was long enough for the weight of Matt's despair to make his head fall forward then she watched as he swung around to face Dave's lackey with his arms outstretched and ready to grab. There was a struggle in the midst of which she was sure she saw a gun but, before she could react, she felt an impact and a strange numbness that quickly gave way to a burning sensation. Then nothing.

A silencer ensured the shot sounded more like a whoosh than the usual loud firecracker but its effect was just as dramatic. As Abi hit the floor, an eerie stillness gripped the room until Matt, as if waking up from a terrible nightmare, threw himself down beside her, oblivious to the thin spray of blood that already covered him.

"Oh my God Abi!" he cried, cradling her head in his lap, leaning over her breathless body, his tears rolling on to her cheeks. "What've I done? What've I done?"

Dave sighed with a look of distain. "Get a grip boy, you're embarrassing yourself."

"She's dead, you heartless bastard!"

"Of course she's dead! One way or another it was the only possible outcome because she was about to take us down. A relationship's one thing but with a copper? You almost ruined us! And you should be bloody grateful I don't kill you for being such a stupid fucking idiot!"

Dave was already heading towards the door. As he reached it, he stopped for a moment and turned back to look at his son, waiting until Matt looked up before he spoke.

"Stop the pathetic whining and clear up your mess."

It wasn't until Matt felt himself start to stiffen that he snapped himself out of the trance he'd slipped into. Until this point, the only motion had been a rocking one as he'd swayed rhythmically backwards and forwards, holding Abi close. There had been so many questions, so much disbelief, so much hurt and such a terrible sense of betrayal that it had been easier to close down and just hold the only woman he'd ever loved but as his mind started to wake up, he knew he had to act.

"Okay, come on Matt, think. What do you need to do first?"

Talking to himself was strangely comforting as if somehow he wasn't alone, and the silence was doing nothing but amplify the manic brain chatter that raged in his head. He lifted Abi's head from his lap and, lying it gently down on the floor, he slowly stood up. He looked at his watch, wondering how long it might be before the police found him too. For a moment he wasn't sure if he cared but then adrenalin took over.

"Upstairs first I think," he muttered, heading straight to the bedroom where he swiftly packed up their clothes and toiletries, leaving himself something to change into before he left. He went into the bathroom and grabbed a disinfectant spray and cloth from the cupboard beneath the sink then started squirting indiscriminately – the taps, surfaces, toilet flush, door handles, anything at all that they might have touched. Intermittently, he stopped to scratch his right eyebrow, gently at first and then with increasing ferocity as the initial shock of what had happened started to wear off, replaced by a gradual swell of panic that he was only able to manage by inflicting an increasing level of pain on himself. With the first beads of blood showing on his brow, he went back to the bedroom and covered the room with an equally liberal layer of disinfectant.

"Good job," he told himself as he surveyed his work from the bedroom doorway. "Very thorough. A very good job indeed."

Picking up their bags he then headed back downstairs. He saw Abi's feet first and felt the sharpest of pains stab at his chest. He dropped the bags and put out a hand to steady himself, not sure for a moment if he was about to throw up or pass out. "What the fuck?" he whispered, fighting to control the stress, the panic and the despair that were generating a deafening sound in his ears, causing every hair on his body to stand to attention and setting every nerve end on fire. It was too much but his only option now was to just keep going.

Taking a sheet he'd brought downstairs with him, he went outside to the car and spread it out in the boot before going back inside for Abi. He carefully picked her up and then taking her outside, he quickly laid her in the compact space. He squeezed his lips tightly shut. There was no comfort to be had now from the sound of his own voice. He found himself fussing over her as if trying to make her comfortable and then, with his eyes closed, he hesitated for a moment before pulling down the boot. Ridiculous as he knew it was, it felt horrible closing her in.

Back inside, he then scrubbed the floor and the stained upholstery until any evidence of the horror that had recently unfolded existed only his mind. He put any rubbish in a black bag to dispose of later and changed into fresh clothes, gathering up the blood-stained t-shirt, jeans and socks he'd been wearing along with anything else that bore Abi's blood and stuffed it all in another bag, again to deal with later. Once he'd put everything in the car he went back inside the cottage for one last quick look around. His expectations of this place had been so incredibly different to what had actually played out and, as he felt a sense of sadness start to seep through his body, he quickly turned off all the lights and locked the door behind him.

Having to concentrate on the road ahead was a welcome distraction but once he was confident of the route there was nothing Matt could do to stop a barrage of ugly thoughts from crashing forward. He couldn't believe how monumentally he'd been played. The idea that Abi's involvement with him had been fake was too awful, too painful, too heartbreakingly paralysing to contemplate for even a second. Did that mean that her friendship with Esther had been fake too? And then it hit him what a massive investment Abi had made in order to get to him but, despite how mercenary it all felt, how cold and calculated, he was still desperate to believe that the intimacy he and Abi had shared had meant something. It simply had to. He'd opened his heart for the first time. He'd made himself vulnerable and taken previously unimaginable risks. She may not have meant to fall in love with him but for his own sanity, he would simply choose to believe that was exactly what had happened.

Tiredness stung his eyes. The lack of street lamps left him squinting, the words on the motorway signs blurring. For a moment he wondered if he should just give into sleep. It felt in the moment like the most efficient way to make the terrible pain and the awful feeling of hopelessness that threatened to suffocate him go away.

He could just close his eyes and wait for it all to end.

Matt had been away for less than half an hour when Ade and Eddie approached the cottage just after eleven o'clock. They drove slowly past and Ade bristled when he saw the place was in complete darkness. He pulled over.

"There's supposed to be a light on," he said to Eddie as he quickly got out the car. "I'm going to take a look."

Eddie got out too and watched as Ade disappeared up the pathway to the front door making sure he kept him in sight. Ade peered through one window then the next and then gestured to Eddie that he was going round to the back.

The second Eddie heard glass breaking he broke into a sprint but when he got to the back door, Ade was already inside. He followed him in, his nose twitching at the overpowering stench of bleach. He could hear Ade moving around upstairs and then a drumroll of thuds as he came running back down the stairs.

"They're not here," he shouted as he reappeared, his voice desperate and disbelieving. "They're not fucking here!"

13

It was thoughts of Esther that had made Matt keep focus. He'd missed the chance to tell Abi everything so maybe it was time to tell Esther? The weight of their past was becoming too much to bear on his own. But first he had to work out what to do with Abi.

Matt knew every camera-free corner of London so chose one on the northern edge of town. He forced himself to accept there was no dignified way to dump a body when it was someone you loved, and neither was it possible to avoid someone having to make the gruesome discovery. He'd thought about just calling the police himself. He didn't care what happened to him but if he'd implicated his father, there was no knowing what that might unleash and he couldn't risk Dave turning on Esther.

In the end, the best Matt could do was a bench on the corner of a park, positioned under the protection of a beautiful tree. If he approached carefully, he was confident he could do so unseen. There were no cameras, no residential properties overlooking him and no bars or restaurants. It was now past one o'clock in the morning and at this time of night, he was as good as invisible.

He pulled the car up as close as he could and then carefully lifted Abi out of the boot and placed her on the corner of the bench, pushing her into a suitable pose, taking a moment to straighten her clothes and smooth her hair, pushing it behind her ears. He worked hard not to look at her face, not wanting to see the haunted look that he imagined was now permanently etched in her eyes. Then he slipped a mobile phone into her pocket that only had Esther's number saved in it. He knew it would be awful for Esther to get a call or a knock at the door but he needed to know Abi would be with someone who cared about her one last time before she was committed to a wooden box; that she would be identified quickly and treated with some respect. Then, with a brief squeeze of Abi's hand, he quickly got back in the car and drove away, defying his instincts to look back one last time.

It was a delivery driver who found her. At first he'd assumed she was sleeping off too much alcohol but a series of badly planned deliveries had him crossing backwards and forwards from one side of the park to the other. Eventually, he'd passed her enough times that he felt the need to stop and make sure she was alright. As soon as he got close enough to see the waxen complexion and lifeless eyes, he raced back to his van for his phone. As he sat waiting for the police a few moments later, he thought of all the excuses he'd given his supervisor in the past for not having completed his assigned deliveries within a designated timeframe. This one definitely trumped them all.

It wasn't long before he could hear sirens in the distance and then a series of cars and vans swooped in, screeching to a succession of halts around him. It was mildly terrifying as he watched the first officers start erecting a tent around the bench with two people dressed from head to toe in white protective suits disappearing inside the second the structure had been assembled.

Detective Constable Eva Carpenter was having an equally surreal morning. Assigned to a new partner, DS Kelly Jackson, following months of barely leaving her desk, she stood for a moment not quite sure what to do at the crime scene of what was increasingly looking like her first murder.

"There's only one number on it." Eva turned with a start to see one of the crime scene investigators holding out a mobile phone in a plastic bag which she took from him. "Here's the number." As soon as Eva took the piece of paper, the white-suited being turned around and disappeared back into the tent.

"What've you got?" Kelly asked, having finished with the delivery driver for the time being.

"A phone," Eva said, holding it up. "With just one number," she added, holding the piece of paper aloft in her other hand.

For a moment they just looked at each other, an air of hopeful expectation from Kelly while Eva stood expressionless with the evidence still held high. And so they stayed until the penny finally dropped.

"I'll call the number," Eva said with great enthusiasm, earning herself a 'we got there in the end' kind of smile from the more experienced officer who then quickly moved on to the tent to hear what the investigative team could surmise from what they'd seen so far.

Eva moved herself away to make the call, running a number of scenarios through her head of what she might say if someone answered. When it went to voicemail, she took a note of the name and then set about finding the address the number was registered to.

An hour later they were on their way to the home of Esther Harrison. Esther invited them in and then Eva could only watch as Esther was told by Kelly, in the gentlest way possible, that there was a body of a young woman they hoped she would be able to identify. Although it hadn't felt that gentle if she was honest but then, what gentle way was there?

Over the next few hours Eva did her best to show compassion and be as supportive as she could be, all the time wondering how she would ever find peace again while images of a woman, shot and then left on a bench like someone taking a brief rest from the world, remained fixed in her mind. And then there were the cries and sobs of this poor dead woman's friend, so raw and heartfelt as she'd stood, holding a pale cool hand, that were like nothing Eva had ever heard before. But despite wanting to put off for as long as possible the moment when she would close her eyes in an attempt to find sleep knowing these images and sounds would inevitably come flooding back to haunt her, Eva had never been more relieved than when the working day was over and she could finally head home.

The next morning, she was at her desk early after the expected patchy night. The office was quiet so she used the time to catch up, checking emails first and then scrolling through bulletins to make sure she was on top of any recent appeals from other stations. And then she stopped, her eyes moving so fast she was barely reading every third word but no matter. The accompanying picture of a young woman, a woman whose image had haunted what little sleep she'd managed to get the night before, told her everything she needed to know. Eva snatched for her phone.

"Hello? Can I speak to Detective Sergeant Adrian Williams please?"

Ade sat at his desk with his head in his hands taking a moment to let the news sink in. She was dead. Abi was dead. And most likely had been for a couple of days now.

Having raced back to London in the early hours of Thursday morning, he'd spent all day trying to find where Abi might have gone and, all the time, she'd been either propped dead on a bench or lying in a police morgue. That was the thought that made him squeeze his eyes shut and bite down hard on his cheeks while he reined in the sudden rush of emotion that made him want to cry big angry desperate tears.

An hour after taking her call, Ade had picked up Eva and was pulling up outside Esther's flat. Jamie let them in and Ade let Eva go ahead of him. She started talking to Esther as they walked into the lounge, asking her how she was and if she'd managed to get any sleep. Ade was struck by how naturally Eva did this, grateful for the sense of calm she brought with her.

"I've brought another officer with me today Esther," Eva told her, making room for Ade to move forward. "This is Detective Sergeant Adrian Williams."

"You?" Esther said as she saw Ade. "I don't understand. I thought you worked at Abi's consultancy?"

"Hello again Esther. I'm so sorry I wasn't completely honest with you when we first met but the truth is I did work with Abi. She was also a police officer."

Esther as good as fell back on to the sofa.

"Would you like some water Esther? Perhaps I could make some tea?" Eva didn't wait for an answer and instead headed for the kitchen.

"You're going to need to explain that," Jamie said, sitting next to Esther and taking hold of her hand.

"Do you mind if I sit down?" Ade asked. Esther nodded and he moved as close as he could to her, sitting on an adjoining sofa. "This is going to be a lot to take in and difficult to hear so I'm just going to get it out as quickly as possible. Please forgive me in advance if any of it sounds insensitive. The last thing I want to do is offend you after everything else you've been through."

"Just tell me what's going on," Esther pleaded.

Ade took a deep breath. "Abi was working undercover." Esther turned to Jamie as if looking for reassurance that she'd heard that right. "The reason she was undercover was part of an operation to get information on your father, David Harrison, and Matt was deemed to be the best route to achieve that."

"Why?" Esther was incredulous. "How could Matt possibly help? We haven't seen my father for years."

"I'm afraid Matt's been working for your father for a very long time using his tech skills to help commit a currently unidentified number of planned robberies and frauds. People have also been hurt and possibly killed, Esther and we think that might include your mother."

"No!" Esther cried. "But he was in prison? You mean he got someone else to kill her?"

"We can't prove it, not yet anyway, but it's thought to be a strong possibility."

Esther shook her head. "I always believed he'd caused her death but I thought it was because of the years of abuse. I never thought he actually killed her. But you've got it so wrong about Matt. There's no way on this earth he'd ever work with Dad. Do you have any idea what he did to him as a child? It's a miracle he even survived."

"I know you don't want to believe it Esther but it is true I'm afraid." Ade opened a folder that he'd been holding since he arrived and handed her a photograph then another and another, each with a different image of Dave and Matt sitting in various cafés or just standing together on a pavement. "I don't want to distress you but these ones were taken on the day Matt and Abi disappeared," he said, handing a set of photographs to Esther that made her wince. "He found out about his relationship with Abi and didn't want Matt getting close to someone in case that person couldn't be trusted. We can't be sure but we think Matt's feelings for Abi were strong enough that he chose being with her over doing as your father wanted which is why they decided to run away. I imagine he thought Abi was in danger which tragically turned out to be true."

Esther put up his hand to stop him. "So just to make sure I've understood this correctly, Abi became my friend for no other reason than as a way to meet Matt?"

"I'm afraid that's right, yes," Ade said.

"And then she started a relationship with Matt, a relationship that got him beaten to a pulp and left him with no choice but to run for his life, just to get closer to our Dad?"

Ade nodded. "Yes, that's also correct."

Jamie shook his head. "I knew there was something about her. She was always poking around, asking so many questions."

"How could she do that to us?" Esther asked.

"She was doing a job, Esther. A job that cost her her life."

Esther glared at him. She was still too hurt and angry to feel any compassion for the woman who she'd just discovered had done nothing but use her, lie to her and betray her.

"Maybe we should take a break?" Jamie suggested.

As if on cue, Eva reappeared with a tray of tea and busied herself handing out mugs, adding sugar as required. There was a tense silence while Esther took a few sips. Ade watched her carefully, trying to judge if he could continue their conversation for just a little bit longer.

"Esther, I need your help to find Matt," he said, deciding he didn't have any time to waste.

"I'm sorry, Sergeant Williams, was it?"

"Yes, but please call me Ade."

"Well Ade, you must be really rubbish at your job," she answered flatly. "Abi waited a year to meet him and I'm sure she must have reported back to you that I never know when he's going to turn up, or where he is between visits. I know nothing about his life as you've just so beautifully illustrated." She shrugged. "So if I'm your best bet to find him then I'm afraid you're completely screwed."

"Do you know who this is?" Ade asked as he showed Esther another photograph, impervious to her scorn.

"That's Pete," she said. "He's an old family friend. He helped us when my Mum died and he and Matt have always been close. He's an old friend of my Dad's. Why are you interested in him?"

"We think he's probably the one who helped Matt and Abi disappear but he also works for your Dad. Are you still in touch with him? Maybe you have a number for him?"

Esther wasn't sure how to react. So harmless old Uncle Pete clearly wasn't as harmless as she'd thought but then pretty well nothing was currently as she'd thought. She reached for her phone and scrolled. "Here," she said holding the screen up to Ade. "I haven't been in touch with him for a million years but feel free to give it a try."

Ade scribbled down the number and then looked at Esther again. "We can't let Abi have died for nothing," he said. "I know Dave is your father but the most likely explanation is that he was responsible for her death. We have to prove what he's done, prove all of it so we can put him away for the rest of his life, and your help to make that happen would be invaluable."

"No way!" Jamie immediately leapt in. "So she can end up in the fucking morgue alongside Abi? Absolutely no fucking way."

"We can protect you," Ade told her, ignoring Jamie and keeping his eyes fixed on Esther.

"Like you protected Abi?" Esther calmly asked him.

"I'm not going to pretend there aren't risks but, whether or not you decide to help us, we do genuinely want to make sure you stay safe until this is all over. We don't know if Dave would ever hurt you, or if he even knows where you are. He clearly has eyes everywhere so it wouldn't be unreasonable to assume he has someone watching you at the very least."

Esther's eyes widened then filled with fear. How many times over the years had she felt like she was being followed? How many times had the phone rung with nothing but an eerie silence on the other end? But her father had never touched her before so why should that change now?

"Well if he is watching me," she said, "then he'll know you're here. So if I wasn't a target before, I guess I probably am now."

"We can protect you Esther," Ade said again. "We can move you to a safe location, just till this is all over. But if you help us, I know we can get the job done quicker." He paused for just a moment. "What do you say?"

14

Esther had needed a change of scenery so she and Jamie had come out for Sunday lunch but she was already questioning whether it had been a good idea after all. She resisted the temptation to down the glass of wine in front of her in one large gulp as she watched Jamie twitch opposite her, his eyes consistently flitting from one side of the restaurant to the other, and then scanning everything in between.

"Will you please stop doing that?" Esther pleaded.

"Doing what?"

"Your eyes are everywhere but on me."

Jamie looked at her and made a real effort to hold her eyes for a moment. "I'm sorry. I'm not doing it on purpose but now that I've seen pictures of your dad, I can't help keeping an eye out. You know, just in case."

The place was buzzing but the number of people was making Jamie nervous, wondering how on earth he was supposed to keep them both safe.

"Worried he might want to check your intentions towards me are honourable are you?"

"That's not funny Esther."

Esther smiled but the moment quickly passed as the enormity of the situation settled back on to her shoulders.

"What are you going to do?" Jamie asked her.

"Well I'm not moving out, that's for sure. Ade has nothing to suggest I'm even on my Dad's radar and the last few days have been unsettling enough without adding leaving my home to the list. Plus, I've got work to do and keeping busy, along with some semblance of normality, feels pretty important right now. So sod my pathetic excuse for a father. I simply won't allow myself to be intimidated."

"Well then I'm moving in," Jamie said in response. "And before you accuse me of taking advantage of the situation, that's absolutely not what I'm doing. I know it's not something you want at the moment and I know how important your independence is but, right now, I'm going to have to insist it's the right thing to do." Esther raised her eyebrows with a smile. "I can work from home," he continued, "and I promise to keep out of your way but you have to let me do this."

"Well if having you move in means you'll stop asking me every five minutes if I'm okay then I suppose we could make it work. Temporarily, of course."

"Of course," he repeated. "And what about helping the police?" Esther thought for a moment but said nothing so Jamie kept going. "I know I was the one shouting 'no way' at the very idea but if you can help find Abi's killer then maybe I overreacted? I suppose she deserves justice just like anyone else."

Esther's eyes shot up. "She used me and she lied to me and if my Dad found out she was working undercover, there's every chance Matt is lying somewhere dead too." Her eyes filled with tears, her words echoing around her head, sounding worse each time they repeated.

"All the more reason to help them then surely?" he said, taking hold of her hand. "If we can find him, we might be able to save him."

"He lied to me too. In fact, I'm pretty sure he's been lying to me for years."

"If that is the case, don't you want to know why? And what about your mother?" Esther flinched. "I know you don't like talking about it Esther but it's obvious you've never really accepted that she died of a heart attack. This could be your chance to find out what happened to her." Jamie stopped. He knew Esther well enough to know he'd pushed her hard enough. "Why don't I get us another drink?"

Esther looked at her empty glass with surprise. She clearly hadn't even noticed she'd emptied it. Jamie headed to the bar, leaving her alone with her thoughts for a moment. When he returned, he was convinced she hadn't moved an inch.

"Here we are," Jamie said as he put fresh drinks on the table. "I got you a large one this time and a bag of those nuts you like."

"Thanks. You really do think of everything."

Jamie sat down and took a sip of his drink while he tried to read Esther's face. "So?" he asked, accepting very quickly that he had no idea what she was thinking. "What's it going to be?"

Ade had never felt such a sense of relief than when Esther called to say she'd help. All he had to do now was work out how she could best do that. If Dave was still planning to break into FutureLab then no one was quite sure how this could be done without Matt and, right now, they didn't have a single lead as to his whereabouts. They'd strengthened the team watching Dave and his immediate circle but not one of them had met with Matt. There were no calls to trace and no financial trail to follow. Ade was convinced it was Matt who had brought Abi back to London and it had now been proven that the cottage was indeed the crime scene. The smell of bleach when they'd arrived was evidence enough as far as he was concerned but forensic experts had now found traces of Abi's blood. Matt had done a good job cleaning the place up but in the emotional state Ade imagined he'd been in, it wasn't really a surprise that he'd slipped up.

"Ade, Esther's here," Eddie shouted over to him.

Ade stood up and Eddie followed him to the meeting room where Esther was waiting. "Thanks for coming in Esther. We'd very happily have come to you."

"It's better here," she said. "I'd rather keep it all away from my home. It's not personal though," she quickly added.

Ade smiled. "I totally understand. This is my partner, Detective Constable Eddie Ferguson," he said as Eddie stepped forward.

"Really good to meet you Esther," Eddie said, offering his hand.

"Someone else who's been skulking around in the shadows," she said as she took his hand then she smiled as she saw Eddie's cheeks flush. "Don't worry Eddie. When I'm not being used as part of an elaborate police operation to bring down the majority of my family, I'm actually quite fun to be around."

"I can't imagine what you've been through," Eddie said to her, his eyes full of compassion. "But the scale of your father's activities is now so prolific I'm afraid this is the only way."

"Well that may be true with regards to my father's endeavours, but I'm not sure there's ever an excuse for messing with people's lives and tricking them into helping you though, is there?"

"Shall we crack on?" Ade suggested, cutting in before Eddie could reply. He sat down and nodded to Eddie to do the same. "Everyone's working really hard to make sure Abi's body can be released at the end of next week so her family are arranging her funeral for the Tuesday after," Ade explained, getting straight down to business. "Will you go Esther?"

"Will her family want me there? How much do they know?"

"They know she was working undercover. There'll be a large police turn out – Abi had a lot of friends and colleagues who'll want to pay their respects so her family won't know who you are, if that's the way you prefer it. You don't have to meet any of them or talk to anyone at all but we'd like you to be there. We'll post the funeral arrangements in a few strategic places so Matt will know about it, assuming he's waiting for the news. And if he does show up, I imagine he'll stay well hidden. You're the only person he's likely to approach which is why we'd like you to come alone. Without Jamie."

Esther took a deep breath and then blew it out. She wanted to say no. She wanted to make it perfectly clear that she didn't sign up for any of this, that it wasn't in her nature to be so duplicitous, so calculating, or so bloody heartless. These people just seemed to see her as a means to an end with no sense of empathy whatsoever. She would see Abi's mother grieving for her daughter and want to hug her, not avoid her. But then she wouldn't be at the funeral in the capacity of mourning friend. She'd be there merely as bait.

"I know what you're thinking Esther," Eddie said.

"Oh you do, do you?"

"That we're just using you without any thought at all for how confused you must be right now. That we're oblivious to the fact you're grieving for someone who, as it turns out, wasn't who you thought they were at all, making it impossible to know how on earth you should be feeling. Am I close?" Esther stared at him but said nothing. "We're not being intentionally insensitive to your situation, we just don't have time on our side. We don't know yet what danger Matt might be in. We don't even know if he's dead or alive...."

"Okay, I'll go," she interrupted, reminding herself that she was the one who offered to help and that she did desperately want to find Matt. "And what do we do until the funeral?"

"We'll continue to watch your father and his associates but it's just business as usual for you," Ade said. "But if Matt gets in touch, we would of course appreciate you letting us know." Ade then hesitated for a moment. "You don't think Matt is a potential danger to you, do you?"

"What? That's the most ridiculous thing I've ever heard!" Esther rolled her eyes. "What is wrong with you?"

"I'm sorry Esther but however hard this might be to hear, until we know exactly what happened, we can't ignore the possibility that it was Matt who killed Abi. It's perfectly reasonable that...."

"No!" Esther threw up her hand to stop him. "You stop right there! If you want my help I have to believe you're not clinically insane which is exactly how you're now sounding."

"I just want you to be safe," Ade said. "And it would be reckless to rule anything out currently, however uncomfortable it might make us. Are you sure you don't want us to move you somewhere?"

"No, I don't," Esther said, unable to stop the anguish she was feeling spilling into her voice. "I'm fine where I am thank you. And I want you to promise you won't have me followed. Helping you find Matt is one thing, but you have to trust me enough not to watch my every move."

"I'll put someone outside your flat any time you feel vulnerable, but that's it."

Esther nodded. "Okay, thanks. I appreciate that." She pushed back her chair. "If we're done?"

"Yes, thanks again for coming in," Ade said as they all stood up. "We're on your side Esther. You do know that, don't you?"

Esther was already out the door. "I'll see myself out," she said, as she hastily walked away.

When Esther arrived at the church just over two weeks later, there was already quite a crowd gathered outside. She was quickly surrounded by a sea of police uniforms as she tried to lose herself amongst the various groups that had formed as people quietly chatted, faces serious, their voices low and respectful. She saw Ade standing on his own on the outer edge, making no attempt to disguise the fact that he was simply watching, eyes constantly on the move. He nodded when he saw her and for a moment she wondered if she should go over and join him but quickly decided not to. And then she stopped, unsure for a moment what she could do to avoid looking conspicuous.

"Hello Esther," Eddie said, suddenly appearing beside her.

"DC Ferguson. Good to see you again," Esther said, surprisingly pleased to see him.

"No one calls me DC Ferguson. It makes me sound like a police officer," he said with a smile. "Eddie'll do just fine. Do you mind if I sit with you?" he asked as people started to file into the church.

"Not at all. In fact, I'd be delighted."

Esther felt more comfortable with Eddie by her side. They sat out of the way, near the back and on the end of an aisle. Esther sought out Abi's parents and her eyes misted over as she watched Abi's mother, head bowed, sadness curling her shoulders, her husband sitting incredibly close as if propping her up. She could only see her side on but Esther thought she looked elegant with Abi's long thick dark hair curling into her neck. And in that moment, something inside Esther changed. She'd been so hurt that her friendship with Abi had turned out to be completely fake that she suddenly realised she hadn't allowed herself to acknowledge how incredibly sad it was that she had died. And it had been such a violent death. Had she known it was coming? Had there been time for her to realise her life was about to be over with just the simple squeeze of a trigger? Esther shuddered and a new realisation of what had happened, and of where she currently was, rippled up through her body and a tiny cry escaped.

"You okay?" Eddie asked.

Esther nodded, unable to speak. It may have been just part of the job to Abi but for Esther, it had felt like a real friendship. It hurt so much because she had genuinely cared for Abi and now she was gone. Esther felt her heart swell with the sense of loss and then there was nothing she could do to stop the tears. Without looking at her, Eddie offered her his hand and Esther gladly took it. Here she was at the funeral of a police officer who had tricked her way into Esther's life, started a fake relationship with her brother and most likely been shot, if not by her father, then by someone ordered to do so by him. Holding the hand of another police officer therefore felt perfectly normal under the circumstances.

The service passed in a bit of a blur with some readings, a few hymns and the traditional prayers, and then it was time to move to the cemetery where a large sinister hole waited to swallow Abi for all eternity. Esther stayed back with Eddie still by her side and let the committal play out in front of them. She imagined Eddie had been assigned to look after her but she didn't have the energy to care, choosing instead to just be grateful for his compassion and discretion.

"Thanks for coming Esther." As everyone started to disband, Esther turned to see Ade. "Can I organise a lift home for you?"

"Thank you but no. I feel the need to walk for a bit and then I'll just find a cab when I'm done. Can I trust you to give me some space?"

Ade looked at her for a moment. "I don't know what you mean."

"Yes you do. You'll want to follow me but I'd really appreciate some time on my own. Matt won't turn up if he knows you're following me, and he will know. And if he does turn up, I'll call you. You do believe that don't you?"

Ade thought for a moment. "Of course," he eventually said, reluctantly accepting she was right. "I'll give you a call tomorrow if that's okay?"

Esther nodded, unsure what they'd have to talk about and then she smiled her thanks to Eddie before the two officers headed back towards their waiting colleagues.

Esther was relieved for Abi and her family that nothing inappropriate had happened but she had seen the strain on Ade's face and knew the pressure was starting to manifest itself, knowing he would be hugely disappointed at the absence of a certain uninvited guest. Oh well. There wasn't anything she could do about that.

Esther took a moment to look at her surroundings, performing a slow complete circle as she tried to decide which way to go. There was a bank over to the left and at the top, she could see a fence that separated the cemetery's grounds from a park. Set just behind this, she was sure she could see a bench, almost hidden from view by a mass of bushes and overgrown shrubbery. Decision made, she then set off through the cemetery towards a gate that she could see would take her up into the park. It wasn't an area she knew but she hoped a stroll through some greenery would help to dissipate the tension of the day.

As she entered the bottom corner of the park, she stopped momentarily to text Jamie, telling him she was fine and just needed a moment to let it all sink in. She then followed the path up through a series of beautiful trees and it wasn't long before she came to the small opening she'd spotted. The bench was perfectly situated, offering a view down to the chapel and the cemetery where the last few people were now dispersing, leaving behind them a visible mound of earth that was smothered in flowers.

It was just the kind of spot she'd hoped to find. She smiled, made herself comfortable and then she waited.

15

Esther had watched at least two thirds of the sun sink behind the horizon before she felt his presence. She stood up and there he was, slowly walking towards her with arms outstretched. She waited until he was right in front of her and then she slapped him hard across the face with all the strength she could muster.

"That's for all the lies you've told me," she said through gritted teeth, "and for making me worry about you constantly, never knowing where you were or if you were okay. When all the time you were with him!" Esther watched Matt press his hand to his face to nurse his stinging cheek but she refused to be put off. "Why didn't you trust me enough to tell me what happened to Mum because I know you know!" And then she sat back down on the bench, so confused, so angry, so defeated by it all that she couldn't even summon up the energy to cry.

Matt waited for a moment and then he slowly sat down next to her.

"And don't you dare tell me you're sorry!" she barked at him.

"Esty please!"

"No, don't say that to me! You don't get to say that, or use that tone with me anymore, expecting me to just forgive you anything and ask you nothing!" Esther looked at him with pleading eyes but Matt quickly looked away. When he stayed tight-lipped, Esther looked straight ahead too, watching the last of the sun disappear. She shivered as it sucked any heat left in the day down with it.

For a while that's how they stayed. A couple of times, she was aware of Matt sneaking a look at her. Then he would go to say something but stop himself. She refused to show him any encouragement. Let him suffer, she thought.

"I knew you'd find my spot," he eventually offered. "You know me too well."

"A place where you could feel you were part of it all and say your goodbyes to Abi without being seen," she said, still staring straight ahead, and then she shrugged as if it were obvious that this was clearly the place she would find him. "How long were you watching me?"

"Since you sat down," he said. "I knew you'd know I was nearby then I just had to be sure you weren't followed. Sorry to leave you sitting here for so long."

"It's fine. I needed a moment to myself," Esther said, finally turning to look at him. She studied his face and then winced. "I think I left a hand print. I'm so sorry, I shouldn't have hit you."

Matt carefully stroked his cheek. "It's okay. I've suffered much worse. And I deserved it."

"Like those new scars I can see? You didn't deserve any of it." She shook her head. "I shouldn't have hit you."

"I disappeared without a word and then left Abi with just your number, knowing how terrifying it would be when the police turned up at your door. Never mind all the other stuff so you have nothing to reproach yourself for."

"You know everyone's looking for you?"

"I needed some time to get my head together. I'm so sorry about Abi. I didn't know what to do but the thought that you might hold her hand one last time made it felt slightly less like I was just abandoning her."

"But none of it was real Matt! She was just using us, and you far more so than me. It was all a big fat lie."

Matt was already shaking his head long before she'd finished. "No Esty, you're wrong. It may have started out like that but Abi had real feelings for me, I know she did."

Esther went to argue back but then stopped herself. "Well I guess we'll never know now will we?" she said quietly. She reached for his hand and for a moment they sat in contemplative silence but there was still so much Esther wanted to know. She waited for as long as she could until it was just too hard to stop the questions flooding forward.

"Working for Dad Matt? What the fuck? How could you keep that from me all these years? And you know they think he killed Mum? In fact, the way they talk about him you'd think he was some kind of modern day Al Capone. So what does that make you?"

Matt released his hand from her grip to pull his coat tightly around him. "It makes me collateral damage. The sacrificial lamb if you will. But don't think for one minute it's a position I put myself in."

"That's just the point. I've no idea what to think."

"It's a long story Esty. Perhaps we should go somewhere warmer before I launch in?"

"Okay but just tell me one thing first. Did Dad kill Mum?"

Matt looked at her with such a pained expression, the like of which Esther had never seen before. His face appeared contorted as he struggled to find the right words.

"He didn't kill her Esty," Matt took hold of Esther's hands. "He did something much much worse."

PART THREE

16

Sixteen years earlier

Matt pulled himself up to full height as the line finally started shuffling forward. He could see those up ahead of him were now slowly filing into the visitors' room and he forced himself to breathe. Slow breaths, in and out, in and out, pushing his shoulders down, keeping his neck long. Anything to appear relaxed and in control.

His eyes were drawn to his father the minute he entered the room. It was nearly two years since he'd seen him and he felt his blood chill as their eyes met. There was no turning back now.

"You made it then," Dave said as he watched his tall lanky teenage son drop into the seat opposite him although there was no noticeable enthusiasm in his words.

"It's not like I had a choice, is it?" The presence of multiple prison guards gave Matt a rare confidence, a feeling he intended to take full advantage of.

"How's my little Esty?"

"She's not yours. You don't own her. You don't deserve her at all. In fact, you don't deserve to even say her name."

"Careful son." Matt immediately sat back in his chair as Dave shot forward, a terrifying look in his eyes that Matt knew all too well.

For a moment neither moved as Dave silently re-established his authority, not moving back until he felt Matt had got the message but Matt was too hyped now to back down so quickly.

"Don't you want to know how Mum is?" he asked. Dave stared at him, daring him to keep going. "Well I'm sure you'll be relieved to hear the scars have faded. I mean they're still there, obviously, just easier to hide with a thick layer of make-up. And this is the longest spell she's had for years without any freshly broken bones or bruising so that's all good news isn't it?"

Dave went to grab him but Matt was too quick, dodging the large hand that swung past his nose as he deftly slid his chair back. Dave may not have made contact but there was enough of a noise to attract a nearby guard who moved closer, making it obvious he was now keeping an eye on them.

"So why am I here?" Matt asked, his voice lowered now.

"Your mother's lucky to be alive. You know she's why I'm in here? She shopped me! My own wife!" Dave did his best to temper the level of his own voice too.

"You're right, she is lucky to be alive," Matt shot back. "But only because of the number of times you beat her to a pulp. Perhaps if you tried looking at life from her perspective you might wonder why it took her so long to make the call?"

Dave swallowed hard, his unblinking eyes never straying from Matt's. "Well it's time she paid. She'll be dead tomorrow."

"Please Dad, no!" Matt cried, seeing nothing but pure evil in Dave's eyes and in no doubt at all that he meant every word. "Why?"

"Because she doesn't deserve to live! She certainly doesn't deserve to have the life she currently has. And the last thing I want to see when I get out is her swanning around, spending my money, living in luxury in my house, laughing at me while I've been locked away in this shithole and all because of her!"

"But what about Esther?"

"She deserves better than that weak treacherous bitch."

"She deserves to have her mother!"

"Well she can pretend to die then and just disappear but she doesn't get to just carry on as if nothing's happened."

Matt wasn't sure he'd heard right. "What do you mean pretend to die?"

They were both leaning in now and the more intense the conversation became, the lower their bodies went, their faces sliding ever closer in an attempt to keep their words inaudible to the nearby guard. Despite the lack of volume, enhanced expression made it impossible to miss the despair in Matt's voice and the malice in Dave's.

"Everyone has to think she's dead." Dave was thinking on his feet. "Yes, this is even better! It's the perfect way for Kate to pay. She needs to move right away and stop all contact with you and Esther. And the only way that's going to happen is if you tell everyone she's dead." Dave paused, wanting to be sure Matt was keeping up, and then his mouth twisted into a horrid sadistic smirk. "If I have her killed it's all over but this way, she'll live a life of misery till the day she draws her last breath." And then he shrugged. "She's dead to me either way. You decide."

"You can't really want Esther to think she's dead? Why would you do that to her?" Matt shook his head, hoping that at any moment Dave would tell him this was all nothing more than a terrible joke but he knew from bitter experience that was never going to happen. "And how the hell would we do it?"

"You'll have to fake her death."

"How am I supposed to do that?" Matt's voice may not have been getting any louder but it was certainly getting higher with every word, a feeling of terror slowly squeezing his voice box making it increasingly hard to speak at all. "What exactly is she supposed to die of? And people will expect a funeral. For fuck's sake Dad please think about Esther! Think what this insane plan will do to her!"

"She'll be better off without her. And she has you. And she'll have me back in her life again soon too."

"Until she finds out what you've done, then she'll hate you more than she does already, assuming that's even possible."

This time Dave was too quick and he grabbed Matt's arm, the vice like grip making Matt gasp. "Let me make myself crystal clear," his voice so low now that Matt had to strain to hear. "You'll go home and tell your mother that if she wants to live she needs to pretend to die and then disappear with no forwarding address. And not at some point in the future, now. I want it to happen now. But you tell her I'll know where she is. I'll always know where she is. You'll be eighteen in a few months so be smart about it and then you and Esther can just stay in the house until I get out."

Dave released Matt's arm and pulled back slightly, his arms resting on the table keeping his body pitched forward. "And now to business. I know your tech skills are off the scale so while I'm in here, you work hard on them. Learn everything you can, buy whatever kit you need. Just speak to Pete, he'll sort you out. I'll be out soon enough and then I'll be lying low for a while, doing whatever I have to do to convince my probation officer that my only ambition is to be a model citizen. And then we'll get started."

Matt's eyes shot up, a swell of nausea propelling him forward. "Started on what?"

"Working together of course! Harrison and Son. Has a nice ring to it don't you think?" While Matt struggled to swallow the rising bile that was now clawing its way up his throat, Dave continued. "We're going to raise our game, taking whatever we choose from the kind of company that will never want to admit someone's hacked their way in, and you're going to get us the access we need to do it."

"And what if I say no?"

Dave slowly leant forward and it took all of Matt's nerve to hold his position until Dave's face was only centimetres from his own.

"If you say no then your mother will be dead. Only properly dead. In the ground dead. And when the time comes, you can make up whatever you like to tell Esther about some great job you've got but you will be working for me and she must never find out. If you ever tell Esther your mother is still alive or you're working for me then again, you'll be planning your mother's funeral for real. And if Kate ever tries to contact you or Esther, or if either of you have a pang of conscience and try to turn me in in the future, I'll kill you all."

"You'd never hurt Esther!"

"Wouldn't I? I'm not messing around here son. Your mother doesn't deserve that beautiful girl after putting me in here so yes, I will kill Esther if it stops your mother going near her. And I will kill Esther if you don't do every job I ask of you. Do you understand?" He waited. "Do you understand?" he said, taking hold of Matt's arm again and giving it a firm squeeze.

Matt winced. "Yes, I get it."

As he fully absorbed the words he'd just spoken, Matt dropped his head, a boy defeated. In the space of less than twenty minutes, Dave had systematically ruined his life, and the lives of his mother and sister. And then he slowly looked up. "But you don't get to come home when you come out of here. If by some miracle I've been able to keep Esther on track, you don't get to walk back into the house and mess it all up again."

Dave looked at him with what almost looked like pride. It certainly wasn't a look Matt recognised. "Haven't quite knocked all the spirit out of you yet then?" And then he chuckled.

"Nothing about this is funny!" Matt suddenly yelled.

"Keep your bloody voice down!" Dave growled, checking the nearby guard to make sure he wasn't interested in them again. When he was confident their conversation was still as private as it could be, he continued. "Fine. But I will want to see Esther and no threat from you is going to stop me but I won't come back to the house. And consider that your first and last concession. You don't get to make any more demands."

"What if Mum won't play along? Have you thought about that? What if she'd rather be dead if she can't be with me and Esther?"

"That won't happen because you'll give her hope," Dave said, suddenly looking smug. "If she's alive, there's always a very slim chance you'll all be reunited." He shrugged. "No chance of seeing you again if she's really dead now is there?"

17

Kate sat quietly letting it all sink in. Only that morning she'd studied her face in the mirror thinking what a good job she'd done with various creams and oils to minimise the scarring over the last couple of years. The last beating she'd suffered had been the worst by far with bruising so severe she'd felt Dave's presence long after the police had handcuffed him and taken him away. But even faded, every time she saw her reflection she was reminded of him, of a specific blow, of a moment when she'd feared she'd finally be broken beyond repair. If there was one thing she thought she would never tolerate it was a violent husband and yet here she was, scarred for life both mentally and physically, permanently afraid even with him locked up, a ghostly shadow of the woman she once was. And now, if she wanted to stay alive, that was exactly what she had to become. A living ghost.

"Mum?" Matt asked, his voice gentle and full of kindness. "Are you okay?"

She smiled at him but her eyes were full of sadness. "I was just replaying the moment the police took him away. I thought I'd won. I thought it was my moment of triumph which is why I whispered in his ear that it was me who'd called them." She paused for a moment. "If I'd just kept my mouth shut." She shook her head. There was little point wallowing in 'what ifs'. All that mattered now was that he was going to punish her for the rest of her life. "Did you believe him?"

"That he'd kill you? Yes, I did believe him. But killing Esther? I find that really hard to believe but are you prepared to take the risk?"

Her eyes filled with tears. "Esther's only fourteen. She still needs me."

"I know Mum and I'll be there for her, always. I know it won't be the same for her but I'll protect her with my life, you know I will."

His words meant everything and nothing. Of course Kate was comforted knowing Matt would look after Esther but she wanted to do it! It was her job, not his! In fact, not a job but a privilege. That's how she'd always considered motherhood and it was so bitterly unfair that the man who had been by her side since they were kids, who had gone on to romance her, been kind and gentle as he'd courted her, had promised her everything, had ultimately delivered nothing but pain and misery.

"And I won't be able to see you either?" The first tears slipped on to Kate's cheeks and she quickly wiped them away. Matt was immediately out of his chair and kneeling in front of her. Kate gently stroked the scars on his face. "I'm so sorry Matt. I tried to stop him so many times."

"I know you did. You distracted him away from me countless times when it was obvious he was looking for a punchbag and I hated that you had to do that."

"None of that compares to the thought of not seeing you both."

"I'll find a way," Matt said with such passion in his voice. "We have to believe we can turn this around. I'll work hard for him, he'll be richer than his wildest dreams and then maybe…"

"Don't Matt. Don't tell me you think he might soften, or suddenly develop a conscience."

"But even false hope is better than no hope, isn't it?"

And then they stopped. An eerie silence descended as both heads went down, lost for a moment to their own thoughts, but someone had to say it and Kate knew that someone had to be her.

"We'd better start planning how the hell we're going to pull this off then, hadn't we?"

Over the next few weeks, they talked through a number of equally ridiculous scenarios and then it finally hit them that the key was to keep it as simple as possible. If they couldn't explain each step in a single sentence they went back to the beginning and started again. It was relentless and exhausting but they felt they were making progress and then suddenly, they cracked it. The final test was to run it past Pete, the only other person who would be privy to the plan.

"Okay," Matt said as the three of them sat down together at the kitchen table. "Let me run through from start to finish to give you the full picture before you ask any questions." Pete nodded his agreement so Matt took a deep breath and then launched in. "Our plan is to say Mum had a sudden cardiac arrest here at home. This would have caused her to lose consciousness and without emergency care, it's perfectly reasonable that she would have died. We've done our research and a sudden cardiac arrest is possible at her age. People will just think it's because of the terrible stress Dad put her under so they'll all say he was to blame which will serve him right." Matt stopped for a moment to regain his composure and then he calmly continued. "I'll tell Esther I called the GP who came and certified the death and that her body was taken away by an undertaker. Esther has a weekend away planned with her best friend's family so we'll do it then. That way I can say I found her when I came home late and it can all play out overnight when there's no one around. The undertaker will be whoever you trust to do the job, Pete. They'll need to have a trolley and a body bag with sufficient air holes in it and then Mum can get out again the minute she's in the van. I'll fake a death certificate but we won't register her death in the hope that one day she'll be able to come out of hiding. We'll have a quiet service at a crematorium so all we'll need is a coffin and something suitably heavy to pass as a body that won't raise any suspicion when it burns." Matt stopped. "I'm so sorry Mum."

"It's fine darling. You're doing really well," she said with an encouraging smile.

Matt took another deep breath. "We'll buy a burial plot and a gravestone. There'll be flowers and anything else you would expect to see. And the timing means it will all happen three weeks after my eighteenth birthday so there shouldn't be any issue with me looking after Esther once the dust's settled."

And then he stopped. Pete reached across and put a hand on his shoulder and gave it a reassuring squeeze. "Well done buddy. It looks like you've got everything covered. I know how tough this is. For all of us." He turned his eyes to meet Kate's and they exchanged a wistful smile. Pete had always been there for them, supporting where he could without putting himself in the firing line. He'd grown up with Dave and Kate, managing to carve a role as Dave's most trusted friend but also as Kate's defender and ally. And he'd always been close to the kids too, but particularly Matt. He'd take him to football training and matches, take him fishing or bowling if he was at a loose end, and was always ready to help with friendship issues or latterly, to offer girlfriend advice. He basically did all the things Dave should have done, but never did.

"What about Dave?" Pete then asked.

"What about him?" Matt said, wondering what he could possibly have missed.

"Will he come to the funeral?"

"So he can literally spit on my grave?" Kate looked horrified at the idea.

"No, that could actually be a good thing," Matt said to her. "Think about it for a minute. If he's going to be there, we can use that as a reason to keep it really small. We can blame the prison. Say there are conditions to him being allowed to attend."

Kate shook her head. "The thought of Dave playing the grieving husband is hard to imagine. But then this whole situation is as surreal as it gets so do whatever you have to do." She stood up. "I need a drink. Anyone else?"

"I'll have one with you," Pete said, "and then we need to talk about…" He hesitated for a moment. "About where you're going to go. Afterwards."

18

The plan worked like a dream and that's how it had felt to both Kate and Matt. Although perhaps more like a nightmare, particularly for Matt who felt like he'd been under the harshest spotlight for days now. From stage managing a visit from a fake GP, to a black unmarked van arriving to load a body bag that had come into the house empty and left with his mother inside, something he'd been unable to watch even though he knew she would be out of it again within a few minutes, to the eerie silence that hit the minute they'd all left, throughout all of it, he'd felt under constant scrutiny.

It was all done by four o'clock on Sunday morning. There was nothing for Matt to do then but wait for Esther to come home from her weekend away, the spotlight waiting menacingly just ahead of him for the moment he would once again be centre stage.

Twelve long hours. That's how long he waited to hear her burst through the door. "I'm home!" she shouted, coming in via the back door and straight into the kitchen. Matt heard her drop her bag as she moved down the hallway towards him in the lounge. "Mum, I'm home!" she shouted again. And then there she was in the doorway, surprised to see him sitting on the floor under the window. "Where's Mum?" she asked him, and then she must have seen something in his expression, seen the anguish in his eyes, or picked up on the tension in his neck because she suddenly rushed across the room, crouching down in front of him. "What's happened? Where's Mum?" She watched Matt's eyes fill with tears. She took hold of his arms and shook him and then she screamed at him. "Tell me what's happened to Mum!"

The only way Esther could cope with the days that followed was to retreat deep inside herself. She barely said a word, kept her eyes down, listened to instructions and did exactly what she was told. She stiffened whenever Matt tried to hug her and walked away if he showed any kind of emotion at all. Her survival strategy to get through this terrible ordeal was to shut down and feel nothing.

Matt, meanwhile, with the spotlight very much still burning down on him, was pulling off the performance of his life. He was a pallbearer alongside Pete, he gave a eulogy, he greeted people, he thanked them for their kindness and provided comfort when friends of Kate's broke down. Dave had come into the chapel once everyone else was seated and the coffin had been brought in, and had sat at the back for minimum disruption. Matt didn't look at him once. He saw Esther's back stiffen when it was very obvious from the gasps and hushed whispers that reverberated all the way up to the high ceiling and back again that Dave had indeed arrived. For a moment, Matt feared she might suddenly lose it and let all that pent up emotion out on a man she would now forever blame for her mother's death. Like many others, Esther firmly believed that her mother's heart had simply been unable to cope with the endless psychological and physical abuse. But Esther didn't move. She barely even blinked.

The service was beautifully respectful and when the moment came for the coffin to disappear behind a curtain there was a flurry of stifled wails, the finality of the moment too much for some to bear. Esther remained rigid, her hands prayer-like against her mouth, preventing any words or cries escaping. Matt stood beside her, his arm protectively around her shoulders and there they waited, with Matt not prepared to move until he'd had some kind of sign from Esther that she was ready to leave.

Pete quietly ushered everyone else outside, directing them towards a nearby pub where drinks and a simple buffet were waiting. The sound of gentle chatter could be heard as the small group of friends and neighbours checked in with each other, making sure everyone was okay and coping with the sadness of the day before they headed off for a well-needed drink. Under more genuine circumstances it would have been a touching moment, Matt thought, one that he might still have taken comfort from if not for the presence of Dave, still lurking at the back of the chapel flanked by two prison officers. There was a brief exchange and then they started to move, prompting Esther to turn and head towards them. Matt looked on, breath held, watching as Dave's eyes started to lift in anticipation, his mouth daring to curl towards a smile at the sight of his beloved daughter approaching. As she stopped in front of him, Dave went to step forward and just as he did, she swung her arm with all the might her fourteen year old body could assemble and slapped him hard across the face. And then before Dave had a chance to take in what had just happened, she ran, out of the chapel and the surrounding cemetery, not stopping until the burning in her legs and her lungs forced her to slow down. She sat on a curb, gasping for air between the violent sobs that now racked her body.

For a moment Matt had remained frozen to the spot and then he raced after her, running through whatever words had flown out of Dave's mouth the moment he'd recovered himself without hearing a single one of them. All he cared about was finding his scared little sister and doing whatever he could to make her feel safe.

When he caught up with her, he threw himself down beside her, wrapping himself around her, rocking her, whispering into her ear that it was okay, that somehow everything would be fine. He squeezed his eyes shut, her pain so intense it took his breath away, his heart tight in his chest. He hoped more than anything that she would indeed be okay in time but he knew that, whatever the future held, he would never ever forgive himself for what he'd just put her through. It may not have been his idea, he may not have wanted to go through with any of it but that changed nothing in his eyes. He felt as responsible as their father and he couldn't imagine ever feeling worse about himself than he did in that moment.

Kate looked at her watch for the umpteenth time trying to imagine exactly what Esther was doing and how she was coping and, each time she did, she cried fresh tears. She'd been in her new home for five days now, a rental property in a small Sussex village. She'd done her best to distract herself shopping for new bits and pieces but she'd barely slept for more than an hour or so at a time, constantly waking with her heart pounding and her hair stuck to her head with sweat thanks to the same recurring nightmare. In it, she repeatedly watched Matt tell Esther that she was dead, witnessed first-hand Esther's shock and disbelief, then saw her ravaged with the most heartbreaking grief, standing close enough to touch her but unable to be seen or felt, unable to offer comfort. Just as it would be for the rest of her life. She would be absent. Impotent. Unable to console or counsel.

She had at least stopped torturing herself about how she could possibly have allowed this all to happen. Having asked herself every minute of every hour of every day that had passed so far, she already knew it was a pointless exercise. It didn't change anything, merely reminded her how powerless she was and threatened to slowly drive her mad. In fact, if it wasn't for Pete, she was sure she'd be certifiable already. Just his presence was a comfort. They sat in silence now at her kitchen table, the doors to the prettiest of gardens open, a gentle breeze washing over them.

"So, this place is working out okay for you?" he asked, waiting for the large mug of tea in front of him to cool.

"It's hard to get excited about anything but yes, it's very lovely. Thank you for finding it for me."

"The least I could do. And particularly attractive because it's about to go on the market. There's no pressure on you at all but, if you decide you like it here and feel like you might like to stay, I'll sort out buying it for you. I've already been in touch with the agents. You'll get first refusal when the owner's ready to get going."

Kate thought for just a moment and then shrugged. "Yeah, why not. Buy it."

"There's no rush Kate. You've got time to really think about it. Time to get to know the area and get a real sense of whether or not you'd be happy living here."

"Buy it," she said again, her eyes gazing out on to the garden.

"It'll be bought outright but in Dave's name. You do realise that?"

"I'm to be a guest in his house, or perhaps prisoner would be more accurate, trapped and beholden for the rest of my life." She rubbed her forehead gently with her finger tips. "Just buy it Pete," she said without looking up.

While there was paperwork to manage, Pete had been a constant visitor and when he left for the last time, knowing he'd stretched the process out for as long as he could, he gave her a mobile phone as a parting gift. "It's not to replace your own phone," he said. "Keep this one just for me. It means we can keep in touch without anyone knowing. Just for emergencies though."

She hugged him tightly, knowing the minute he walked away, that was it. She would be on her own, cut off from everyone she loved with only guilt and a sense of hopelessness for companions.

And then as the weeks limped past after the funeral and there had been no calls to say it had all gone horribly wrong, or that the plan had been blown wide open, Kate knew she had a decision to make. She could either wallow in a bed of misery and die a slow painful death from her broken heart, or she could accept that she was in an unimaginably tragic situation but resolve to make the best of what she had. And most importantly, she could choose to believe that she would one day find a way back to her children.

She of course chose the latter.

19

"Is there anything to eat?"

Matt gulped, aware that his eyes had spontaneously filled with tears. It was the first time Esther had spoken since the funeral which was now almost two weeks ago. The day after the service, he and Esther had buried Kate's ashes alone. Matt had read a poem but Esther hadn't said a single word. Neither had she cried. It was like she was completely numb, vacant almost, having shut down so efficiently she'd become desensitised to everything.

Suddenly hearing her voice again made Matt immediately step towards her with his arms outstretched causing her to take a large step back. He put his hands up by way of an apology and instead just smiled at her.

"Why don't we go out for something? A burger at that new place maybe?" Matt could see Esther was seriously considering it. "I hear they do amazing puddings." The mention of desserts caused a slight flicker and Matt thought his heart would burst when she slowly looked at him and quietly nodded her consent.

It had been such a challenging couple of weeks. Everyone around them had gone back to their normal day to day lives while Matt and Esther had been left to carve out their new normal. Matt had been so worried about Esther who'd retreated so far into herself he'd been unable to reach her at all. He'd almost called for help a number of times but was terrified of drawing attention to them in case some do-gooder decided Esther would be better off with a foster family. He'd run away with her if he had to. Whatever it took to stop that happening.

Not wanting to give her time to change her mind, Matt whisked Esther straight out for dinner and within half an hour their burgers were ordered, there was a sugary fizzy drink in front of each of them with the promise of the biggest ice cream sundae on the menu still to come.

"So how was school today?" Matt asked with the lightest tone he could manage. He'd felt it was too soon when Esther appeared in the kitchen in her school uniform within days of the funeral but she'd been quietly determined.

"Okay," she said with a shrug. "But people don't really know what to say to me."

"That's because they're worried about saying the wrong thing, or upsetting you, either of which would be better than saying nothing at all." Esther looked at him, surprised that he knew exactly what she was thinking. He smiled at her. "People don't know what to say to me either."

Her eyes went down for a moment and then, when she'd found enough courage, she looked up again. "How will we survive? Where will we get money from?"

"There's plenty of money Esty so you don't have to worry. We get a monthly allowance and if we need more for anything, I just have to ask Pete."

"But where's it coming from?"

The truth was Matt had no idea. He was starting to realise that despite various fronts to convince them otherwise, their father had clearly never done an honest day's work in his life. He grew up believing he worked in insurance but he'd never been interested enough to ask about it. All he knew now was that whatever their father was doing he was clearly very good at it due to the endless funds that seemed to be readily available without question.

"I guess Dad worked harder than we realised. Is there anything else worrying you?" Matt then asked, keen to change the subject.

"You haven't talked about university."

"What about it?"

"Where you'll be going? When you'll be going?"

"But I'm not going to university. I thought you knew that?"

A huge surge of relief made Esther's chin quiver and Matt immediately reached for her hand.

"Oh no!" he said with real anguish, horrified that he could be the cause of Esther feeling yet more vulnerability. "You thought I was going to leave you? Esty, I'm not going anywhere! I'm so sorry that wasn't clear."

"So what will you do?"

Matt was about to leave school and hadn't yet planned what he was going to tell Esther about work. He silently kicked himself for his lack of forethought but as she was now waiting for an answer, he had no choice but to just make it up as he went along.

"I decided an apprenticeship was more me. There's a few I'm looking at in IT. It'll be perfect Esty. Something more practical that'll allow me to develop my skills and earn money at the same time. And of course, most importantly, I don't have to go anywhere."

"I don't want to hold you back."

"Of course you're not holding me back!" Matt told her, still with a tight hold of her hand, his eyes pleading with her to believe him. "It was already something I was researching long before Mum….."

"Before Mum died. It's okay to say the word Matt."

It was months before Matt felt Esther was really starting to adjust. He knew she'd never be the same again. He knew she visited Kate's grave on a daily basis and that her grief was something she would carry with her forever but slowly a little spark reignited and he felt hope for the first time.

She celebrated with him when he received a letter, that he had in fact created himself, confirming his appointment as an apprentice with an IT firm at an imaginary location just far enough outside their town to avoid Esther making any impromptu visits.

In reality, Pete had set Matt up in the back of a pawnbroker's that Dave had owned for some time. What started as a large empty room had quickly filled with state of the art computer equipment that Matt had handpicked, regularly providing Pete with a shopping list of the most advanced technology available. Dave had told him to get whatever he needed so Matt had decided to not only take him at his word but make sure he had the absolute best of everything.

As soon as Esther started the new school year, Matt began his daily commute into London. He was on a train the minute Esther left for school and always home in time to make sure they had dinner together. It was all a bit of a scramble and meant he was permanently shattered with one eye always on the clock but he was determined to make sure Esther continued to come first.

Fortunately for Matt, Esther was far too busy studying to even think about surprising him at work. Concentrating on her school work gave her the focus she needed, having decided that if her head was full of algebra and medieval history, there was less room to think about how incredibly lost she felt.

It was a year later when the news reached them that Dave was to be released early from prison and put on probation for six months, and of course he wanted to see them.

"What are you thinking?" Matt asked Esther as they sat at the kitchen table. It was Saturday at least so neither was in a hurry to be anywhere.

"I was just thinking how successful I've been at convincing myself he was gone forever and I'd never have to see him again. I'd chosen to forget that he'd come back again at some point."

"You don't have to see him. And you know he's not moving back here."

"So where will he be?"

"Pete said he's organising a flat for him, half way between here and London. He's clearly going to move to London as soon as his probation period is done." Matt stopped for a moment. "But I suppose we have to think tactically. If we play ball and have regular contact with him that might tick some boxes with his probation officer. Anything that helps him to the point where he packs up and moves away for good has to be worth it, doesn't it?"

When the time came, Esther decided to see Dave on her own, an arrangement Matt was distinctly uncomfortable with. She'd allowed him to drop her off but only on the understanding he left immediately and came back again an hour later. She didn't want the pressure of knowing he was lurking right outside.

"Esty!" Dave opened the door and immediately wrapped himself around her, only to feel her body stiffen. He quickly released her. "Come in, come in," he said, ushering her inside, trying his best to hide the fact he felt flustered and uncomfortable. No one else had this effect on him. She was the only person who required effort on his part, who didn't just fall in line. She was the only one who mattered.

Esther stood awkwardly in the hallway as Dave closed the door behind them.

"This way," he said, heading for a large open-plan living space. He stopped at a kitchen island. "Why don't you sit on one of those?" he said to Esther, nodding towards some high stools. "I wasn't sure what you'd like so I've got fruit juice or all sorts of fizzy drinks," he said, opening the fridge to show her what was on offer.

"Some juice would be fine, thank you."

"And what about something to eat?" Dave said as he poured her a drink and then placed it in front of her. "I've got crisps and biscuits and some chocolate bars too." He opened a cupboard, pulled out various items and then spread them on the counter top.

"I'm fine thank you."

Dave went to object and then stopped himself. He hadn't expected to feel quite so on edge. He watched as Esther took a sip of her drink, taking a moment to really look at her. "You look so grown up Esty." She'd been just twelve years old when he'd started his sentence and it had been three years since he'd seen her apart from fleetingly at Kate's funeral. Three years when she'd gone from a child to showing the first glimpse of the striking young woman she was set to become.

"Losing Mum forced me to grow up." She held his eyes as she spoke, her expression cold and determined.

"It must have been very hard for you," was all Dave could manage. "Which is why it was easy to excuse the fact you slapped me at the funeral. Emotions were running high."

Esther continued to stare, only now she could feel something bubbling deep inside her causing her body temperature to slowly increase. "I'm sorry that's your overriding memory of the day," she said, her voice quiet and calm, "rather than the fact that your wife and my mother was lying dead in a box."

For a moment Dave didn't say anything but neither did he so much as flinch, offering no clue as to what he was thinking or feeling. "It was a difficult day for all of us," was eventually all he said. There was a moment's pause and then in an attempt to lighten the mood, Dave forced his shoulders down and smiled. "Why don't you tell me about school? Are you still playing the piano? And netball? Are you still the one scoring all the goals?"

Esther took a deep breath and then decided it was easier to just play along so she answered his questions, feeling herself start to relax as she did so. He looked genuinely proud when she told him about the consistently high grades she'd been achieving and they even shared a laugh together as she recounted tales of angering defenders on the netball court with her nimble moves, smashing all school records with the number of goals she'd scored along the way. And then they stopped, coming abruptly to the end of the conversational line. An awkwardness circled.

"So where do we go from here?" Dave asked with a smile, desperate to end on a high. "Perhaps I could take you out next week? To the cinema maybe, or for something to eat?"

Esther felt herself flush and for the first time, her eyes went down. She could hear Matt's words about doing what was needed to get Dave through his probation and out of their lives forever but it felt disloyal to their mother to spend time with him. And with all of this filling her head, it was impossible to know if somewhere deep within she might be harbouring a tiny yearning to spend time with him. He was her only living parent after all which had made her feel drawn to him in a way she hadn't expected.

Esther slowly looked up. "The cinema would be good."

Dave smiled. "Great. Have a look and see what's on and then I'll book us some tickets."

The doorbell sounded to announce Matt's return. "Have some more juice if you want, or one of those chocolate biscuits. I just need two minutes with your brother," Dave said as he headed out of the room, closing the door firmly behind him.

"Is everything alright?" Matt asked, the minute Dave opened the front door.

"Oh relax, everything's fine. Esther's perfectly happy in the kitchen," Dave said, waving Matt in. "Come in here a sec. I need a word." Matt followed him into the lounge. "Pete says you're all set up which I should bloody well hope so after the amount of money you've spent. And you've had more than enough time on the payroll sitting around doing nothing."

"That's not quite how I'd put it. And I might still need more kit. It depends what you want me to do."

"I thought a bit of basic hacking just to cut your teeth. I'll send you a list of companies. Steal their customer data and then see what you can get for it on the dark web. Pick two companies and do it next week. If you get caught, I'll hang you out to dry. And if you don't, then the fun can really start."

20

Matt didn't get caught. In fact, the exercise was so successful, he banked a small fortune but not before he'd shaved off enough to comfortably see Esther through university when the time came. Helping himself wasn't something he planned to make a habit of but Dave would never know. It was a paltry amount by comparison.

For phase two, Dave told him to steal data but then offer it back to the company he took it from for an even more mouthwatering sum of money. If the company complied, no one would be any the wiser but if they refused, it would be on the understanding the data would be sold to the highest bidder with enough information made public to ensure their customers would feel immediately vulnerable and undoubtedly leave in their droves. They knew what the black market was prepared to pay now which made it easy to be ballsy. The first company they targeted didn't take anything like the twenty-four hours offered before they agreed to pay up. The thrill Matt felt when he realised the plan was going to work was unimaginable. He'd never felt a sense of power like it.

And so their business model started to take shape. Dave assigned a team to do the initial research to identify targets and Matt would then steal something valuable without so much as forcing a lock, never mind actually breaking into a building. Whatever he took would then either be sold back to the company it was stolen from or taken to market.

Without even noticing, life had found its new rhythm and the weeks and months ambled by. Esther still regularly visited Kate's grave, often starting with a silent apology for having been out with Dave. She liked spending time with him. He was different when he was with her, especially when there was no one else around. There was no threat of violence, in fact no tension at all, and having him around made her feel like it was still okay to be a child just for a little bit longer.

Esther secured herself a place at university and then before she buried her head in revision for her exams, there was her eighteenth birthday to celebrate.

"To my Esty!"

"To Esther!" rang out the cheer as Dave led the toasting.

Esther would party with her friends at the weekend but for tonight, she was surrounded by her extended family which basically meant Pete and his wife, a selection of Dave's 'colleagues', who were a surprisingly friendly crowd despite their tough leathery faces and burly physiques, and just enough of her closest friends to keep the average age below fifty. They were a generous crowd and she had been showered with gifts of jewellery and cash so hadn't stopped smiling for hours.

"Now it's my turn," Dave said as he handed over a large envelope.

Esther took it with her eyes full of anticipation but when she pulled out a stack of documents, she couldn't make any sense of them at all. "What is it?"

"I thought you might like to go to university knowing you can afford to buy somewhere to live when you're finished so, now that you're eighteen, I've put the house in your name. You can sell it whenever you like but I'd like you to buy a home with the money and not just fritter it away on sex, drugs and rock 'n' roll."

"As if that would ever happen!" Esther was still struggling to take it all in and then she put her arms around Dave's neck. "Thank you so much Dad," she said as she hugged him tightly. "I'm completely blown away. But what about Matt? Surely he should have half?" she then asked as she released him.

"Don't you worry about him," Dave said. "I'm looking after him in other ways."

Esther sold the house two years after she finished university. The large family property had been bought decades earlier in an area that had enjoyed much investment over time, comfortably sitting within the commuter belt for those wanting the best of both worlds – one foot in the capital, the other firmly planted in a pretty rural oasis. With no mortgage to repay, Esther had struggled to swallow her shock in one exhilarating gulp when an estate agent told her what it was now worth.

She then poured over the internet looking at flats she could afford to buy in London which was where her first steps towards becoming a graphic designer had taken her. On the day the house sale completed, she turned up at Dave's place with a bottle of champagne and some property details she wanted to share with him. As far as Esther was concerned, Dave now owned a chain of high end pawnbrokers dealing in expensive jewellery and antiques, a business that was clearly going very well for him.

When she arrived outside the ridiculously large gated property he now lived in, one of Dave's employees was just on his way out. Esther smiled as she saw him.

"Hello Esther. Do you want me to let your Dad know you're here?" he asked, holding the front gate open for her.

"No thanks. My visit's a surprise so your timing's perfect."

"Well in that case, let me open the front door for you too."

Esther followed him back down the short gravel driveway and then with a big smile to say thank you as he opened the door, she quietly slipped inside the house but she'd only taken a few steps when she stopped again, aware of a raised angry sounding voice. She stood for a moment while she tried to work out where it was coming from, quickly deciding it was Dave's office. She headed down the hallway and then, convinced her arrival would immediately put paid to whatever nonsense was riling him, she threw open the door. She had imagined a loud 'ta da!' by way of a greeting but the words stuck in her throat, momentarily choking her. There in front of her was Dave, standing with his thick hands wrapped tightly around Matt's throat whose own fingers were desperately clawing at Dave's as he tried to loosen his grip, a look of absolute panic in his eyes. His nose was bleeding, one of his eyes was already swelling and he was clearly unable to breathe. She couldn't believe what she was seeing and for a split second she simply froze. And then a rush of terror swept through her body bringing her right back into the moment.

"Dad, stop!" she yelled.

The unexpected sound of her voice was enough to make Dave release his grip. Matt dropped to the floor and Esther raced to his side.

"What the hell are you doing?" she screamed, spittle flying from her mouth in a perfect spray as she whipped her head around to face her father. The look of pure hatred in her eyes was enough to make him step back. Esther held his eyes until she was confident he wasn't about to take a step towards them and then she turned back to Matt. "Can you get up?" she asked him, her tone immediately gentler and full of concern.

Matt nodded and Esther helped him to his feet and then she carefully steered him towards the door. He was heavy but fear made her strong and determined to get him to safety.

"Esty, please! Let me explain what happened," Dave pleaded.

Esther encouraged Matt to keep going which he did in small shuffling steps using the wall to keep himself upright. As soon as she was sure he was stable, she turned around again.

"I think what happened is pretty bloody obvious," she said to Dave, her words strong again, her stare fierce. "I grew up in a house full of fear because of you and yet, despite that, I was prepared to try to build a relationship with you. I totally opened myself up to you because I believe everyone deserves a second chance, but no one, and that includes you, ever deserves a third. So that's it. You and I are well and truly done."

Dave took a step towards her and Esther put her hand up to stop him. "No! You stay there!" Dave found himself obeying, not recognising this fearsome steely version of Esther. She took her phone out of her pocket and held it up in the air. "One more step and I'm calling the police." She waited for a moment until she felt sure Dave believed her and then put all of her energy into getting Matt out of the house.

As soon as they were on the pavement outside, Esther grabbed some tissues from her bag and gently wiped the blood away from Matt's nose. "What the hell happened?" she asked. "No don't tell me," she quickly added before he could answer. "I don't need to know. I don't want to know. I'm done with him. First thing tomorrow I'm going to change my number and I suggest you do the same. We tried Matt but enough is enough! He's never going to change and I was crazy to think he had."

Matt said nothing. What could he say? Other than spout more lies that he would be walking away right behind her without so much as a backward glance when he would really be patching himself up and presenting himself back at work first thing the next morning. He'd rather just remain silent than add to the long list of fairytales he'd already told her.

"Come on, let's get away from here," she said, taking his arm.

"I'm fine, honestly Esty. I'm okay to walk."

"We should just call the police," Esther said. "Why do we continue to let him get away with this barbaric behaviour?" Matt glanced at her but the question was thankfully rhetorical. "He needs help. Or better still he needs to be locked up with the key thrown into the deepest part of the Thames," she continued, head shaking with anger, her words muttered low and fast. And then she shot her arm out as she spotted a taxi.

"Where are we going?" Matt asked her as the cab pulled in.

Esther opened the door and waited for him to get in. "Anywhere, as long as it gets us away from him."

21

Esther remained true to her word and first thing the next morning she cancelled her mobile phone and got herself a new contract and a new number. She then went back to the flat she'd been renting long enough to give notice and pack everything up.

Dave's house was south east of the city centre so she headed north, putting a good twelve miles or so of busy city between them which was about as good as she could hope for. She took a short-term let on a fairly basic flat and then put all her energy into a new search to find the perfect place to buy having ditched the properties she'd planned to show Dave for being way to close to him.

When she stepped into the ninth flat, she knew immediately she'd found it and four months later, she and her minimal belongings moved in. Property in London came at a price but she was still able to afford a spacious three-bedroomed flat, one of which she would use as a studio, in a beautiful mansion block on a smart quiet street.

"Very nice indeed," Matt said as he took his first look around. "Some furniture would be good though."

"Did you know it takes three months to get a bloody sofa? And anyway, I want to take my time and make it all completely perfect."

Matt smiled. "I've no doubt it'll be stunning when you've finished."

Esther watched as Matt wandered over to the large bay window in the lounge, looking one way and then the other.

"That's the third time you've checked outside. What's going on Matt?"

"I'm just familiarising myself with the area."

Esther continued to look at him but Matt was unable to make eye contact. "Matt?"

"Everything's fine, really."

"Has Dad been in touch? Has something happened?"

Matt forced a smile. "Nothing's happened. Relax Esty, it's all good."

The luxury of walking away from Dave clearly wasn't an option for Matt. The worst part was he wasn't even sure what had suddenly made Dave attack him but what he did know was that he absolutely couldn't go back to living in fear of the next beating, wondering every time he saw Dave if he would leave with his face battered and his spirit crushed. So, on the morning after the attack, when Esther had leapt into action to make sure Dave had no means of contacting her, Matt had gone back to his house to confront him.

Dave was sitting in a high backed chair in his study when Matt walked in. When Dave looked at him, Matt was convinced he saw his left eye twitch in an otherwise emotionless face. Or maybe that was just wishful thinking on Matt's part. A desperate need for a sign that somewhere buried deep within, Dave might care enough about him to generate even a tiny muscle spasm when he saw the results of his latest moment of madness.

"It can't happen again," Matt said to him, his words confident and clear. Dave looked at him, his lips held tightly together. "I don't want to talk about it," Matt continued. "I don't want to know why I seem to make you so angry. I don't want to try to work out why our relationship has always been so broken. I just want it to stop. I need it to stop."

Matt waited. He didn't want to offer ultimatums that would just anger Dave all over again. Neither did he want to embarrass or humiliate him, or do anything that might spark another violent outburst which is why he spoke very matter of factly with as little emotion as he could manage. He also knew his swollen face and the marks left by Dave's hands around his neck were inflammatory enough without him adding overly emotive language into the mix.

"I've already made you a shedload of money and we've barely scratched the surface," Matt continued, "but I can't continue to do that if I can't see, or use my hands, or worse, if I'm no longer breathing." Matt waited again. "Do you think you can do that? Can we agree it will never happen again?"

Their eyes locked but Dave's mouth remained firmly closed. "I'm going to take that as a 'yes'," Matt said as he turned to leave. "Good talking to you," he shouted over his shoulder as he left.

After several months of meeting with Dave and leaving with his face intact, Matt slowly allowed himself to relax. He stopped tensing up when Dave chose to stand or sit close to him, and stopped hyperventilating when his anger started to swell.

"Can you wait for a moment Matt?"

A briefing meeting had just finished as they neared their next job and Matt now stood by the door watching everyone else file out. Dave waited for the last person to leave before speaking. "So how's Esty?"

"She's good. Still looking for just the right flat," he lied. The last thing he wanted was Dave asking for her address.

Dave thought for a moment. "She changed her number."

"She's angry with you."

"How long's that going to last?"

Matt looked at him wondering how on earth he could continue this conversation without risk to his own physical wellbeing. "I don't know what to say to you."

"I want you to be honest."

"Then I think it's going to last forever."

Dave busied himself tidying papers on his desk. "Maybe you could talk to her?"

"You made it quite clear I was never to tell her I was working with you. As far as she's concerned, we're not in touch now either." Matt watched Dave's jaw clench and he tried not to panic. "There's nothing I can do Dad. Not because I don't want to but because I'm in an impossible position."

Dave suddenly stopped what he was doing. "Well if I can't have a relationship with her then neither can you."

Matt immediately felt sick to his stomach, a horrible metallic taste flooding his mouth and making his eyes water. He slowly counted to five and then looked back at Dave. "Then she'll have no one. Is that really what you want?"

"I always felt like you, Esther and your Mum were this tight little unit. Do you have any idea what it felt like to always be on the outside looking in? And now it will be the same with you and Esther. Well I won't allow it."

Matt shook his head. "It was a protective bubble and we were protecting ourselves from you! And if you feel shut out by Esther and me it's because you locked yourself out! Surely you can see that? And even now as I'm talking, I'm trying to be honest because that's instinctively what I want to do and what feels right but at the same time I'm wondering which are the words that might just tip you over the edge and make your fists tighten? You can blame me all you like Dad, you can beat me till you kill me but it won't change the fact that I'm not actually to blame, and neither is Esther, and yet still you keep punishing us both!"

"This conversation is over." Dave sat down at his desk, turning in his chair until Matt could only see the back of his head.

For a moment Matt paced up and down, full of nervous energy, not sure if he should offload it while he had the chance, or just take it home with him. "I just want to look after her Dad. I need to look after her. Please let me do that!"

In one swift movement Dave swung back around to face Matt, placed his hands down on his desk and propelled himself forward. "Get out!" he bellowed. When Matt didn't move, he banged his fist down hard on his desk. "I said get out!"

Dave managed almost three years before the urge to know about Esther's life became too prevalent to ignore. He was a belligerent stubborn old mule with eyes constantly forward, refusing to never so much as glance back and admit that maybe he'd acted in haste and caused himself to suffer as a result. No, there would be no self-reflection here but that didn't change the fact he wanted a window into Esther's life.

Dave left his desk and headed to the kitchen. While large sections of his home remained strictly off limits, there were parts of his house that were always occupied by at least a few members of his team. They came and went as they needed, using the kitchen as their hub and then a small number of rooms accessible from this point for meetings, research or just catching up.

Dave went straight for the coffee machine and topped up the mug he'd brought with him, pleased to see Bill sitting at the large kitchen table with a mug of tea and a newspaper. Bill was one of the original team, running around with Dave and Pete as kids and causing trouble everywhere they went. You wouldn't think it to see him now though. Money had given him a desire for elegance, or at least his interpretation of elegance, which meant sharp suits and always with a waistcoat, highly polished shoes, cufflinks and a perfectly placed handkerchief in his top pocket, all stretched across a rather portly frame, the result of years of decadence and overindulgence.

"What's that posh nephew of yours up to?" Dave asked as he sat down opposite him.

"If you mean Jamie, he's launching a new magazine. But on the computer. That's the way these days isn't it? People are giving up on actual magazines that you can hold in your hands and flick through from page to page."

Dave was already waving a hand to hurry him along. He had no interest in a chat about the demise of the printed word.

"What kind of magazine?"

"One for men," Bill said, his pride obvious. "You know the kind of thing? Full of chiselled jaws, glossy six packs and moisturiser."

"Well tell him I have a designer for him."

"Last time I saw him it sounded like they were all sorted."

Dave looked at him, his eyes narrowing slightly. "I don't think you heard me right. Tell him I have a designer for him. In fact, better still, get him to come in to see me. And as soon as possible. I've a very special job for him."

22

Being in one place made Matt feel vulnerable. Like a resident punch-bag available for a quick whack whenever the need might arise. The anxious child in him grew up believing that if Dave knew where he was then he wasn't safe so, even as an adult, and despite being in contact with Dave on an almost daily basis, putting down roots simply wasn't an option.

Instead, he was permanently on the move. He had plenty of money so he would flit from a short-term let to a hotel suite then to another apartment for just a month or so, swinging from one side of London to the other. He wasn't one for possessions so everything that mattered to him could easily be transported in one medium sized holdall; a watch that had belonged to his maternal grandfather, a photograph of himself with his mother, some toiletries, a minimalist wardrobe, his laptop and any other pertinent technology he might feel it necessary to carry with him. Anything he couldn't carry was left in a cupboard in his office at the pawnbroker's.

Since the day after Dave had been hell-bent on strangling him, Esther's name had not been mentioned. It was like she didn't exist. Or worse, as if she'd never existed. Matt didn't know what had motivated Dave to cut her dead, wondering if he was embarrassed that Esther had witnessed him losing control again, or if he was upset that she'd cut off all contact with him, or jealous perhaps that Matt and Esther had such a strong relationship, something he appeared to be incapable of nurturing. Whatever it was, Dave stopped asking if Matt had seen her, stopped asking how she was doing and reacted so badly when someone else mentioned her name that very quickly, everyone around them stopped doing so. She was officially persona non grata.

While Matt hugely preferred a world in which Dave and Esther had no contact, the silent rule of not acknowledging her had made it impossible to have any further discussion about whether Matt might be able to continue seeing her. Matt wanted to believe that Dave had just overreacted in the heat of the moment but bringing the subject up simply wasn't an option so, as always, he now had to consider the consequences of being caught acting against Dave's wishes. He therefore had no choice but to accept his relationship with Esther was now on a new course. And one that would mean he would barely see her.

Matt sat in his current hotel suite, a half-eaten plate of food to his left, a half empty bottle of wine to his right, his laptop open on the table in front of him. The screen was split in two; live footage of Esther's road on one side thanks to a camera he'd installed himself (he found simply putting on logoed overalls pretty much gave him permission to do whatever he wanted), and a map of the surrounding roads on the other. As he did every night, he used his keyboard to move the angle of the camera so he could see up and down the street, checking the parked cars for anyone he recognised. Without their knowledge, he could track every mobile owned by Dave's gang and the map confirmed that none of them were in the vicinity. Stifling a yawn, he then crawled off to bed, leaving his laptop where it was so he could check again first thing in the morning. He'd promised Kate he would look after Esther and while this current set-up may not have been what either of them had imagined, it was now the best he could do. He'd said he would protect Esther with his life and that was now quite literally what he was doing.

The next morning Matt was finding it hard to settle. Work was quiet while he waited for confirmation of the next company to be targeted and until then he had little to occupy him. He ordered himself some breakfast and checked Esther's road a few times for any unwanted attention and then, unable to think of anything better to do, he headed for his office at the pawnbroker's where he wasted away the afternoon with some online gaming. It was a pastime he loved for the anonymity it gave him. He regularly hooked up with the same people, all masked by unique gaming monikers that gave no clue to their real identities or lifestyles and, in an otherwise solitary existence, they were the closest thing he had to friends. His only problem was that he kept winning which on some days he hugely enjoyed. Today, it wasn't long before he got bored and left them to it.

An hour later he was in a bar, nursing a whisky and coke. He liked to sit at the bar where he could enjoy the banter between the barman and his customers, catching snippets of conversations as people ordered drinks before moving on to find a table. It made him feel connected and sociable without actually having to talk to anyone.

"Can I get you another one?"

Matt looked up with a start to see a young woman staring at him. She was dressed in a suit but looked harassed and a little crumpled around the edges as a result.

"You look like you need a drink even more than me," Matt said with a smile. "Bad day at the office?"

"The absolute worst."

"Well let me buy you a drink then," Matt said, slipping off his stool.

"No, please let me get you one. I've had to be really tough on people today. A random act of kindness might help redress the balance."

Matt conceded and the woman, Alison, ordered them some drinks and then pulled up a stool next to him. An hour or two slipped by easily with a few more drinks along the way and then Matt started to feel uncomfortable. It had been amazing to switch off from everything for a while but it was never long before reality swept back in.

"Sorry Alison, but I'm going to have to go."

"Oh," was the short reply.

Having spent the last few hours getting to know her, Matt doubted Alison was used to picking up strange men in bars so she was clearly unsure how to handle the situation, wanting him to stay but not knowing if it was appropriate to let him know that.

"Maybe I'll see you in here again?" she asked.

"Maybe." There was no point making false promises, even if he quite liked the idea of meeting up again. "Take care of yourself, Alison."

Matt walked quickly away, a heavy heart threatening to slow his escape. He'd accepted a long time ago that it was pointless developing relationships of any kind, from the platonic to the romantic, that would inevitably be built on lies. It never took long before there were questions he didn't want to answer and demands on his time that he couldn't satisfy. It wasn't unusual for a relationship to hit a crossroads but for Matt, the road could only ever lead to a dead end. Once he'd accepted that, there was no point even trying.

As he stepped outside, Matt checked his watch. It was almost nine thirty. He stood where he was for a moment, thinking how it had been several months since he'd seen Esther, the longest stretch yet without spending time with her. He looked at his watch again and then decided it had been quite long enough.

He took a short bus ride, getting off a few stops early and then walked the last part of the journey to Esther's flat. He was able to follow the tracking devices on his phone and as he got closer, he checked the immediate area first and then everyone's current location so he could be absolutely certain no one was following him. It was impossible to know if Dave was even interested in knowing where Esther was but Matt was determined not to be the one who brought him to her.

A few moments later he was ringing the bell bracing himself for a frosty reception, knowing Esther would be hurt as she always was by the lack of contact, remaining ever hopeful that one day he'd be able to explain why he had no choice but to keep away.

23

Initially Kate kept in touch with Pete at least once a week, ignoring the fact he'd told her the phone was for emergencies only. Sometimes it was more often if she found herself really struggling but she knew what a risk he was taking so fought a constant battle between wanting to have a full debrief on a daily basis and knowing she had to be mindful of keeping him out of trouble.

The passing of time stretched it to snatched messages every few weeks which was just enough for her to keep on top of how Esther was doing at school. Pete didn't say much about Matt's work. He knew how distressing it was for Kate that Matt had been sucked into Dave's world against his will. She also knew it was as dangerous for him to share information as it was for her to know it.

In between updates, Kate did her best to build a new life. She kept herself to herself at first but as the months and then years rolled by, her confidence began to grow and she started to be more proactive. She enrolled on a floristry course and secured herself a part-time job at the local florist's. Over time, she dropped her guard enough to make a few genuine friendships, quickly realising how much she'd missed the warmth and security that came with human contact. She invented a far less colourful past for herself and, ever so slowly, it started to feel that some sense of happiness and contentment might actually be achievable if she was willing to allow it.

"Morning Kate. How are you today?"

Kate started her day as she always did with a large milky coffee from the village café. She'd become such a regular that the owner, Pat, was already reaching for a takeaway cup to make Kate her daily latte without the need for instruction. Kate smiled warmly at her. "I'm good thank you Pat. Busy morning?"

"The sun's brought everyone out early. I haven't stopped."

"Busy is good!" Kate told her, picking up her coffee. "I'll be back later to freshen up your flowers."

Kate took her coffee and stopped as she always did to sit outside for five minutes before heading for work. Taking her phone out of her bag, she then went straight to Instagram. When Esther had gone off to university, she'd created a fake account so she could feel a part of Esther's journey. She loved the reels of Esther's design work, all increasingly impressive as time passed, and the pictures of friends and significant moments captured in one beautiful image after another, all leading up to a selfie of her and Matt to mark her graduation which had been a bitter sweet day. In that single moment, Kate had felt like she could burst with pride, with regret, with joy and sadness too but instead, she looked at the happiness on her daughter's face, gazed into eyes that were so full of jubilance and her own confused emotions had simply ebbed away. Her daughter was happy and doing well and that was all that mattered. And she had her big brother by her side, his arm tightly around her, protecting her as always.

Esther had now moved into her own flat and Kate scrolled through the recent posts for the umpteenth time, trying to imagine what the cushions Esther had clearly been so happy with would look like on the sofa she'd posted about the week before. The curtain fabric had been stunning and if she closed her eyes, she could imagine the vintage wine glasses lined up perfectly on the thick wooden shelves in Esther's kitchen.

Kate smiled as a new post popped up. The drawing desk Esther had been waiting for had finally arrived. She felt her heart swell, grateful every day for this tiny little window into Esther's life.

But pictures of Matt were rare. When she asked Pete about him, he'd just say he was doing fine and keeping his head down. Kate hoped that meant he was doing what Dave needed of him and was avoiding any violent attacks as a result but she knew there could be no joy in his life and that always shrouded her in a deep sense of sadness that she would carry with her for days at a time.

The worry was so constant she wore it like a second skin but regardless, life continued to slowly build momentum. Having finished her first foundation diploma in floristry, Kate moved on to get her technical certificate, finishing off with a distinction in the advanced technical diploma which meant she was taking on more and more project work at the florist's. The place had never been busier, or more profitable.

When Kate walked into work one typical Friday, she stopped to check her watch when she saw that Beth, the shop's owner, was already there ahead of her. Beth was slowly drifting towards retirement so Kate always did at least the first couple of hours on her own. It was rare to see Beth much before lunchtime.

"I thought I was late for a moment!" Kate said with a smile. "I'd have picked you up a coffee if I'd known you'd be here."

"I've had way too much caffeine already this morning but thank you anyway. Come and sit down," she said, ushering Kate into the back of the shop and into one of only two chairs before she sat down herself. Kate waited for her to say something.

"Is everything alright Beth?" she eventually asked when no words were forthcoming.

"I've decided it's time," Beth then blurted. "Time to retire. And as soon as possible. But I want you to buy the business. This place has your stamp all over it now anyway, and I know you could do so much more if you had a free rein. What do you say?"

Kate was immensely proud that she'd been able to motivate herself enough to just get out of bed every day, never mind obtain qualifications in something she loved and then help build a business that was flourishing under her care. Taken aback as she was, it was only seconds before she said yes.

Paperwork was drawn up, a business plan was written, there were meetings with the local bank and in no time at all, Kate was implementing new ideas, introducing new stock and employing staff to help facilitate the flood of corporate and event orders. So, with so much going on, it was hard to pinpoint exactly when she started to feel unsettled. To identify the moment when, despite being busier than she'd ever been and more fulfilled than she'd ever imagined possible, it was simply no longer enough to take whatever crumbs Pete threw her way which were falling way short of satisfying her increasingly insatiable appetite for information. Maybe it started with an uncomfortable fleeting thought? Or a moment of unimaginable sorrow? Or maybe it was more specific, like the moment she quietly acknowledged it was fifteen long years since the day the world believed she had died? Whatever started it, the thoughts and sense of unease grew over time until they became a permanent fixture, still pushed to the background but there nonetheless.

She ignored the disquiet for as long as she could and then one nondescript day, despite being exhausted after a full day of work, Kate just couldn't get to sleep. She'd been in bed for hours, shattered but alert, her head throbbing. She got up to find some headache tablets and when they didn't work, she got up again to open a window hoping some fresh air might help. She tried reading but couldn't concentrate, turning several pages before she realised she hadn't taken in a single word. Her mind was simply too wired, too plugged into what big plans Esther might need her help to refine and too switched on to the idea that Matt would never have the life he deserved if she didn't at least try to intervene.

She put the book down and, picking up her phone, she headed straight to Instagram and then she gasped, out of bed in an instant and pacing the room. Esther had posted a painting she was clearly incredibly proud of. It was a portrait of Kate and it was breathtaking. Kate was a modest woman but she was completely mesmerised by it, by the colours, by the sheer beauty and by the love that had clearly flowed through Esther and onto the canvas. It was a sign. It had to be.

By six o'clock the next morning Kate was already showered, dressed and ready to go. She drove herself to the nearest mainline train station and by eight, she was sitting in a café just a whisper away from Esther's flat. She had no idea at all what Esther's plans for the day might be or if she would even leave the flat at all. She might not even be at home but it didn't matter. Kate was physically closer to Esther than she'd been for over fifteen long years and she hadn't felt so alive since long before this sorry saga began. Every nerve end tingled with a mix of fear and anticipation. She was breaking the rules but right now, it definitely felt worth it and she was too excited to really care.

She didn't see Esther that day, or the next time she came and then she tried a Friday, thinking Esther might be more likely to be out and about. She was back early as always, this time choosing a different café to avoid the risk of anyone getting used to seeing her face. As the shops around her started to open, she had a little browse, buying a very pretty teapot and a set of vintage tea spoons that she immediately loved and couldn't possibly leave behind, and then she saw her. Just like that. She walked out of a shop, paused for a moment on the pavement while she decided where to go next, and there Esther was, walking towards her on the other side of the street. Kate froze, unable to breathe, her eyes the only part of her that were able to function as she watched her beautiful daughter glide past her in lovely confident strides. Kate was oblivious to everything else around her. Every sight, every sound and every smell evaporated with all her senses focused solely on Esther. And then suddenly she was walking away. The brain chatter that started the minute Esther turned her back to Kate was deafening. She looked well. Her shoulder length hair shaped softly around her face suited her perfectly. Her green eyes were as bright as ever. Her clothes were simple but stylish and there was definitely a bounce in her step so she must be happy. The barrage of thoughts and silent comments were relentless as Kate replayed every detail she'd seen, making sure every nuance was captured, recorded safely to memory, knowing she would want to relive this moment again and again and again.

As soon as she was able to gather herself, Kate headed along Esther's path until she could see her up ahead. She continued to observe as Esther picked up some food and then headed to a café where she took a table outside. With only a slight hesitation, Kate sat down a few tables behind her. She couldn't even see her face but she could smell her perfume on the breeze, a scent she immediately recognised because it was the one she wore herself. Just knowing Esther chose to wear it was enough to make her press her hand to her chest where she could feel her heart pounding, powered by the most intense and joyous love.

Over the next few weeks and months, Kate got more and more attuned to Esther's routine making it possible to get the most from every visit. On one occasion she allowed herself to brush past Esther. The temptation to just take her in her arms had been enormous but she had, of course, resisted. She was horribly aware of the risks she was taking but convinced herself that as long as she didn't approach Esther or engage with her in any way then she was merely bending the rules rather than breaking them.

But then inevitably, the moment came when once again, she needed more than just the occasional glimpse of Esther. Getting hold of her mobile number had been easy. Esther was working freelance now so had a website showcasing her work and there it was, readily available for anyone looking for a graphic designer or artist. Or for an estranged mother perhaps, desperate to hear the sound of her daughter's voice.

Using the burner phone that Pete had given her, it took several weeks for her to build up the courage to call but when she finally dialled the number she'd already memorised, she could only listen for a moment and then hang up, too scared to speak, too terrified of what might happen to both of them if Dave found out. She vowed never to do it again but of course she did. Every few months in moments when she felt hopelessly lost, she would make a call, listen, say nothing and then when her brain caught up with what she was doing, she would quickly hang up.

It was February 8th, Esther's birthday. Kate looked at the present and card that sat on her kitchen table and then as she did every year, she picked them up and took them to a box stashed in a cupboard in the spare bedroom. She placed the gift inside, the sixteenth present she had lovingly chosen and wrapped, each one a reminder of another year lost. And of course she'd done the same for Matt. Just another one of the ways she kept hope alive that they'd all one day be reunited. When that day came, she certainly couldn't have her beloved children thinking she'd ever let a birthday go by without acknowledgement.

Kate went back downstairs, poured herself a large glass of wine and turned on some music then she quickly turned it off again. She needed quiet so that she could focus. She took a few sips of wine and felt her body relax and her thoughts start to align.

Sixteen presents. Sixteen years. She may have been able to reassure herself from a distance that Esther was flourishing but what about Matt? She was no closer to rescuing her older child who had gone from boy to man weighed down by more misery and secrets that anyone should ever have to bear.

Well enough was enough. She'd more than served her time. Kate finished what was in her glass and poured herself another and then she smiled. Dave had put a noose around her neck and then held on to the rope, ready to squeeze out her last breath if she ever tried to stray too far from the prison he'd banished her to. Well no more. It was time to plan her escape.

PART FOUR

24

Now

"So she's still alive? All this time I thought she was dead and she's alive?"

Matt nodded. "Just tell me you understand there was no other option? You do get that don't you? He would have killed her! And possibly you too. I didn't have a choice!"

"Of course you had a choice!" Esther said, not able to stop her voice rising, fuelled by the most insane mixture of anger and pure joy as she struggled to process the news that her mother was still alive. "You could have told me! That was what you should have chosen to do!" Esther put up her hand to stop Matt interrupting. "And before you spout some ridiculous bullshit about the fact I was too young, it was too big a burden to carry, it might have affected my school work, or whatever other fucking bollocks you were about to throw at me, NO!"

Esther and Matt had swapped the park bench for the privacy of a room in a cheap roadside hotel but the walls were thin and Matt flinched as the volume of Esther's voice continued to swell until her last word came out as a piercing scream.

"Get a grip Esther!" His voice, by comparison, was now deliberately low and calm. "If you just want to attract attention to us then let's at least go somewhere where we can enjoy some more comfortable surroundings." The room they currently occupied was basic to say the very least with little more than a bed, a tatty looking dressing table and a stained armchair.

Esther walked over to the window. She had no idea what to do with all the information she'd just been given. It was like there was a crowded bottleneck in her brain with too many thoughts and questions fighting to get through the narrow gap. It was simply too much to cope with in one outburst.

"Three weeks ago my brother and my friend disappeared off the face of the earth without a word," she said with her back to Matt who sat perched on the end of the bed. "Three days after that I had to identify the body of that friend only to then discover that she wasn't my friend at all but a police officer, and that my dear gentle brother is actually a criminal of some magnitude. And then, just when I allowed myself to believe that was more than enough for anyone to have to deal with, on the day I watched my friend lowered into the ground, I discover that the mother I've missed every single day for almost sixteen years is actually alive after all." She swung round to face him, her eyes now full of tears that spilled onto her cheeks, forming mascara-stained streaks as they ran down the length of her face. "So please don't tell me to get a grip," she cried, "otherwise you'll leave me with no choice but to believe you're the heartless bastard that my head is currently insisting you must be."

Matt looked at her for a moment. "Can you even begin to imagine how petrified I was of him?" he eventually asked, his voice shaky and quiet. "As a kid I would be paralysed by fear when I heard him coming through the front door wondering where he'd go first. If he went to the kitchen and started shouting at Mum I'd feel relieved for a moment and then I'd hate myself for not being able to protect her, and for being glad his attention was on her and not me. Or if he walked up the stairs, I'd hold my breath until he either passed my bedroom door or burst through it." He stopped for a moment. "The truth is there's absolutely no way you can even begin to imagine what it was like so please don't insult me by telling me I had a choice. I've had no life of my own at all but you're still alive and Mum's still alive so throw whatever you like at me but I'm never going to apologise for doing what I had to to keep you both safe."

Matt's voice cracked and he bit down hard on his lip. Esther immediately sat down next to him and took hold of his hand. "I'm so sorry Matt. It's such a lot to take in and I can't get a clear picture from my own perspective yet, never mind trying to understand what it's been like from yours."

"If there'd been any other way Esty!"

"I know," she said, stroking his hand. And then she smiled. "So where is she?"

"I don't know. But I'm pretty sure Pete does."

"I wonder what her life's been like? If she's happy?"

"I'm sure the only thing that's kept her away from a large bottle of pills is the hope of one day seeing us again."

"We have to ask Pete where she is. Do you think we can see her?"

"I don't know if it's safe. Or if it ever will be."

They sat quietly again for a moment, Esther still battling to align all this new information alongside all the many questions she still had about their past.

"Why didn't losing Mum bring us closer together?" she then asked. "Once I moved to London you virtually disappeared from my life. It was like losing Mum all over again."

"Why do you think I stayed away?" Matt replied, a sense of desperation creeping into his voice that Esther still wasn't getting it. "You remember the last time you saw Dad when he had me by the neck? Well after that he told me I was never to see you again. He'd made enough threats by this point about what he would do if I didn't toe the line that I had no choice but to keep away. And yet despite the risk, I just couldn't do it. But every time I came to see you, I tracked every one of Dad's gang to make sure they weren't following me, or you. In fact, I did that constantly, day and night, to make sure he wasn't after you. I've never known if Dad knew where you were, or if it even mattered, but I had to at least try to keep him away. I wanted to see more of you, of course I did, but every decision I've made as an adult has been based on a risk assessment of what Dad might do if he found out." And then he stopped. "Until Abi."

"Did Dad kill her?"

"No, but he was there."

Esther's lips parted to say something but her mouth was suddenly very dry. She swallowed hard. "Were you there?" she asked and then watched as Matt slowly nodded, his eyes filling with tears.

"We walked back into the cottage I'd rented and he was just waiting for us. Him and one of his animals. Then he took great pleasure in telling me she was a cop before he got the brainless thug to shoot her. I saw him lift his forefinger. It's a sign I've seen numerous times to signal it's time for whatever violent act he's deemed necessary. I tried to grab the gun but I wasn't quick enough."

Esther put her arms around him. "There's nothing you could have done to save her."

"But that's just it," he said, standing up, agitated as he relived it. "In the moment, all I could think was what have I done, bringing her into such a terrible world where decisions are made on the whim of a complete psychopath? What the hell was I doing Esty? I might as well have killed her myself!"

Esther took hold of his arm and pulled him back to sit on the bed. That might have been true of someone else, but not Abi. Matt didn't bring her into his life, she purposefully manipulated her way into it but there was little to gain from reminding him of the fact. "I'm desperately sorry things turned out the way they did," she said instead, "but there really was nothing you could have done. Dad's responsible for all of it. He's the epicentre of all the misery and of course I can see how much worse it's been for you. And to finally fall in love and think you've found a way out, only for it to end in the most heartbreaking way." She shook her head at the sheer magnitude of it all. "So yes, I absolutely get it."

She thought for a moment and then reached up to pull his face gently towards her until their eyes met. "Maybe it's time to make him pay?"

25

"Everyone's staring at me," Matt said under his breath, as they followed a young officer through a very quiet police station.

"No they're not," Esther said, although the stillness of the office was putting her on edge a little too. It was true no one was looking at Matt although she sensed everyone they passed wanted to. She clocked a series of eyes quickly averting, desperate not to be caught showing any interest at all in someone who was obviously the talk of the entire building.

Esther was relieved to finally see Ade up ahead, his arm already outstretched. "It's good to finally meet you Matt," he said, shaking Matt's hand.

"I'm not sure how I feel about it yet to be honest," Matt replied.

"Well I'm really grateful you're here," Ade reassured him, "and thanks for calling me again Esther. I know it was another big ask," he said as he led them into a meeting room where they all sat down. "And the news about your mother is absolutely mind-blowing."

"Have you found her yet?" Esther asked.

"No, but we will."

Esther had never felt a level of nervous anticipation like it, accepting she would be unable to relax until she knew Kate was safe. "Sorry for the fact I'm still in my funeral attire," she said, suddenly remembering she was still wearing her sombre black dress. "I stayed with Matt last night so haven't been home yet. Matt, this is Eddie," she then added as Eddie came into the room. "Eddie held my hand while I sobbed my way through Abi's funeral yesterday."

"Thanks, I really appreciate that," Matt said, shaking Eddie's hand.

"It was the least I could do after everything we've put Esther through," Eddie said, his cheeks flushing.

"Esther's been incredibly helpful and we're very grateful to her," Ade said, "and if you're willing, that mantle is now coming your way Matt. So, let's start with the good news. If you're prepared to give us your co-operation we can offer you full immunity. Once I was able to explain to my superiors the terrible circumstances that led to your involvement, it was a pretty easy decision."

"So you can save him from a jail sentence but can you save him from our Dad?" Esther asked, taking hold of Matt's hand. "He'll have Matt killed. Or what if he has my Mum killed before we even get to see her? If you end up putting him away for life, he's hardly going to care about another murder charge or two, is he?"

Knowing her Mum was alive and yet still out of reach had been the worst part for Esther but they couldn't risk anything happening to her now. All she could do was focus on getting Dave behind bars as quickly as possible so they could finally plan their big reunion.

"Let's see how this plays out," Ade said. "We may have other options but if there's no alternative, we can always discuss putting you in the witness protection programme. You, Matt and your mum."

"What about Jamie?" Esther asked.

"Leaving loved ones behind is hard," Ade said, "but there'll be plenty of time to discuss the detail," he added quickly in response to the sudden look of panic on Esther's face. "So are you interested Matt?" he asked him, moving on swiftly before there were any more emotionally charged questions. "With your help, we can bring an end to years of...."

Matt put his hand up. "I'll do it," he said, saving Ade from the need to provide any additional reasons why he should comply.

"Good decision," Ade said, certain he could now feel the table in front of them vibrating as Eddie's foot tapped furiously on the floor.

"So what do you need?" Matt asked him.

"We need to record a full statement covering as far back as you can go but we'll also need physical evidence," Ade told him. "I've talked to the surveillance team who've been watching the pawnbroker's and if we're careful, we think we can get you in there to access any files, or is that something you can do remotely without triggering any suspicion?"

Matt put his hand inside the neck of his t-shirt and pulled out a long silver chain with a memory stick on the end of it. He slipped it over his head and placed it carefully in front of Ade. "Everything you need is on there. Documents, emails, plans – you name it, it's all there. And right back to the first job I was involved in. My Dad makes sure everything is deleted the minute a job is done but I always made sure I had copies first. An insurance policy if you like, for a moment just like this. And there's recordings too of various meetings. Audio only but enough to identify key voices."

Ade's jaw dropped slightly. "Wow," he said, handing it to Eddie who was already standing up ready to deliver the innocent looking storage device to their tech team.

"Every associate who's linked to my Dad will be mentioned somewhere," Matt told him. "Every job is catalogued. There are copies of coded text messages detailing 'problems' having been successfully removed or dealt with, and copies of bank statements too. Some of it he didn't even know I had access to. The only thing I could never find was an address for where Mum is but I know Pete's been in touch with her over the years."

"And it's just been hanging around your neck for all to see?"

"I tried keeping it in a safety deposit box but I couldn't sleep imagining what I'd do if it got lost. I checked on it every day for a week and then got paranoid I might be followed. And it constantly needed updating." He shrugged. "Just seemed easier to hide it in plain sight."

Ade's eyes remained wide with disbelief. Not only that the memory stick had never been spotted but at the realisation that if the information was as thorough as Matt said it was, he'd just been picked up from the back of the race and dropped a short sprint from the finishing line.

Ade gave himself a little shake and tried to remember where they'd got to. "I think it might be time we brought Pete in if you've got an active number for him? We got one from Esther but it's no longer in use."

"No," Matt said. "Don't bring him in. Pete took a beating when Abi and I left. He's done too much for me to risk the same again or worse. Let me meet him. You'll see from all the information I've given you that he doesn't have a significant role in any of it. He was my Dad's school buddy and is one of the few people he's ever looked out for until he found out he'd helped me get away, but he wasn't involved in any of the jobs. He's more of a…I don't really know how to describe him. He's like the housekeeper, or maybe a personal assistant, booking and ordering stuff, but not doing anything more scandalous than making sure the fridge is always well-stocked." Matt thought for a moment. "In fact, if you want a recorded statement from me, I'm going to have to make it a condition that you leave him out of it."

Ade paused while he considered Matt's request, knowing he really had nothing to lose by waiting to see what evidence they had from Matt before deciding whether or not they needed to speak to Pete. "Okay, let's meet again in twenty four hours by which time we'll have worked out exactly how we want this to move forward from here. And if what you say about Pete is proven in the documents then I can assure you we won't be wasting any time on him. In the meantime, Matt, we'll take you somewhere safe."

"No, I'm not going anywhere. I've done pretty well keeping out of everyone's sights and I'm way more vulnerable locked away. You're going to have to trust me," he said. "I've already given you more than enough to put my Dad away for the rest of his life, and put another dozen or so people in the dock alongside him. I need to meet Pete and I'm safer looking after myself. And why would I disappear on you now?"

Ade was tempted to point out he was famous for his frequent vanishing acts and the fact that he'd already handed over so much was exactly why he might now choose to disappear without trace. What the hell would he tell DI Baker if that happened? But if they were to continue moving forward, it might just be worth the risk.

"It's all very unconventional," Ade said, "but I'll go with it if we can do your interview now. It would be good to get it done and it'll mean we can move quicker towards making arrests. The sooner we can do that, the safer everyone will be." Ade decided not to mention that it would also soften the blow slightly if Matt did decide to do a runner, and it would give Eddie and the tech team time to make sure the memory stick was indeed packed with the history they'd been assured it was before Matt left the building.

Ade immediately stood up. "I'll get us some coffee and then we can get started."

Esther waited for Ade to leave the room and then she turned to Matt. "You okay?"

"I'm not sure I know what that is."

"This is the only way out of this. Getting Dad locked up is the only chance we've got to actually live our lives. Without fear or danger. And with Mum!"

She smiled at him, her eyes glistening. "I know," he said, his tone suggesting he couldn't quite visualise this nirvana as efficiently as Esther just yet. "What are you going to do about Jamie?"

Esther sighed. "I don't know. I might go and see him now while you do your interview. He's working in my flat and getting increasingly irritated by how little I'm sharing so whatever happens, we need to talk. I guess now is as good a time as any."

"You do realise there's a chance we may have to just disappear? No warning, no forwarding address. Literally vanish of the face of the earth." He looked at her, not sure if she'd fully accepted what it would mean if they stepped into the Bermuda Triangle that was witness protection.

"It's okay, I get it." She stood up. "What are you going to do when you're finished here? Where will you go?"

"I'm going to catch up with Pete and then I'll see what Ade has in store for me next." He stood up too to give her a hug. "Nearly there Esty."

"Sorry, am I interrupting something?" Ade said as he came crashing back in, using his elbows and feet to negotiate the door, a coffee in each hand and a packet of biscuits under one arm.

"It's okay, I was just going," Esther said as she picked up her bag and coat. "You'll let me know what the plan is?"

"Of course," Ade said. "Try to keep it low key tonight if you can. Be silly to take any chances at this point. And I think it's time to put someone outside your place, just to be on the safe side."

26

At least a couple of minutes had limped past since Esther had sat down at one side of the large kitchen island with Jamie looking incredibly distant sitting opposite her. She knew the silence was quickly becoming uncomfortable but she wasn't being deliberately obtuse or insensitive. She genuinely had no idea what to say to him.

"I take it there's no point asking you what the hell is going on?" Jamie eventually asked. Esther looked at him and when she said nothing, he picked up his phone. "Let's have a little recap shall we?" he said as he opened his text messages and then clicked on her name. "So yesterday, you go to Abi's funeral, alone. Couldn't have me getting in the way of Matt seeking you out, could we? Did he by the way?" Her eyes went down, shoulders hunched to protect her from the vicious edge to his tone. "Of course, you can't tell me! I wait all day, wondering how you're coping then finally a text. 'All fine. Just need a little time to let it all sink in.' I text you back but there's nothing more until eleven. Eleven o'clock Esther! At which point you tell me you won't be home. No explanation. No information at all. And then I've had to wait until…" he checked his watch, "almost midday for you to just stroll back in without a word all morning. What the fuck Esther?"

"I'm sorry."

Jamie's eyebrows shot up as his jaw dropped slightly and then he waited. "You're sorry? That's it? That's all you're going to say to me?"

"There's nothing else I can say." She shrugged. "That's just the way it is. Not my choice. In fact, none of this is of my doing. I mean look at me. Do I look like someone in control? Do I look like someone who's having anything even close to a good time right now?"

"So let me help! Let me be some comfort to you but that means you have to share first. You've got to talk to me, properly, not just snatched bits here and there to shut me up, you have to go back to the beginning and tell me everything. And if you can't, then…."

"Then what?" Esther asked, feeling her shoulders slowly moving backwards as her back straightened in preparation for whatever was coming next.

Jamie looked at her for a moment. "I had a visit a few months ago from a couple of your Dad's thugs."

Esther gasped. "What do you mean?"

"They…..encouraged me into the back of a car for a… chat." Jamie chose his words carefully but the meaning was crystal clear, his emphasis of certain words leaving her in no doubt how this had played out.

"Where were you? And what did they want? And why the hell didn't you tell me at the time?"

"Just around the corner from here, and they wanted information. They wanted to know about you and your life. Wanted to know when Matt had last been here and if an older woman had come into your life recently. And I didn't tell you because I didn't want to scare you."

Esther suddenly felt very hot, her palms clammy with sweat, her heart tripping over itself as it started to race. "What did you tell them?"

Esther then jumped as Jamie banged his hand down hard on the kitchen surface. "What do you think I told them?" he yelled at her. "I didn't tell them anything! For fuck's sake Esther, of course I didn't tell them anything! But do you know how hard that was? How terrifying it was, wondering what might happen if I refused to help? And despite me risking who knew what to try to protect you, your assumption is still that I would've told them anything they wanted to know!" He sat back, his hands up and rubbing his forehead as he slowly rocked backwards and forwards.

Esther watched him. What could she possibly say? She felt the knot that had been sitting in the pit of her stomach for days now tighten until the pain and discomfort caused her eyes to fill with tears. She sniffed loudly in an attempt to draw the liquid back in. She could cry later once he'd gone.

"You don't trust me," he eventually said.

"I find it hard to trust anyone."

"But I'm not just anyone!"

Esther shook her head. "No, you're not. But a lot has happened to me. As a child. As an adult. And the last couple of weeks since Matt and Abi first went missing have been terrifying, surreal, mind-blowing." She continued to shake her head, not sure how best to capture what she had just lived through.

"So tell me what's going on and let me help you?"

"I can't."

"Can't or won't"

Esther looked at him. "Does it matter?"

"Yes, it does! Of course it does! It matters to me!"

Esther paused for just a moment. "I think it's best if we just leave it here Jamie."

"So when are we going to talk?"

"No," she said quietly. "Leave our relationship here."

Esther watched the colour drain from his face. He went to say something but then stopped himself and instead he quickly gathered up his laptop and phone and left the room. Esther heard him go into the bedroom where she assumed the muffled sounds were him putting his things into the bag he'd arrived with just under three weeks earlier, then more footsteps followed by the sound of the front door opening. She held her breath while she waited, anxious for a moment that he was about to come back in and tell her she was making a terrible mistake and then there it was, the finality of the door closing.

Esther sat where she was until the silence became too much and then she stood up and headed straight to the bathroom, suddenly feeling in desperate need of a shower. She peeled off the black dress she'd worn for Abi's funeral. Had that really only been yesterday? Her head throbbed with the amount of information she'd taken on board since then and her skin felt claggy, a whole new suite of questions, hopes and fears now blocking every pore. She stood under a hot jet of water, taking the full force in her face, not moving until she started to feel the tension wash away.

Pulling on some joggers and an oversized sweatshirt, her hair left loose and damp, Esther then went straight to the fridge and pulled out a selection of cheeses. Next she opened a cupboard and grabbed a packet of crackers, and then a second cupboard for a large glass that she filled generously with red wine. Putting her selection of treats on a tray, including the opened bottle of wine and a large bar of chocolate for good measure, she moved into the lounge, turning the television on before she sat down. She opted for a channel that would offer her back-to-back reality shows. Not her normal genre of choice but perfect for the occasion; just the right amount of distraction with very little focus required.

She ate and drank her way through the afternoon and then when she started to feel fidgety, she got up and walked around the room for a moment before wandering over to the large bay window to look out on to the street. Just as she was about to walk away again she spotted a familiar car parked diagonally opposite. She went back to the sofa for her phone and then dialled as she came back to her chosen vantage point.

"Everything okay Esther?"

She saw Eddie's face peering up at her flat from his car window and she gave him a little wave.

"I thought that was you," she said with a smile.

"Good at this undercover lark, aren't I? I saw Jamie leave. Is everything okay?"

Esther's jollity immediately faded. "We had a chat about trust which was never going to go well. He ended up offering me a way out so I took it. There was no point building bridges only to blow them up again if we end up having to disappear into oblivion."

"I'm sorry to hear that. You've had a lot to deal with these last few weeks."

"In all honesty, the relationship wasn't really going anywhere. It was just easier to wallow in denial. None of my friends like spending time with him. Abi certainly didn't warm to him. And he knew what Matt went through growing up and yet he constantly joked about wanting to hit him. Who does that? Talking about the possibility of moving away and cutting all ties made me realise I'd quite like a fresh start. The thought of leaving him behind should have bothered me much more than it did."

"As long as you're okay?"

"I'm fine, thanks. Other than wondering why on earth I'm telling you all this!"

"There aren't many people you can talk openly with at the moment so I'm very happy to listen whenever you need to talk."

"Well thank you, I appreciate that," she said, surprised that she could feel herself blushing, and then she remembered the news Jamie had shared earlier. "One thing of potential interest," she told him. "Jamie mentioned he had a visit from a couple of my Dad's lynch mob a few months ago, wanting information about me and Matt and wanting to know if there was a new older woman on the scene."

"Shit. That means they definitely know where you live and they're looking for your mother. But in London? I'd better let Ade know." He paused for a moment. "Are you sure you're okay?"

"I'm fine, honestly."

"I'm expecting someone to come and take over from me any minute so I can be back in the station when Ade finishes with Matt, otherwise I'd come up and see for myself."

Esther smiled. "Is that an offer to hold my hand again?" Esther then laughed as Eddie stuttered and stumbled over a suitable reply. "I'm just teasing you Eddie but I do really appreciate your concern."

She watched as his face appeared at the car window again and she smiled, hoping he could see in her face how genuine her appreciation was before she hung up.

27

When Matt left the station after giving his statement, he felt like he'd shed a skin, and a heavy one at that. He felt purged, experiencing such an overwhelming sense of relief and feeling so light as a result, he thought he might actually take off.

He left the station via an underground car park and then melted into the hordes of people who were spilling out of every surrounding office building at the end of the working day. He'd chosen a random bar for his meeting with Pete in a quiet corner of town where he was as confident as he could be that they wouldn't run into anyone they knew. That didn't stop him employing his usual tracking devices though, just to be sure. The ramifications for Pete if they were seen out together were something Matt would do absolutely anything to avoid.

He chose a booth towards the back of the bar and had been there for half an hour when Pete dropped into the seat opposite him. There was always something reassuring about having Pete around and Matt felt himself immediately relax the minute he was in the presence of his friend and protector.

Pete took off the cap he'd been wearing. "Hello young sir."

Matt's response was to gasp as he took in the fresh scars Pete still wore from the punishment he'd been served for helping Matt and Abi get away. "I'm so sorry Pete."

"Oh don't be," Pete said, waving his hand as if batting away the apology. "It was bound to happen at some point. It's a miracle I got away with helping you for as long as I did."

"Well that doesn't make it any better, or stop me being sorry."

"Well it doesn't look like you fared much better?" Pete said, clocking the new scars on Matt's face too.

"Already long forgotten," Matt said. "You know Abi's dead? I should've known it was completely ridiculous to think he'd let me go."

"What can I tell you?" Pete said with a shrug. "He's never going to let your mum off the hook and that means you're hanging right up there with her. His ability to hold a grudge knows no bounds."

A loud noise behind them made Pete whip his head around, his eyes suddenly wide.

"I know it's risky you being with me so let's keep it brief," Matt said in response. "I need you to do two last things for me. I need Mum's address and I need you to take a holiday for a week or so. My treat. Take Evie and get yourself some sunshine."

Pete had now squeezed his hands together so tightly his knuckles had turned white. "What the fuck are you planning?" Matt looked at him, eyebrows raised, lips tightly shut. "Whatever it is," Pete continued, "it won't work. You must know that?"

"Just give me Mum's address and fuck off as far away as you can."

"Matt, please!"

"Mum's address?" Their eyes locked and Matt held his breath until finally Pete pulled a pen out of his pocket, grabbed a napkin and scribbled something down, then he pushed it across the table.

"I messaged her a couple of days ago but I haven't heard back."

"Is that normal?" Matt asked, trying to ignore the seed of fear that had just planted itself in his gut.

Pete shrugged. "Well let's put it this way. It hadn't concerned me until now."

Matt picked up the napkin and stood up. "Thanks Pete. For everything." A surge of emotion suddenly overwhelmed Matt causing him to choke on his words as he realised this might be the last time he ever saw Pete if the witness protection programme turned out to be their only option. While he'd wondered earlier if Esther had really grasped what it would mean to have to sever all ties, now here he was, facing a man he truly loved, who'd helped and supported him through unimaginably tough times, knowing he was possibly leaving him for good, and yet he was unable to say goodbye. Instead, he pulled Pete out of his seat and hugged him tightly. Then with a final slap on the back, he forced himself to let him go.

"Now go and get Evie to pack some bags and tell her to meet you at the airport."

28

It took Ade more than six hours to get everything he wanted from Matt. The factual accounts of one job after another had been one thing but the first-hand account of how Matt had planned his mother's funeral, how he'd comforted a fourteen year old Esther and continued to do so for years, how he'd then played the role of brother, parent and provider, and how he would have done anything to protect her, had left him with a throbbing head and a heavy heart.

As soon as they were finished, Ade quickly checked his phone and found a message from Eddie. He'd been keeping in touch with the tech team from outside Esther's place and was now back and waiting to update him but wanted him to know as soon as possible that the memory stick was clearly rammed with more information than they could ever have hoped for so, with only a slight twinge of anxiety, Ade had let Matt go.

When he walked back into the office, it was a hive of activity.

"Here's the first lot," Eddie said, handing him a large bundle of papers. "We're going to be here for hours but it'll definitely be worth it. And we're going to need more white boards," he shouted over his shoulder as he walked away to rejoin the tech team to see what gems were coming next.

A few hours later, a series of white boards were creating a temporary wall running the full length of the office. Ade had worked his way through the initial pile of print-outs which were now perfectly displayed on the first board in a series of paper flowers. At the heart of each was a company name, the target of whichever job was being outlined, with all the accompanying evidence attached like petals. A number of officers had been tasked with finding pictures of anyone mentioned along the way and these were added as they were found while someone else started researching the names of anyone who seemed to have been 'dealt with' or 'removed', again with the information pinned to the boards as it was uncovered.

The jobs were presented in chronological order dating all the way back to a year or so after Dave was released from prison, just as Matt had promised, and each one perfectly told a story. It was a painstaking process but one that was undoubtedly made quicker by Matt's incredibly organised brain.

When the last piece of information had been added, Ade took a step back, his tired eyes narrowed, his vision blurred around the edges. He'd gradually let people go as time had slipped by and was now alone, the only one left to appreciate this spectacular display. It was like a modern day tapestry depicting a tale of conflict and criminal artistry.

"Fuck me!"

Ade's head shot round at the sound of DI Baker's voice who had just walked in with a senior member of the Crown Prosecution Service.

"Impressive isn't it?" Ade said, only adrenalin now keeping him upright.

"Ade, this is Patrick Robbins from the CPS." The two men shook hands before they all walked to the first board and slowly worked their way along. Ade talked them through the process, taking his time to go through every piece of information for each job, outlining what additional bits they'd already added and what they were still waiting for. As he talked, he updated Patrick on Matt's story following their interview and any additional anecdotal stuff Matt had passed on relating to the cases spread out in front of them.

"Where is Matt?" DI Baker then asked him.

"Oh he's safe. You don't have to worry about him," Ade said, based on the fact he was doing more than enough worrying about where Matt might be for all of them.

"I've never seen anything like it," Patrick said, his head blown by the amount of detail and the sheer volume of information he was seeing.

"Wait till you hear the audio recordings. I want to call them the icing on the cake but I'm not sure that does them justice."

"It seems a rather ridiculous question under the circumstances but I have to ask," DI Baker said, turning towards Patrick as they reached the last board. "Do we have enough to make the arrests?"

"That would be a resounding yes," Patrick replied without hesitation. "Go knock yourselves out."

"Excellent," DI Baker said, her eyes alive with expectation. "We'll get the team in for a briefing first thing tomorrow."

29

"So what time did you finish last night?" Esther asked as she climbed into the passenger seat of Eddie's car.

"I left the station somewhere in the early hours."

"Don't you ever sleep?"

"Sleep is for wimps," he laughed as he pulled away, "and to be honest, it's hard to switch off at the moment."

"I guess we're all too wired to sleep right now," Esther said after another fitful night herself.

They sat in a comfortable silence for a while as Eddie negotiated the morning rush hour traffic then, as the silence started to stretch to a point where its tension could clearly be felt, Esther stole a glance at him. There was something calming about Eddie. She felt safe in his company which wasn't something that happened often for her. She wondered if she should suggest stopping for a coffee along the way. They had plenty of time until they were scheduled to meet with Ade so why not? And then suddenly he was looking back at her, the car conveniently stopped at a traffic light. He raised his eyebrows, inviting her to share whatever was on her mind and she blushed, bringing her eyes swiftly back to face the front again.

"You okay Esther?" he asked, as they started to move again.

"Yes, I'm just fine thanks," she replied, keeping her eyes fixed firmly forwards.

Ade had stayed at the station until the sun was threatening to show itself while he desperately tried to get confirmation that Kate was safe. It had been hugely unnerving to hear from Eddie that Dave clearly thought she was in London so the minute Matt had text him with her address, he'd had local officers trying to track her down. The officers had been to her house but there was no one home. A neighbour had told them she owned the local florist's but it had been closed for hours by this point and when Ade eventually went home, there was still no news. The local officers would go back again first thing and her mobile phone would be tracked for any recent activity but all of this took time.

Ade wasn't sure why he'd bothered going home at all. He certainly didn't get any rest but there was so much adrenalin coursing through his veins he felt more alert than he ever had despite the sleep deprivation and not having eaten a proper meal for days.

He was back at his desk by seven o'clock and then spent an hour or so walking up and down the office, scanning every piece of information on the white boards again and again, just to be sure he hadn't missed anything. Despite the need to constantly check and re-check, he was confident they had everything covered and a subsequent plan was now starting to take shape. As long as Matt turned up.

He felt a familiar burning sensation in his chest and he winced, reaching into his pocket and popping another antacid into his mouth. He then tossed the empty box into the bin, took a fresh packet out of the drawer and put it safely in his pocket. He was averaging at least a packet a day at the moment and was praying the almost constant gnawing discomfort in his ribcage would stop once they finally had Dave in custody.

Ade went back to his desk and buried himself in paperwork. When he looked at his watch again, it was eight thirty and the office was now full. He knew Eddie had already picked Esther up which would give them plenty of time to talk her through the plan before he briefed the team at ten. It was vital that meeting went well. They had little more than twenty four hours before they were all systems go and this would be the last opportunity for Ade to make sure everyone knew exactly what was expected of them both individually and as a team. There would be one final meeting with DI Baker tomorrow but it would be way too late by that point to address any problems. That had to be done today, now, with every potential issue discussed and planned for, and every concern raised and addressed.

Ade reached for another antacid and then almost jumped out of his chair as two hands came down heavily on his shoulders.

"Sorry Ade, did I startle you? Anyone would think you weren't expecting me back," Matt said with a wink.

Ade felt every last muscle in his body relax. He then fought the urge to give Matt the tightest hug he could manage, so grateful was he to see him.

"Not at all," he said instead. "I just wasn't expecting you this early, that's all."

"Well I can go away again if you like?"

"No, please don't do that," Ade said as he stood up. "Come on, I'll get us some coffee."

As they headed into the corridor towards the kitchen, Esther and Eddie came around the corner to face them.

"Aahh, look at that," Esther said with a smile. "Our little dysfunctional family is all back together." She headed straight for Matt, drawing immediate comfort from the strong arms that he immediately wrapped around her.

"Why don't you two head into the meeting room?" Ade suggested, happy to give them a moment alone, "We'll get the drinks."

Esther led Matt to the room that already felt like an extension of home and closed the door behind them.

"So Jamie and I split up," she said, the minute the door was shut.

"No!" Matt said, with genuine surprise. "What happened?"

Esther shrugged. "It was the right thing to do. The relationship was already over, we just hadn't admitted it, so it's definitely for the best."

Matt studied her face as he took hold of her hand. "I think you're right. A clean break will be easier for you both in the long run. And a fresh start will be good for all of us Esty."

"Did you hear he got roughed up by a couple of Dad's mates somewhere near my place?"

In a flash, Matt's demeanour flipped from warm and supportive to defensive and protective. "No I didn't. When did that happen? What did they want?"

"A couple of months back. Maybe that's why he became so suspicious and mistrusting of you?"

"But what did they want?" Matt asked again.

"Information, about me and about you. And they wanted to know if an older woman had suddenly come into my life."

"Mum?"

"Not sure who else they could have been talking about." And then she gasped, her eyes wide. "If Mum's been coming to London do you think it's her who's been watching me? And calling me? Maybe it was her presence I could sense?"

"Shit! So they're looking for her in London?" Matt said, ignoring her questions. "I've got her address. I need to go there now."

As Matt turned towards the door, Ade and Eddie were just coming in.

"No Matt, we can't let you do that I'm afraid."

"I don't need your permission!" Matt squared up to Ade, a sense of panic puffing him up like a balloon.

Ade stayed calm, giving Eddie a moment to close the door behind them. "Matt, please. Just sit down for a moment. I spoke to local officers last night. They haven't made contact with her yet but as soon as they do, they'll be calling me so you racing off isn't going to help. And your focus has to be Dave. We've got no time to lose now and arresting him is without doubt the quickest and most effective way to guarantee your mother's safety." He waited for a moment to let that all sink in but wouldn't hesitate to take a tougher line if he had to. The reality was Matt had given him sufficient information to arrest him any time he chose, and if Ade suddenly decided the safest place for him was a cell, that's exactly where he'd put him. He really didn't want to have to threaten him with that prospect though, hoping Matt would work out for himself that they needed to stick to their agreed plan.

Matt's head then went down, his torso deflating as he reluctantly accepted Ade was right. Feeling that the immediate threat of him bolting had passed, Eddie chose this moment to sit down and Esther followed his lead.

"Right," Ade said, not wanting to waste another moment. "Here's what we're going to do."

30

Once Ade had finished with them, Esther had been driven home again while Matt chose to just slip out on foot. Esther wanted him to go with her but he'd made his excuses and insisted, once again, that he was better on his own, needing to mentally prepare himself for the next and final stage.

Matt had spent the previous night in a pretty fancy hotel but on the off chance the next few days didn't go as planned, he chose to head off in the direction of the most luxurious hotel he knew of, deciding he might as well have a night of obscene indulgence. An hour later he was checking into a decadent suite and ordering some room service.

Once he was settled, Matt sat with his laptop, combing back through the footage from outside Esther's flat. Jamie had said he'd been approached a couple of months ago and increasingly it had niggled Matt that he could somehow have missed that some of Dave's men had made it into the vicinity of Esther's place without him noticing. He knew being with Abi had made him relax and possibly take his eye off the ball but surely not to the point where he would render Esther vulnerable?

He started from four weeks ago and worked back from there, looking for the alert that should have been activated the moment either a number plate was picked up by the camera he'd installed, or an active mobile phone had crossed the boundary he'd set up. He sipped on a glass of ridiculously expensive red wine as he searched and by the time he'd worked his way back through eight weeks of footage, which took him to three months ago, his eyes were stinging and barely open. And he'd found nothing.

He stood up, grimacing as he stretched every inch of his stiff body and then walked out on to the suite's terrace. The air was cool and he shivered, the drop in temperature waking him up in a flash. What was he missing? Apart from any evidence at all that Jamie was telling the truth. Matt rolled that around in his head for a moment until the obvious finally hit him. The reason he couldn't find anything was because there wasn't anything to find.

Matt came back inside, wide awake now, adrenalin revving up, his brain already firing on all cylinders as he reminded himself what it was that had made him mistrustful of Jamie in the first place. He'd never understood why Dave had started having him followed, and then Abi too. That must have been when Dave had found out Abi was a police officer but what, or who, had made Dave suspicious in the first place?

It had to have been Jamie. Matt had often wondered why Dave had never tried to reconnect with Esther, or was able to resist asking how she was. If he'd sent Jamie into her life, there would have been no need to ask. He would have known everything about her and in the fullest possible detail.

Matt topped up his wine glass and swallowed a huge mouthful, taking a moment to be sure his imagination wasn't running away with him but this was his father which meant, of course, it was all perfectly plausible. If he was right, he realised that meant Jamie had played his part in Abi's death too. He must have voiced doubts which prompted Dave to have them both tracked and once Dave knew her true identity, she was a dead person walking. And if he was following Matt, maybe that was how Dave knew Pete had helped him which meant Jamie was responsible for his beating too.

Matt looked at his watch. It was almost one o'clock in the morning. He leapt up, rummaged in his holdall for a baseball cap and then, pulling it low over his eyes, he left the room. A few moments later, he was walking out of the hotel heading south on foot. It would take him nearly an hour to get there but it would be worth it. He would make sure of that.

Jamie lived in a modern apartment block near the river. Matt had always wondered how he could afford it and now he knew. It was all thanks to the Dave Harrison Special Projects Fund. It took Matt less than three minutes to bypass the security pad that required a code to gain entry and then once inside, he found Jamie's name amongst a sea of postboxes in the foyer and headed quickly up the stairs.

When Jamie woke with a start a few moments later, it was with Matt's gloved hands wrapped tightly around his neck. The immediate sense of panic was huge.

"Wherever you live, whatever security systems you install, I will get in," Matt spat through gritted teeth, his face only inches from Jamie's. "I will keep coming whenever the thought of you deceiving my sister so spectacularly becomes too much to bear. Or when I remind myself that it was you who set off the chain of events that would lead to Abi being shot to death in front of my fucking eyes!"

Jamie thrashed his body and kicked his legs, his hands tugging at Matt's as he desperately tried to free himself from Matt's deathly grip.

"You are the scum of the earth," Matt continued, his voice low and gravelly, "the absolute lowest of the low. And the reason I know that is because I've been on the receiving end of violence all my life and never once have I physically attacked someone until now. That's what you've driven me to. That's how truly disgusting you are."

Jamie suddenly stopped fighting and looked at Matt. His eyes were full of regret and sadness and self-reproach, none of which Matt had expected to see and, for a moment, he loosened his grip.

"I'll never stop coming back to scare you, to remind you what you did, and maybe one of those times I'll decide you don't deserve to live."

With that Matt roughly let him go and Jamie coughed and gasped, gulping in as much air as quickly as he could. By the time he found his voice, Matt was already heading out of the room.

"I just didn't know how to make it all stop," Jamie called after him, his voice sounding strained and raspy.

Matt stopped in the doorway and turned back to face him. He was surprised to feel a strange sensation overcome him, realising quickly that it was pity. No, worse than that, it was empathy. No one knew better than Matt what it felt like to be imprisoned by Dave, to have him as your puppet master with no choice but to dance to his tune.

"What did you tell him?" Matt asked.

"That there was something about Abi I couldn't put my finger on. That I didn't trust her. She was always asking questions and pushing for information." Jamie sat on the edge of the bed now, his head in his hands. "But I didn't know he'd kill her," Jamie said, keeping his head down, his words quiet and still full of cracks, heightened emotion crippling what little voice he currently had.

"So why tell Esther you got roughed up?"

"It was the only way I could think of to encourage her to talk to me. Dave's been pushing me harder and harder for information about what Abi knew but it didn't work. Esther didn't tell me anything."

"Esther said you encouraged her to work with the police. Why would you do that?"

"It was just another way to try to find out what they knew. By that point I could feel his presence everywhere. His patience was running out and I didn't know what he was going to do to me if I didn't deliver."

"You mentioned an older woman? Are they looking for our mother?"

"I don't know the background but someone thought they'd seen her near Esther's place. I thought she was dead?"

Matt chose to ignore Jamie's question, pausing for a moment instead. There was certainly no satisfaction in discovering he'd been right that Jamie was just another of Dave's pawns, but that paled into insignificance knowing that his mother could be in danger if Dave thought she'd tried to see Esther.

Jamie looked up at him. "Will you tell Esther?"

"No," Matt said without hesitation. "She's been through enough without knowing you were a fake too."

"I'd have fought much harder for her if things were different but letting her finish things with me felt like the only way to break free from Dave. That has to be best for Esther, doesn't it?"

"So you're no use to my Dad now?" Matt watched a new surge of fear flood Jamie's eyes. "Well I might decide you're too pathetic and insignificant to turn up uninvited again. But I can't say the same for him."

31

Kate stared out of the window but saw nothing but a blur of green that slowly turned to grey as the train transported her from rural surroundings to urban, and all in just under an hour. She wore sunglasses to soften the glare as a cool sun sat half up and half down on the horizon as if undecided which way it was going to go. Apart from shielding her eyes, the glasses also made her feel as if she was disguising herself, helping her to keep a suitably low profile. She certainly didn't want anyone to catch her eye and start talking to her.

On the one hand, she felt fully prepared for today. She was on top of Dave's daily routine, knowing exactly what time he appeared every weekday morning for a brief stroll. She knew what newsagent's he went to to pick up his newspaper and which café he then went on to for his daily coffee, always ordering it in a takeaway cup so he could drink half of it while he flicked through the news pages of his paper first before flipping it over to get his daily sports fix then drinking the remainder as he ambled home via a park.

She wasn't daft enough to have done this research herself. No, she'd paid someone else to do that who had followed him over a number of days and weeks until he was confident he had his schedule totally pinned down.

Today would be the first time in sixteen years that she'd seen Dave in the flesh. The last time had been in a court room when his eyes had been fixed on her for the duration and had burned into her soul. She'd only gone for the first day of his trial. Even in a room full of police and security guards she hadn't felt safe. She shuddered now as she did every time she was reminded of the level of fear she had once lived with, every minute of every waking hour. She had been on high alert constantly, heart forever racing, eyes permanently startled.

Today, however, there was a welcome steeliness to her demeanour. She had expected to spend the journey doing breathing exercises, putting herself into a meditative state in an attempt to stay on an even keel but she was perfectly calm. She was confident she was doing the right thing and determined to take control of her life. She was excited about the future for the first time in longer than she could remember and, perhaps most importantly, she felt fully prepared and fired up for the day ahead. Whatever obstacles were thrown her way she would either overcome them, or die trying.

32

The silence on the other end of the line was horribly unnerving, and then finally he spoke.

"Well I'd like to say this is unexpected but I knew you'd come crawling back at some point."

"I've been compliant for years without complaint. Surely I can be forgiven one moment of madness?"

"That's what we're calling her is it?"

Matt bit down hard on his lip and took a deep breath. "Call her what you like. It's history now. I just want to come back. We've got a job to do haven't we?"

"We've lost weeks thanks to your antics."

"Then let me back Dad so I can make it up to you!" Matt held his breath for a moment. "At least meet me? I never got the chance to bring you fully up to speed with where I'd got to. It'll be an easy decision once you see what I've got. Get the team ready and we can go straight to brief them afterwards. That's how confident I am you're going to be blown away by the new info I got just before…..I temporarily lost my focus."

Matt could almost hear Dave's brain whirring on the other end of the phone and then finally he spoke. "Go on then. Out of sight though. I'll see you at the old briefing room at three then if that goes as well as you seem to think it will, we can come back to the house to meet everyone else."

"You won't be disappointed," Matt said but Dave had already hung up.

Matt swung round and looked through the glass wall of the meeting room to where Ade and Eddie were sitting with headphones on. Ade immediately gave him a thumbs up but, relieved as Matt was to have that first part done, it was impossible to slow his heart or stop himself shiver as his body temperature plummeted leaving an uncomfortable layer of cold sweat behind. He shook his arms as he paced for a moment, so charged with nervous energy that he couldn't keep his body still.

"Well done Matt," Ade said to him as he came into the room. "You did really well."

Matt raised his eyebrows, interested to know what the appropriate definition might be of doing well in these circumstances. If it meant securing an invite to a potential deadly meeting then yes, he'd done very well indeed.

"That was the venue the firearms unit was hoping for," Ade said in an attempt to reassure. "It came up a number of times in all the notes and like lots of other places, they recce'd it yesterday. It's pretty remote so perfect as far as they're concerned."

"Yes, perfect for my Dad too. If he decides to pummel me to death, no one will hear me scream."

"We won't let that happen. There's a team already on their way to make sure they're in position first. It's like I said, too many people in one place is messy and hard to control. By coaxing Dave away, we've got the best possible chance of getting him which is the absolute priority."

"Everything just feels so rushed."

"You're not to worry. It's all in hand, I promise."

Matt raised his eyebrows. He knew it was his own anxiety that was making it all feel like a runaway train. He'd just have to accept that fast moving didn't necessarily mean out of control. He glanced at the large clock on the wall. "So what do I do for the next five hours?"

"There'll be a final briefing meeting at one o'clock but we can go over the plan again before then if you like?"

"No, the briefing will be enough."

"Another coffee then? Or something to eat?"

"I couldn't eat if I wanted to."

Ade watched as Matt paced up and down, backwards and forwards, the hypnotic perpetual motion making his head spin. "Well you need to try to relax."

"Can I go for a walk?"

"I don't think that's a good idea."

"Can I go anywhere?"

"No, not really."

There was a pause while Matt considered his options. "Maybe I'll have that coffee then?"

Esther's briefing had been just that. Brief. Ade had basically told her to go nowhere and do nothing other than let Eddie in who would call when he was outside so she could be certain it was him.

"So you drew the short straw again?" she said when he arrived. "You never did tell me what terrible thing you did to be punished with the job of babysitter. Or is it so bad you can't bring yourself to share?" she asked as he followed her into the kitchen.

"Have you seen recent pictures of your dad and his known associates? Have you not heard what they do to people? This wasn't punishment. I volunteered."

Esther laughed. "Coffee?"

"Yes please. Just the two sugars today, I need to pace myself."

Eddie watched her as she busied herself making drinks. "It's okay not to be okay Esther."

She stopped for a moment and looked at him, the spark in her eyes immediately evaporating. "I'm so anxious I don't know what to do with myself. I feel so useless, so helpless. Everyone's got a role except me."

"Well that's not true. Without you we'd be nowhere."

"But I didn't exactly play an active role did I? It's not like I was a willing participant. I didn't actually know I was helping. I've been used and manipulated. It doesn't do much for a girl's self-confidence."

"I'm really sorry you feel like that."

"And it's not just today. Life's been so awful for Matt and somehow I've just coasted through."

"Well that's not strictly true either. Your childhood wasn't exactly without trauma."

"But it was nothing compared to what Matt went through. You know some people call it the Cinderella Phenomenon when one child is singled out for abuse. And there's apparently no obvious reason for it. Maybe Matt reminded my Dad of himself in some way? Or of his own father which would've been worse."

Eddie thought for a moment. "So, if Matt's Cinderella? Who does that make you?"

Esther gasped. "An ugly sister! For fuck's sake! Is there no end to it?" And then she laughed, loving how beautifully Eddie had put the brakes on her journey towards the kind of dark place she really didn't need to go, today of all days.

"Right, come on. Help me carry this all through."

Esther handed Eddie several packets of biscuits and then put the coffees and a plate of pastries on a tray.

"Well we certainly won't be hungry," Eddie said as he followed her through to the lounge but when he saw what was waiting for them he immediately stopped. "What the fuck?"

Esther put the tray down on the coffee table. "We've got Monopoly, Cluedo, possibly not quite right for today," she mused, "Connect 4 and everybody's favourite, Mouse Trap," she said, picking up each board game in turn. "Plus a selection of card games and here's a list of my favourite films," she said handing him a piece of paper.

"And I need to know this because….?"

"In case we fancy watching a movie of course! It's going to be a very long day and we need to keep busy. I need to keep busy."

Eddie smiled at her. "So Matt's preparing to face your father, we've got practically every armed officer in London scattered around the capital on 'Dave-watch', not to mention Ade in a bullet-proof vest somewhere in the middle of it all and meanwhile, we'll be watching…" He stopped to look at the list of films he'd just been handed. "A World War II movie but one with lots of singing and a family dressed in curtains?"

Esther let out an exaggerated gasp. "I thought everyone loved The Sound of Music?"

Ade looked through the glass wall into the meeting room and could see Matt sitting back in a chair, leaning against a wall, eyes closed with headphones on. He was obviously listening to music, his foot gently tapping, his head swaying slowly and rhythmically from side to side. The movements suggested something calm and soothing and Ade hoped it was doing the trick. It was hard to imagine how he must be feeling. Dave was intimidating enough without the violent history the two Harrison men shared. It had taken huge amounts of restraint not to react to some of the accounts Matt had shared with him about his childhood, all needed for background and clearly incredibly challenging to recount without reliving some of the emotions felt by the six, seven, eight, nine year old and beyond. There was going to be something incredibly satisfying about reading this horror of a man his rights. He'd got to know Esther and Matt well enough that it felt personal now. He needed to do it for them and, of course, for Abi. She was enough on her own for him to want to see Dave hanging from a rafter, stripped of all dignity. He sighed. He knew he couldn't bring Abi back but he could give Matt and Esther a freedom pass, a ticket that would grant them the reunion they never thought could happen, and the fresh start they deserved.

Ade snapped himself out of his reverie to see Matt staring at him through the glass, eyebrows raised in question. Ade jumped up and a moment later was opening the meeting room door.

"You okay?" Matt asked him.

"Yes, sorry, lost in thought there for a moment. How you doing?"

"Wondering if it's possible for time to pass any slower."

"Not long to wait now. Dave's still at home and has everyone gathered already. As soon as we know he's on his way we can get ready to leave. Can I get you anything?" Matt shook his head. "I could get you hooked up with Esther if you like? She and Eddie are playing Monopoly if you want to join via a video call?"

Matt looked at Ade with complete incredulity. "I'm literally preparing to walk into the lion's den and they're buying up London with paper money?" Ade grinned at him and as he went to say something, Matt put his hand up to stop him. "And if you're about to make some crap joke about a get out of jail free card then think again my friend."

Ade winked at him and closing the door, he quickly retreated back to his desk.

33

There was nothing random about the date Kate chose to make her move. It was sixteen years to the day since her daughter had been forced to stand in a church and mark the supposed end of her life, changing Esther forever. Her attitude to relationships, her confidence, her outlook, everything about her had been set on a different path in that moment at an event that was as distressing as it was unnecessary. The follies of a mad man too used to getting his own way, and too brutal to be challenged.

Kate had arrived in London early and had walked the streets for an hour enjoying how still everything was, a city not yet ready to wake up and start a day that felt full of hope and opportunity. The train had delivered her into London Bridge station and from there it was impossible not to marvel at the sights around her as she crossed over the River Thames, the majestic Tower Bridge to her right and St Paul's Cathedral sitting just as grandly over to her left while in between, an array of new architecture towered over old. Bleary-eyed shift workers with creased and tired-looking clothing yawned as they passed her as chatter spilled from cafés from those who were bright and bushy-tailed, their days just beginning.

There was an unfamiliar sensation deep in Kate's gut as she walked that she chose to interpret as excitement. There was certainly no room for fear today. She could smell change in the air and she drew it in in long deep breaths, filling her lungs with strength and courage.

At eight o'clock on the dot, Kate was in the agreed spot waiting for the car and driver she'd hired for the day, the partner of the private investigator she'd used to track Dave's movements. She wanted someone who would understand her desire for discretion, who wouldn't ask questions or try to engage her in banal conversation. Someone who would take instruction without question. She knew the investigator had assumed she was trying to trap a philandering husband and that suited her just fine. She was happy to let him make up his own back story particularly as he'd done such a good job for her. She would have employed him again today but she was worried that if Dave clocked him, he might recognise him. He'd followed Dave for long enough that Dave must have registered his face at some point even if he'd be unable to remember when or why. And even if the chances of Dave remembering him were remote, it simply wasn't worth the risk.

A few moments later, a dark blue saloon pulled up beside her and she quickly checked the number plate was the one she was expecting before she opened the back door. "Good morning," she said as she climbed in. "You must be Gerald?"

"Yes, that's right. Is it okay to call you Kate?" he asked, their eyes meeting via the rear-view mirror. He watched her nod before continuing. "Great. Well, good morning Kate. Where would you like to go first?"

Kate handed him a piece of paper with an address on it. "The house has a gated entrance. Just pull up somewhere out of the way where we can still see the entrance please." Kate then sat back as Gerald pulled away and joined the steady morning flow of traffic, clutching her bag tightly to her lap.

It was just over forty minutes later when they pulled up outside Dave's house. Gerald found a space a comfortable distance from the front gate and pulled in.

"In the next ten minutes or so, a man will come out and follow the route you should already have been told about."

"Yes, I know exactly where he'll be going and how to play it so I can confidently hide in plain sight. I'll be totally invisible to him."

"Any clues about how he'll be spending his day are what I need if at all possible otherwise we'll just have to go wherever he takes us."

"No problem. I'll get to the café first so I can be seated ahead of him. I understand he's got a regular table so I'll make sure I'm close." Gerald then undid his seatbelt as he saw Dave come through the large iron gates. "Here we go. I'll see you in a while."

Kate watched him go and then concentrated on keeping her breathing deep and slow. It could be an anxious wait if she let her imagination run wild but, before she had the chance to settle, she was distracted by the iron gates opening again as a car pulled up. She gasped, recognising the face of the passenger. She couldn't see the driver but his companion was definitely a face she remembered. Someone who had sat around her kitchen table as part of Dave's gang, plotting and planning who knew what. Over the next hour, the gates were in constant use as more people arrived. She counted at least eleven visitors, a number of whom she also recognised as she tried to squash a growing sense of unease that something significant must be brewing.

Kate jumped as the car door opened and Gerald got back in. "Does the old briefing room mean anything to you?"

"Yes it does," Kate said, that sense of unease now firmly taking hold. "It's on the site of the old Woolwich Dockyard."

"He took a call while he was having his coffee. I can't be sure of the time but he's definitely just arranged a meeting there for some time later today. I want to say three o'clock but I can't be certain."

"Let's just head off now then. I'd like to be there first. I'll direct you when we get closer. There's a back way in but I can't remember the name of the road. I'm sure I'll recognise it when we get closer."

Gerald started the car and pulled away without question but, as they got closer, and after a number of furtive glances at Kate in the rear-view mirror, he started to sense a tension building.

"Is there anything you can tell me about this place? Just so I can get a feel for the layout," he asked. "You know, in case I need to…..come and find you, or something."

Kate recognised the 'or something' as a catch all for whatever currently unexplained event was likely to happen there as he desperately tried to work out what role he might be needed to play.

"I don't know what shape it will be in now but Dave's grandfather worked there," Kate told him. "He had a small export business and we used to hang out there when we were kids. When his grandfather retired the business kind of fell apart and I never knew what happened to the ownership of the place but Dave carried on meeting there long after the electricity was switched off and the windows started to crack. Made him feel like a big man when he was gathering his minions and playing the godfather, plotting the stuff of nightmares." Kate stopped suddenly, a burning heat rising as she remembered where she was and who she was with. She clamped her mouth shut. She'd said way too much already.

They sat in silence until Kate started to recognise where they were, giving clear instructions until Gerald pulled up at the end of what looked like a terrace of old red-bricked factory-style buildings. There was a number of boards up suggesting the site had been bought by a developer but there was no sign of any activity.

"This is fine here," she said, knowing she could work her way through to what Dave called the briefing room at the far end of the block. She could do it unseen from here but Gerald didn't need to know that. The less he knew the better.

As the car came to a stop, Kate leant forward and handed Gerald an envelope full of cash. "This is to cover the rest of the day and a bonus too for your….." She hesitated for a moment. "Kindness," she eventually added.

"You want me to leave you here? I'm not sure that's a good idea."

Kate was already getting out of the car. "I'll be fine, thanks." And with that she closed the car door and disappeared inside.

34

"Okay everyone, let's get started please!" DI Baker shouted above the noise. She waited, not prepared to begin until she had complete silence and the full attention of the room. As soon as that moment came, she kicked off.

"For those of you who haven't been formally introduced, this is Matt Harrison." A few nods and mumblings aimed in Matt's direction followed and Matt instinctively sat up straight doing his best to look like part of the team rather than the criminal hired hand that he was. He knew every person in the room was now intimately appraised of his life to date. That had made him feel uncomfortable initially but it had inspired a quiet respect. However unexpected this was, it certainly made his presence in the room easier.

"If you don't already know the minutia of what is about to unfold then you should probably leave the room. That said, I'm going to ask Ade to run the top line for us one last time. If you've any questions this is your last chance to ask. Doubt and hesitation are our enemy today and could cost lives so do not exit here with any uncertainty."

Matt's eyes scanned the room. If anyone did have any questions, he strongly doubted they'd let that be known. This feisty woman hadn't exactly created the kind of atmosphere that was conducive to opening up and sharing worries, or asking for elements of the plan to be repeated without fear of retribution. He hoped they'd all been paying sufficient attention before today or they were all in a whole heap of trouble.

"Ade, over to you."

"There's a firearms team already in situ at the old Woolwich Dockyard," Ade said, taking centre stage. "They're on the inside and the outside too and there's a control unit parked up on the east side away from the natural approach to the building. That's where DI Baker and I will be with someone from tech, and we'll have camera access from the lead officers on site so will be able to see everything they can. Tim will drive Matt there in a black cab and they'll arrive just before three o'clock by which time we expect Dave to already be inside. Information on how many people are with him will be shared once we know. Matt will be carrying a mic the size of a small button in his pocket and we'll be ready to strike quickly if Dave has plans that we're not aware of." Ade glanced at Matt briefly. Matt would know what he meant as did the rest of the room without him being any more graphic. "The moment to move will be on DI Baker's command. That command will also apply to Stacey's team who'll then apprehend anyone and everyone who's gathered at Dave's house. So far there's been eleven arrivals throughout the morning plus any staff in the house and three gang members who arrived last night. One of them has already been identified by Matt as Abi's killer." Ade paused for a moment while a series of gasps and whispers swept around the room. "The information Matt gave us that you've all worked so hard on so quickly has allowed us to build a phenomenal list of charges against an extensive network of criminals. This is an unprecedented operation we're about to blow wide open, and Dave's reign is about to come to a rather abrupt end. We've got all the evidence, now we just need to bring them in."

The room erupted with a boisterous adrenalin-fuelled rush of energy that manifested itself in a series of loud affirmations of 'let's do this!', 'we've got this!' and similar along with some back slapping, several fists in the air and even the odd roar. Matt watched quietly thinking this bunch weren't that dissimilar to Dave and his posse, just younger and a little less rough around the edges, and definitely better looking.

"You okay Matt?" Ade asked, appearing back by his side. "I'll be heading off in a minute and then Tim will be waiting around the corner for you at exactly two o'clock."

"I'm good. I wouldn't mind calling Esther before I go if that's okay?"

"Of course. Head back to the other meeting room. You'll get some privacy there." He hesitated for a moment and then he put out a hand that Matt took hold of firmly. "I'll see you later then," Ade said with the most reassuring smile he could manage, his stomach now so full of antacids he was sure everyone could hear him fizzing.

"Let's hope so," Matt said and then, with a brief nod, he let go of Ade's hand and headed for the door.

"Esty, it's me."

"Matt! Are you okay? I've been so worried about you."

"I haven't done anything yet! And is that fucking Edelweiss I can hear in the background? Bloody hell Esty, Monopoly and The Sound of Music? You really know how to show a guy a good time."

"Eddie's perfectly happy, aren't you Eddie? There you are, he's smiling and nodding."

"Of course he is." Matt smiled, feeling comforted just by having the line between them open.

"What time are you heading off?"

"In about half an hour or so."

"Eddie has a walkie talkie but I might have to leave the room till it's all over." She paused for a moment "You know today's the anniversary of the day we buried Mum. Or not, as it turned out."

"Yes. I realised as soon as Ade said today was the day. It felt befitting somehow."

"Yes, I thought so too."

"It's just a shame it took sixteen years to get us to this point." Matt paused for just a moment and then to avoid them both getting overly emotional, he decided it was time to go. "I'll call you later, okay? And for goodness sake, give Eddie a break."

"How do you know The Sound of Music isn't his favourite film too?" Esther asked, glad to be talking about anything other than the potentially dangerous events that were now just ahead of them.

"Trust me," Matt said with great confidence. "I just know."

35

Kate made her way carefully from one building through to the next, the layout of this old terrace of industrial buildings slowly coming back to her with every step. It had been an exciting place to hang out when they were kids. Now it just felt tired and neglected and, if she was honest, darker than she remembered, and more than a little threatening but, as she entered the last building, she was surprised to find it in pretty good shape. The space was clearly still being used and she wondered if the sold signs she'd seen outside were nothing more than a ruse to make it look like development was coming while unthinkable business was going on inside.

She stopped just short of the old briefing room, a rather grand name for an almost empty space with just a table and two chairs in the middle. As Kate looked in, it was hard to work out how long it had been since someone had been there. If it was set up for anything, the atmosphere and surroundings certainly felt more conducive to interrogation than collaboration. It was separated from the main factory space by a paper thin plasterboard wall that looked like it would disintegrate if a large gust of wind chose to blow through. She felt her blood chill slightly as she stepped inside.

There was a second space off the briefing room that Dave used to call his private office when he was a fourteen year old boy. Kate almost smiled at the memory until the image of grazes on his knees and bruises scattered all over his body, left by the hands of a brutal father, started to come back to her but the abuse had inspired big dreams that he'd claimed would take them away from it all, from a life of nothing to a future where they would have everything they'd ever wanted and more. Sadly, the only way he knew how to make that happen was by following the example set by the adults around him; by cheating the system, by taking what wasn't his, by creating fear in a community willing to pay to be left alone, and by removing anyone who got in his way.

Kate quietly moved into this second room and then crouched down in the near corner. For a moment, all she was aware of was her heart pounding and then she started, convinced she could hear footsteps running somewhere on the other side of the building. She froze, terrified of staying where she was but equally terrified of moving. Maybe it was just very large rats? She shivered, not sure if that would be better or worse. She checked her phone was on silent and then looked at her watch. It was half past twelve. If Gerald had heard correctly, she had two and a half hours to wait. She sat down fully on the floor and stretched her legs out in front of her, accepting that this was about as comfortable as it was going to get. No matter. It would all be worth it in the end.

"Where to mate?" Tim's smile quickly disappeared as he clocked Matt's expression in the rear-view mirror. "Sorry, not the time for jokes clearly," he muttered as he pulled away from the kerb in the borrowed black cab.

Matt fixed his eyes outside the window trying to visualise his way through the next couple of hours, imagining his father making an eloquent confession to it all and then men dressed in black swooping in and whisking him away forever. He sighed. Of all the ways this could go, this cosy smooth scenario felt like the most unlikely. And then he gave himself a shake. He could do this! He had to do this. And anyway, what was the worst that could happen? Aside from Dave killing him obviously. Apart from snatched moments with Esther and a handful of magical weeks with Abi who'd been so brutally stolen away from him, his life had been completely empty. A perfect hollow, absent of feeling, without hope or purpose. He'd come to realise that death was actually preferable to such a miserable existence which is why he was prepared to take the risk of losing his life in an attempt to save it. So, let Dave do his worst. He'd got nothing to lose and absolutely everything to gain.

He was distracted from his thoughts by Tim talking on a walkie talkie, the intermittent crackling making it difficult to hear exactly what was being said.

"Was that Ade?" he asked, waiting till he was sure they were finished.

"He was just checking we're running to time," Tim replied, his eyes flitting between the road and Matt via the rear-view mirror. "He also wanted you to know Dave has just gone in. He arrived in a car with blacked out windows which is still parked outside. He got out of the passenger seat and it's impossible to tell if there's anyone in the back. Another car pulled up a few moments later on the other side of the building. Again, difficult to say how many people are inside. Either way, both cars are covered by the firearms unit."

"Did my Dad go inside alone?"

"Yes he did and they have eyes on him too. He's sitting at a table. There's a chair waiting for you on the other side."

"How very civilised." Matt looked away again, his eyes drawn back out of the window by a need to soak up daylight as if drawing badly needed energy from a sun that was only partially visible which just made him focus his eyes even more sharply. He just wanted it over with now. The day had limped by so painfully slowly that he was desperate for the torture to end.

"How long?"

"We're here," was the answer.

Matt felt his stomach deftly tie itself in a knot as they pulled up outside. Having felt like he was trapped in the day that would never end, he suddenly felt like everything was happening too quickly. He took a long slow breath in an attempt to squash the rising swell of panic as Tim brought the car to a stop and then turned around to look at him.

"If you tell me how much I owe you I swear I'll swing for you."

"Even I'm not that stupid," Tim said with a reassuring smile. "This is a really great thing you're doing," he added. "And we may look like a bunch of idiots but we're a good team. We won't let you down."

Matt looked at him, his emotions so confused and his heartbeat so chaotic that he wasn't sure in the moment if he wanted to hit Tim or hug him, deciding quickly that it was probably best to do neither.

"If you think that'll earn you a tip then you really are an idiot," Matt said as he opened the car door.

"You're a bit early," Tim said.

Matt got out the car. "Just make sure you're here when I come out."

Even though she couldn't see him, Kate knew it was Dave who had strode into the room and then paced up and down a few times before pulling one of only two chairs back to sit down. It was the smell that floated in with him that was so unmistakably Dave. He'd been wearing Aramis since he'd pinched a bottle from his uncle as a teenager and the classic citrusy, leathery aroma had become part of his DNA. He'd read something at the time that described the scent as 'sophisticated, classic and distinctly masculine' and had assumed he would adopt these qualities simply by splashing it liberally on his face. It may not have done any of the above but it certainly made him easy to identify, for her at least.

She checked the time again. It was twenty to three which gave her twenty minutes at most assuming there was a meeting scheduled for three. Was twenty minutes even long enough? She quickly decided she didn't have time to think about it or the answer would rapidly become irrelevant. Her chance would be over should anyone else arrive but, however nervous she might be, however scared, she knew that missing her chance to act was something she simply couldn't let happen which gave her all the courage she needed to seize the moment while she had it.

By the time Dave saw her, Kate had drawn her gun and was holding it with both hands, arms outstretched, her body strong and rigid, her nerves suddenly made of steel. She'd never felt more alive.

"Hello Dave," she said, her voice as steady as the weapon he now faced. He tried to stand up but his chair was positioned so close to the table that his thighs merely bounced off it, pushing him back down again. He had no choice but to look like he was comfortable staying where he was even though his eyes suggested something very different.

"You look a little unnerved?"

"Just surprised to see you, that's all," he said.

Kate waited for a moment. "Aren't you going to say what a lovely surprise it is?" She moved slowly around the table until she stood right in front of him and then held her position.

"It's been a while. How've you been?" he asked.

"How have I been? How do you think I've been?"

"Why don't you put the gun down and we can talk properly?"

Dave put his hands on the table and went to slowly push back his chair but Kate stepped forward.

"Don't you fucking move!" she screamed at him so loudly that she didn't hear Matt step into the room behind her.

"Mum, no!" he yelled above her piercing words.

And then she released her first bullet.

"What the fuck?" Ade leant forward desperately trying to make sense of the image in front of him, a grainy depiction of the unfolding events broadcast via the closest firearms officer to the briefing room.

"This is Command," DI Baker boomed over her walkie talkie. "Please identify who that is with the target."

"IC1 female. I think she's armed," came the crackly reply over the radio.

"No fucking shit Sherlock," Ade gasped. "Where the fuck is Matt?"

"This is Command," DI Baker said again. "Who has eyes on Matt?"

"Heading closer to the briefing room now Guv."

"Mum, no!" Matt's cry filled the command unit and everyone held their breath until the sound of a gun firing reverberated throughout the van, propelling DI Baker into action.

"Go, go, go!"

The volume in the control unit exploded as the firearms officers leapt out of the shadows and made their presence known. At exactly the same moment, both the car that Dave had arrived in and the second vehicle that had pulled up on the other side of the building were surrounded by officers. For a few seconds, all of the screens in front of Ade were rendered useless with each view blurred by a swarm of black uniforms distorting every angle.

Ade did his best to track what was going on but it was a few minutes before the situation started to take shape. Kate had been disarmed and put in handcuffs. Matt had also been cuffed which he hadn't been expecting so was putting up quite a fight. An ambulance that had been on standby had now pulled up and paramedics were on their way in to attend to Dave with a firearms officer already having confirmed he was still alive.

"We got him," DI Baker said, a smile slowly spreading across her face. "We bloody got him!"

36

The atmosphere back at the station was like nothing Ade had ever experienced. The only thing that was missing was bunting and a bowl of punch. It certainly felt like a party. There was a huge cheer when he walked in and he smiled graciously with cheeks flushing then DI Baker walked in behind him and the attention immediately switched to her. She allowed the revelry to last for a minute or so and then started barking orders as she reminded everyone there was still plenty of work to do.

Ade had heard on his way back that fifteen arrests had been made at Dave's house with those apprehended taken to five different police stations to be processed to ensure it was all done as quickly and efficiently as possible. If you added Dave, his driver and two men from the second car, and then threw in Matt and Kate for good measure, that was a grand total of twenty one arrests. Various members of the team were now spreading out across the capital eager to start their interrogations, each armed with huge folders full of copies of the various documentation that would ultimately see the entire gang charged. And the moment they all realised their fate, deals would be offered in exchange for any statements declaring Dave as their leader, the metaphorical final nails required to ensure the case against Dave was incontrovertible.

Meanwhile Dave had been taken to hospital but was expected to be discharged at some point very soon with nothing more than a flesh wound. He would then be brought to the station where Ade and DI Baker would be waiting. By that point, information would already be filtering in from their colleagues which would make their own interview even more satisfying.

Ade headed for the kitchen in need of some caffeine and bumped straight into Matt.

"Well done mate," he said, taking hold of Matt's hand and shaking it firmly.

"As it turned out I didn't really do anything, thanks to my gun-wielding mother. Where is she? I've been asking the whole way back but no one would tell me anything."

"She's fine, but there's a process. There's paperwork to be completed and we want to make sure we've done absolutely everything by the book. Any idea where she'd have picked up a gun?"

"Pete would be my best guess. She's not in any trouble is she?"

"She shot your father."

"It was an accident. And it was my fault. I made her jump."

"Matt, it'll be fine. The CPS won't press charges but she had to be arrested." He put his hand up in anticipation of Matt's protests. "I haven't let you down yet, have I?" he said calmly to Matt. "You're just going to have to bear with me for a little while longer."

"And what was the deal with cuffing me? That was an experience I wasn't expecting."

"We wanted Dave to think you were being arrested too so it had to look genuine. Unexpected was therefore the only way I'm afraid," Ade said with an apologetic smile.

Before Matt could object further, Esther came around the corner and clamped her arms around him from behind. "I'm so relieved to see you!" she cried. "I've been so worried. Are you okay?"

Matt gently pulled her arms loose enough to allow himself to turn around and face her. "I'm fine Esty, really. Did Eddie tell you what happened?"

"Yes! Mum was there! And with a gun! What the hell was that all about? And where is she now?"

Matt turned to Ade to let him explain. "She's been taken to another station," Ade said. "I've already told Matt that your mother won't be charged but there's still a process. And she'll need to be interviewed too."

Esther stepped forward, her face suggesting she was anything but happy about the situation but Matt put his arm out to stop her. "Esty, she had a gun and she may not have hurt him badly but she did actually shoot Dad."

"Since when did you become such a purveyor of the law? And she should be given a medal for what she did, not be put in a police cell." Esther took a moment to calm herself down. "I just want to see her, that's all."

"I know Esther, and I promise you we're doing everything we can to make that happen as quickly as possible," Ade told her. "But for now, let's just be grateful Matt and your mum are okay and that we've got your dad in custody."

"Yeah, way to kill the mood Esty!" Matt nudged her with his shoulder again and then again until she frowned at him, her eyes narrow, but a smile wasn't far behind.

"Sorry Ade, I didn't mean to spoil your big moment."

"Absolutely nothing to apologise for. In fact, I'm sure you must have seen enough of this place to last you a lifetime so now that you've seen Matt's okay, why don't I get someone to take you both home? If it's okay with you, I can come over and update you later. How does that sound?"

"Will I get to see my Mum any quicker if I stay here and annoy you?"

"No, you won't."

"I guess we'll see you at mine later then."

37

Matt pushed the door open and waited for Esther to go in.

"Ade kept quiet about the gatekeeper," she said as she closed the door behind them, leaving an officer outside the door. "What if I want to go out?"

"Then you can," Matt said as he followed her into the kitchen. "The minder's for me. I'm not exactly a free man Esty, am I? It's all been very nicey nicey so far but anytime I don't play ball they can just arrest me for my part in all this and put me in a cell with the rest of them."

"Ade wouldn't do that to you!"

"Wouldn't he?"

Esther thought about that for a moment. "Well let's make sure we don't give him any reason to want you behind bars then," she said, desperate not to add worrying about Matt going to prison to her long list of current troubles. "Would a drink help?" she asked him, already reaching for wine glasses and then offering up a bottle of red wine.

"Yes please," Matt said as he sat down on a kitchen stool. "It's definitely time to blur the edges."

They worked their way effortlessly through the bottle with an assortment of crackers, cheese and crisps consumed along the way to soak up at least some of the intoxicating liquid. The conversation had been sparse, both spending large chunks of time lost to their own thoughts which occasionally spilled out into the room.

"Do you think Abi loved me?" Matt asked from nowhere.

"Yes, I do," Esther said without hesitating, knowing that whether she believed it or not made no difference to her but it meant everything to Matt. He nodded slowly and repeatedly, pleased to have received the affirmation he needed, and with such conviction.

"What if Mum had killed him?" Esther said after several more minutes had stretched across another pause in conversation. "What if, after all that's happened, we'd ended up burying him and visiting her in prison?"

"Let's just be grateful that didn't happen."

"Or what if one of the armed officers had shot her and then we'd have been burying her for real, knowing she'd been alive for years but never getting the chance to see her or talk to her again?" Esther's eyes filled with tears.

"For goodness sake Esty!" Matt laughed. "Stop with the what ifs! Haven't we had to contend with enough actual shit without you conjuring up an even worse set of scenarios? Enough already!"

Another lingering silence.

"Your eyes look heavy," Esther then told him. "Why don't you go and lie down?"

"What will you do?" he asked as he stood up, the thought of sleeping suddenly incredibly attractive.

Esther shrugged. "I'll find something to keep me busy."

Matt looked at her for a moment wondering if he should stay and keep her company but the weight of his eyelids was becoming unmanageable. "Wake me if you need me," was all he could offer as he walked away in the direction of the spare room and a large soft bed.

Esther sat where she was, pouring the very last drops of wine into her glass and savouring the final mouthful. She took her time clearing everything away and then headed for her work room. She had no expectations of actually doing anything useful but she felt calm there and would be able to distract herself by sketching or even just doodling. It didn't really matter as long as she was able to put a stop to the increasingly alarming brain chatter and the physical twitching that was also now completely out of her control as the anxious wait to hear news of her mother continued.

When there was a knock at the front door, Esther imagined it was the police officer needing to use the bathroom but when she opened it, she was surprised to see Eddie.

"Sorry to arrive unannounced," he said with a huge smile.

Before Esther had the chance to speak, Eddie stepped to one side and the most beautiful sight imaginable appeared in his place. Esther slowly reached out with her hand, eyes wide and disbelieving, desperate to confirm that the vision in front of her was real and not cruelly conjured up by her over-stimulated imagination. Her eyes took in every detail of the face she had gone to sleep dreaming about every night and when her fingers finally reached soft flesh she gasped.

"Hello Esty."

And there it was. The voice that had soothed, encouraged, reassured and made her feel so loved. For a moment, Esther felt frozen to the spot and then, as the grief and sadness she'd carried with her for all those years melted away, she threw herself into her mother's arms and clung to her, terrified of letting her go.

"Well there's a sight I thought I'd never see again," Matt said as he appeared at the door. Kate put her hand out to him and Matt took hold of it firmly, the relief to be reunited evident in every feature of their faces. "Why don't you come inside?" he asked, holding on to Kate with one hand and gently pulling Esther towards him with the other one. As they crossed the threshold, Esther let Kate go and Kate immediately took Matt into her arms. Esther looked at Eddie, her eyes blurred with tears, only able to nod her gratitude but he didn't need thanks. Just to witness this incredible moment was more than enough for him.

Esther didn't trust herself to speak. Instead, she simply blew him a kiss and then slowly closed the door.

38

As soon as Esther and Matt had left the station, Ade had gone straight back to his desk, eager to see if there were any updates on the interviews that were already underway. He expected Dave to be in a cell in the station's basement within the next hour or so but he didn't want any conversation with him to take place until they'd got a clear picture of what everyone else was saying. The more his loyal followers could be persuaded to turn on him, the harder it would be for Dave to do anything other than put his hands up to it all.

Ade looked at his watch. It was already almost seven o'clock. He reluctantly conceded that Dave's interview was unlikely to start until the morning now but no matter. He'd keep everyone else hard at it so that within minutes of turning on an interview tape, he'd have Dave backed so tightly into a corner that he'd be firmly wedged there until he'd given a full and complete confession.

When he received a text from Eddie to say Kate had been safely reunited with her children, Ade let Esther know he'd see them tomorrow. There would be time enough to update them without crashing into the middle of their first evening back together. He'd tried many times to put himself in both Matt's and Esther's shoes and imagine what their lives must have been like and each time he'd had to accept his imagination simply wasn't equipped to get him even vaguely close to understanding what they'd been through. But what he did know was that they all absolutely deserved the night to talk and just be with each other without interruption.

By nine o'clock the next morning, Ade had received enough feedback to know that every single member of Dave's gang had accepted that a jail sentence was now unavoidable. Once that first milestone had been achieved, it hadn't been long before they were forming an orderly queue to point the finger at Dave if it meant a few years might be shaved off their imminent incarceration.

Half an hour later, Ade and DI Baker were sitting opposite Dave and his lawyer, an equally heinous character who was almost as accomplished at manipulating the law as the client sitting beside him. Ade set the tape running, announcing who was present and then immediately, there was a knock at the door.

"For the purpose of the tape, Detective Constable Ferguson has entered the room," Ade said, neglecting to mention that he was pushing a rather large trolley loaded with fifteen boxes. He nodded at Eddie. There was nothing like a bit of theatre to get proceedings underway.

"For the purpose of the tape, Detective Constable Ferguson has now left the room," Ade said as Eddie disappeared again leaving the trolley behind.

Ade stood up, taking his time to pick up the first box and then, placing it carefully on the table between them, he retook his seat. "Each one of these boxes represents a year of your life Dave. The contents of each outline the detail of every robbery you masterminded including emails, copies of text conversations, blueprints of buildings. You get the idea,

I'm sure. We also have bank statements and copies of orders to remove 'obstacles'. And so it goes on. Is there anything you'd like to say at this point Dave?"

Ade had been staring at Dave while he spoke, searching his face for any clue that he might be even slightly perturbed but of course his poker face was world class. Ade wasn't worried. He'd barely got started.

"My client won't be making any comment," Dave's lawyer cut in.

"Fair enough," Ade said as he removed the lid from the first box and removed the first folder. "Let's take a trip down memory lane then shall we?"

Over several hours with only one short break, Ade went through every single piece of information. Every time he laid something in front of Dave, he asked him if he recognised it, and each time he was told he had no comment.

"Can't we speed this up?" Dave's lawyer asked for the umpteenth time. "We get the picture. So you have a stack of paper that we don't even know is genuine. This is a completely pointless exercise."

"But I don't think you do get the picture," Ade replied. "It's important you understand the breadth of evidence we've got which I can assure you is all completely genuine. And before you ask, copies are already on their way to your office. But if you really had a sense of the big picture, you'd be advising your client to start talking. And we haven't even got to the audio recordings yet, or the point where we get to discuss how your client had my friend and colleague shot. I'm looking forward to hearing what he has to say about that."

The lawyer looked at Ade, his stare rigid, his mouth set in a patronising smirk. He opened his hand towards Dave, inviting him to say something, while his eyes stayed fixed on Ade.

Dave leant forward, resting his elbows on the table. "No comment," he said.

"Do you think he plans to keep going all night?"

Patrick Robbins had been watching the interview from behind a glass screen for almost two hours now. He'd left the air-conditioned offices of the Crown Prosecution Service with the expectation the interview would be almost done, but Ade clearly had other ideas. He pushed a finger into his shirt collar and pulled in an attempt to release some hot air, or let some cool air in. When neither happened, he roughly undid his tie and unbuttoned his shirt and then he sighed. "He's obviously not going to say anything."

"Ade's just trying to make life easy for you," Eddie said. "Surely the more convincing he is presenting this stuff, the greater the chance of Dave pleading guilty?"

Eddie had been dipping in and out all day and was slightly in awe of Ade's patience, but he knew it was important Dave understood exactly what a mountain of evidence he was facing. The more impenetrable it appeared, the less likely he was to think he could find a way around it.

"Do you know his lawyer?" Eddie asked.

"Unfortunately, yes. Harry Lewis. He defended Dave the last time he was in court and was responsible for securing him that ridiculously small sentence. He's an unscrupulous slimy bastard."

Eddie smiled. "Of course he is."

"Well thank goodness for that," Patrick said, quickly picking up his jacket and his bag as his eyes were drawn to the sudden flurry of movement through the glass marking the end of the interview. "About bloody time! I need to have a cosy chat with the slimy bastard."

As Patrick left the room, he ran straight into Ade. "Are you going for some kind of record?" Patrick asked him. "You've been locked in there for hours."

"And we'll be doing the same again tomorrow. Can we have a quick word?"

"Two minutes. As long as you don't let the lawyer leave till I've spoken to him."

Ade took him into a smaller interview room where there was no chance of being overheard. "As the clock's ticking," he said, "I'll get straight to it. I'm really hoping you'll agree to leave Matt out of it all. We have so much detail here and pretty much every gang member is ready to say whatever it takes for them to be shown leniency. If they all turn on each other and, most importantly, turn on Dave, you'll have more than enough to secure a lengthy sentence. I mean, take the guy who shot Abi. He's already given a statement to say it was on Dave's order in an attempt to reduce his sentence."

"Why are you so keen for him not to give evidence?"

"Because if he does, he'll never feel safe again. He'll be the one with the life sentence. And Esther and Kate too." Ade studied Patrick's face as he ruminated. "And let's not forget we're only in such a strong position because of Matt," he added. "Never mind the money and hassle we'd save with three less people in witness protection."

Patrick put his hand up. "Okay I get it. It's too early to be making any promises but I'll see what I can do."

An hour later, Patrick was surprised to find himself in a private drinking club with Harry Lewis as his companion but it had been the only way to secure a chat. He watched Harry relax in a large leather chair, an incredibly expensive whisky in his hand that Patrick would no doubt be paying for, sporting the same patronising smirk that seemed to be permanently tattooed on to his face.

"He'll get life if we go to trial. You do know that don't you?"

Harry shrugged. "I know that the public are a fickle unpredictable bunch. I also know how very persuasive I can be."

"And brown envelopes stuffed with cash makes you even more so."

"Now now Patrick." Harry narrowed his eyes, the threat in his voice unmistakable.

Patrick looked at him, refusing to be intimidated. "Maybe you're right," he said. "Maybe it is worth taking your chance with a trial, during which I'll have the absolute time of my life. The physical evidence is overwhelming. We made twenty-one arrests which means there's a whole choir of gang members ready to sing their criminal hearts out. Not to mention their written statements, all of which incriminate your client."

"Does that include Matt? And Kate? She bloody shot him!"

"Yes, they were both arrested but when a jury hears what your client did to both of them, they'll hate every inch of him. They'll be disgusted and horrified by a man who made his wife choose between faking her own death or being killed. Never mind the years of physical abuse they both endured."

"Well, that's how they remember it."

Patrick shook his head in disbelief. "And that's before we even consider the robberies, the use of weapons, the murder of a police officer."

"Well all that crap we've been forced to wade through must have come from Matt?"

"I know you seem to have your own highly imaginative narrative running in parallel to what's actually going on here but, just to be clear, Matt's actually the only one who hasn't offered to stand witness against your client." Patrick shrugged. "But then I suppose Dave's been attacking him all his life. Why stop now?"

Patrick then sat forward and downed his drink in one satisfying gulp. There was only so much slimy bastard he could take in one sitting. "Why don't you have a long hard think and we'll talk again in a couple of days? Twenty five years with the chance of parole is the best you can hope for but at some point, I will be giving you a deadline, after which I'll happily see you in court and watch your client be put away for the rest of his life with no chance of coming out until he's carried out in a box."

Patrick stood up. "A pleasure as always Harry," he said as he walked away, leaving the bill behind him.

39

It was late the following afternoon when Ade turned up at Esther's and he could feel the nervous energy as soon as he arrived.

"I imagine you've had a lot to talk about," he said to Kate and Matt while Esther busied herself in the kitchen making tea.

"Yes, it's been completely magical, like a dream," Kate beamed, sitting close to Matt on the sofa and holding his hand tightly as if afraid to let him go. "I'm still pinching myself."

"Well you can rely on Ade to bring us crashing back to reality, isn't that right Ade?" Matt asked.

Ade thought Matt was looking particularly agitated but before he had a chance to respond, Esther appeared.

"So do you have good news for us?" she asked, coming into the room with an overladen tray. Ade jumped up to help her as she nervously continued, her voice higher than normal, anxiety having taken a tight hold. "I wasn't sure what everyone would want so I've made a pot of tea and there's a bottle of wine too if you prefer. Or I could make coffee? Would anyone prefer coffee?"

"A cup of tea would be great Esther, thank you," Ade said, his voice gentle and reassuring by comparison.

"Come on then Ade. Put us out of our misery," Matt said as Esther continued to fuss over drinks.

"Well I definitely have news," Ade said as he accepted a mug of tea from Esther. "We've spent the last two days presenting all the evidence we have to Dave but he made no comment throughout. His previously loyal disciples have all turned on him so we have testimonies now as well as the physical stuff."

"I feel a but coming," Matt chipped in.

"No but," Ade said, doing his best to keep the mood positive. "Our man from the CPS met with Dave's lawyer yesterday and offered him a deal. Twenty-five years with the chance of parole for a guilty plea. If he accepts, and he'd be insane not to, then there won't be a trial."

"So we wouldn't have to testify?" Kate asked, not ready to believe this might all be nearly over.

"No, you wouldn't have to testify," Ade confirmed with a smile. And then he looked at Matt. "You okay Matt?" he asked, unable to read his expression.

Matt continued to bounce this fresh information around, his head moving slowly from side to side as he did so. "But where's he pointing the finger?"

"Patrick from the CPS told his lawyer you were the only one who hadn't offered to testify against him."

"So Dave thinks it was me who provided all the physical evidence? Otherwise why did the CPS guy feel it necessary to tell him that?"

"We've been consistently saying the information came from a number of sources and your statement makes no mention of the memory stick."

"But as soon as his lawyer realises I'm the only one not in jail, it won't matter what you've said or done. It'll be bloody obvious it was all down to me."

"It's perfectly reasonable that you're not in jail because of the extreme circumstances that led you to being involved with him in the first place."

"And as for accepting the deal," Matt continued, not ready to give any room to Ade's counter arguments, "you're choosing to ignore the fact that he is absolutely insane so anything could still happen."

Ade looked at him for a moment. Despite his reassurances, Matt was right of course but he didn't want to admit that. "Why don't you all just talk it through this evening? And if you still feel there's a very real physical threat then we can get the witness protection team to come and chat through how that would work." Ade stood up. "The CPS will give Dave's lawyer a deadline tomorrow so I'll let you know as soon as there's an update."

Ade said his goodbyes and Esther followed him towards the front door. As he went to open it, she put her hand on his arm, making him immediately stop and look at her.

"Can I see him?" she asked in a hushed tone.

Ade look momentarily confused. "See Dave?"

"Yes, and the sooner the better."

"He's being moved to a prison tomorrow so I suppose you could see him before he goes." Ade was thinking on his feet. "I'd have to speak to the CPS though."

"Please Ade. I wouldn't ask if it wasn't important."

"What's this about Esther?"

She shrugged. "It just feels like the right time for a chat."

40

Patrick had arranged for a special visit in a small meeting room. The guard who brought Dave in, who was waiting to escort him to prison, made a huge deal about the fact he would be right outside if Esther needed him which did little for her confidence. She nodded her thanks, working hard to appear calm. It had been a battle to secure some privacy so she was desperate not to look intimidated as Dave lowered himself into the chair opposite her.

The door then closed behind the guard and they just looked at each other for a moment.

"It's good to see you."

"Is it?" Dave hadn't expected to hear that from his estranged daughter. "Well I'm certainly very pleased to see you. It's been a long time Esty."

Esther felt a wave of nausea sweep up from her gut. She swallowed hard, giving herself a little shake as she tried to focus. She'd been rehearsing what she wanted to say all night but now that they were facing each other nothing she'd prepared seemed even remotely appropriate. She wanted so desperately to shout at him, call him every disgraceful name she could think of before telling him how much she hated him. She knew it would change nothing though, but getting him on side just might.

"I had a whole speech planned," she eventually said.

"I can imagine," Dave said, attempting a reassuring smile.

Esther was immediately reminded how different his demeanour was when he was talking to her rather than Kate or Matt which was enough to get her back on track.

"I just need to know who you're going to blame for this? Someone has to pay, right Dad?" She watched his jaw stiffen. "Will it be Matt? Or Mum?"

"I think we both know I wouldn't be here if it wasn't for your brother."

"I can certainly see why you'd want to think that," she said, ignoring the deferred responsibility. "You've been torturing him physically and mentally his entire life. But the truth is lots of people had access to the information the police now have and anyone could've recorded conversations. Why is that so hard to accept?" Dave looked at her, his face set to neutral but there was a flicker of something currently indiscernible in his eyes. "Just let him go Dad, please! And Mum too. Haven't they suffered enough? I don't even know why you've been so fixated on punishing them all these years. And me too."

"I never hurt you!"

"You made me think my mother was dead for sixteen years!" Esther watched as Dave's eyes widened and she felt herself pull back. The room suddenly felt oppressive, the atmosphere suffocating. "Actually I don't need to know why," she said, her words heavy with the weight of dark painful memories that she forced to the back of her mind. "We can't change the past but you've got the power to decide what happens from here. You can accept that you are in fact guilty of every charge against you which means that what's happening right now is no one's fault but your own. So stop looking for someone else to blame! Take responsibility, accept the deal you've been offered and let us all get on with our lives without fear of pointless retaliation."

Esther watched Dave's head slowly lower. His hand came up to his face and he rubbed his forehead. Kate had opened up about Dave's childhood and it had been brutal to say the least but Esther wasn't here to psychoanalyse. Neither was she hoping for apologies or explanations. She just wanted it to stop.

"I just want to be able to get on with my life without being terrified every time the phone rings, thinking something might have happened to Mum or Matt," Esther continued when Dave remained silent. "And I want them to be able to go about their lives without constantly checking over their shoulders."

Still he said nothing. Esther took a deep breath and slowly exhaled. She hadn't expected this to be easy and she certainly wasn't ready to give up. It was time to show her hand.

"Despite everything, I've missed having you around. I want to be able to see you." Dave's head shot up, mistaking the tears in Esther's eyes as longing and not the result of having to force out such unnatural words that wanted to choke her, her brain knowing she had to push them out, her heart desperate to keep them in at all costs. "I haven't forgotten the tender moments," she said, her speech slow and deliberate. "Watching a scary film with you and burying my head into your shoulder, feeling safe with your arms wrapped around me. Simple things like you taking my hand when we crossed a road, or going out for a sneaky ice cream before tea. And chewing the fat with you about what my future might look like. I definitely wouldn't be working for myself without you making me believe anything was possible." She stopped for a moment until she was confident Dave was now reliving the memories with her. "But seeing you is impossible while your relationships with Mum and Matt are so....strained."

Esther slowly reached across the table and took hold of Dave's hand, her skin crawling at the very touch of him. He seemed hesitant at first, the physical contact unexpected and alien to him but when she made it obvious she wasn't about to let go he reciprocated, taking her hand between his own.

"If it could all just stop Dad, maybe we can all start again? I've spoken to the CPS about where you might end up and they've promised me they'll keep you close so I can visit regularly. And I really want to. I want to feel like something good has come out of all this but that's only possible if I know Mum and Matt are safe."

Dave continued to stroke her hand as Esther studied his face, searching for any hint that she was getting through to him.

"Please Dad. Do it for me."

Patrick told Dave's lawyer his offer was only available for another twenty four hours after which he'd see him in court but it hadn't taken that long.

Within an hour of taking the final call from Patrick, Ade was ringing Esther's doorbell. Her expression when she opened the door made Ade laugh. "Well that's a lovely welcome! You look absolutely horrified to see me," he said as he stepped inside.

"I'm so sorry," Esther said, struggling to control the adrenalin that had been pumping furiously through her body since she'd visited Dave. She was running on caffeine and every part of her was twitchy and uncomfortable as a result while she waited to hear if her visit had worked. "We're all just trapped in a horrible limbo," she said. "Will Dave take the deal or won't he? Will Matt and I have to face him in court? Will we have to disappear and start again somewhere?" She shook her head. "It's mind-blowing."

"Is everyone here?" he asked as he followed Esther into the kitchen. She automatically switched the kettle on and started to gather mugs together. "You don't have to make tea Esther. It's just a short visit."

"Oh, okay," she said, unsure if this was a good thing or not.

"I thought I could hear your voice," Matt said, appearing in the doorway. "Mum's in the lounge."

Once they were all seated, Ade jumped straight in, aware of the tension his presence was causing. "So I told you a deadline on the deal was offered and I've just heard back from Patrick that Dave has accepted. It came with an assurance from Dave himself that he fully accepts responsibility and isn't looking for anyone else to blame."

"Then we're free?" Kate asked.

"Yes, it's all over."

"But why would he say that? Why would he want us to know he's not coming after us?"

Ade thought for a moment. "I really don't know. But I think Esther might."

41

Esther was still getting used to the idea that she could spend the day with her Mum. That she could jump on a train, turn up at the florist's to find Kate looking relaxed and happy and so wonderfully confident as she chatted with customers, many of whom she considered to be friends, and then take her out for lunch and a chat, enjoy a stroll around the picturesque village she lived in and still be home before sundown.

She was also still struggling with the fact she now had a phone number for Matt, that he was living just twenty minutes away and working freelance on legitimate projects. But this was the new normal and one she celebrated every minute of every day.

After a lovely lunch with Kate the day before, she'd had her head down all day making up for the lost hours at her desk, and it was well into the evening when she finally felt she'd caught up. As she stretched her neck in various directions in an attempt to relieve the day's tensions, she walked into the lounge and headed for the window but as she went to close the curtains, she momentarily froze then immediately started searching for her phone.

"Has he gone mad and escaped?"

"Who?"

"My Dad! Has he decided he wants us all dead after all and escaped?"

"No, of course he hasn't."

"Does that mean someone else is after me?"

"Esther, no one is after you."

Esther took a moment to let that sink in. "So what are you doing here then?"

"What can I tell you? Old habits die hard."

A huge smile spread across her face. "Do you want to come up? It's movie night."

"Don't tell me, it's number two on your list?"

"Yes it is! Love Actually!"

"Isn't that a Christmas movie?"

"Oh come on Eddie! Where's your sense of adventure?"

Acknowledgements

Book three done! And what makes this page really special is the fact I'm thanking the same amazing group of people for the third time. So once again, my enormous heart-felt thanks go to Tammy Kempinski and Emma Carboni for reading the first post-edit draft, providing essential feedback that shaped this final version. My husband, Steve, is also a crucial part of the early reading team but he got to read it with me sitting next to him, scrutinising every facial expression and challenging him every time he dared to make a note. His perspective always spots something different so I am incredibly appreciative of your input, even if it didn't always feel like it at the time!

To Alison Parkin, who went way beyond the awesome task of proofreading, high-lighting subtle disconnects in character traits and plot timelines, I am hugely grateful as always for your precision and care. And I feel so privileged to have another stunning cover designed by the super talented Anita Mangan. Once more you have perfectly captured the heart of the story in one striking image.

If you've bought this book, my biggest thanks are reserved for you. I really hope you've enjoyed it and if you have, you can find out what I'm up to next on Instagram (@elaine_robertson_north) and Facebook (facebook.com/elainerobertsonnorth), with apologies in advance for my intermittent posting. And if you felt inclined to post a review on Amazon or Goodreads that would be great. It really does make a difference.

About the Author

Elaine spent twenty-five years working in marketing and publicity in the media and entertainment industries. This included seven years marketing national newspapers and a variety of senior executive roles in TV, radio and film.

I've Been Waiting For You is Elaine's third novel. Her previous novels, I Can't Tell You Why and Bring Me To Life are also available.

Elaine lives in North London with her husband and their two sons.

Printed in Great Britain
by Amazon